## KINDRED SPIRITS

Keith eased away from her, and she felt a loss such as she had never felt before. She also felt the air on her body where her shirt had been. She shook away the fog clouding her mind. Her shirt was in Keith's hands. She frowned. *How did he do that?* She looked down at her own body and let her gaze follow the trail being made by his gaze.

It settled on her breasts—her tightened, sensitive breasts. Her lace bra revealed as much as it covered. Or more. She glanced up at him. His gaze was stuck on her breasts. She felt her fullness tighten even more, as if his hands were touching her rather than his gaze. Her tips swelled and pushed against the lace as if waiting for him.

## BOOK YOUR PLACE ON OUR WEBSITE AND MAKE THE ARABESQUE ROMANCE CONNECTION!

We've created a customized website just for our very special Arabesque readers, where you can get the inside scoop on everything that's going on with Arabesque romance novels.

When you come online, you'll have the exciting opportunity to:

- View covers of upcoming books

- Learn about our future publishing schedule (listed by publication month and author)

- Find out when your favorite authors will be visiting a city near you

- Search for and order backlist books

- Check out author bios and background information

- Send e-mail to your favorite authors

- Join us in weekly chats with authors, readers and other guests

- Get writing guidelines

- AND MUCH MORE!

# Kindred
# Spirits

*Enjoy the romance*
*Alice Wootson*

### ALICE
### WOOTSON

ARABESQUE
★BET
BOOKS™

**BET Publications, LLC**
http://www.bet.com
http://www.arabesquebooks.com

ARABESQUE BOOKS are published by

BET Publications, LLC
c/o BET BOOKS
One BET Plaza
1900 W Place NE
Washington, DC 20018-1211

All Kensington Titles, Imprints, and Distributed Lines are available at special quantity discounts for bulk purchases for sales promotions, premiums, fund-raising, and educational or institutional use. Special book excerpts or customized printings can also be created to fit specific needs. For details, write or phone the office of the Kensington special sales manager: Kensington Publishing Corp., 850 Third Avenue, New York, NY 10022, attn: Special Sales Department, Phone: 1-800-221-2647.

BET Books is a trademark of Black Entertainment Television, Inc. ARABESQUE, the ARABESQUE logo, and the BET BOOKS logo are trademarks and registered trademarks.

First Printing: June 2004
10 9 8 7 6 5 4 3 2

Printed in the United States of America

# ACKOWLEDGMENTS

Thanks to Jonathan, Jeff and Donna of Orange Blossom Balloons in Orlando for giving me a necessary up-close look at the balloon and basket that figure so prominently in a key scene. It was fascinating to take part in the whole process of inflating the gigantic balloon. (They look so much smaller when they are in the air and I am on the ground.) It was worth getting up at dawn and going out in the chilly morning.

A special thanks to Ronnie for sharing his special ops expertise with me so I could get it right.

Many thanks, again, to my agent, Deidre Knight, for her gigantic efforts on my behalf. A special thanks to my computer expert sons: Randy for a crucial bit of information and Tony for being my Web master. To my third son, David, for creating a great work space, and, as always, to Ike for following my dream path with me.

# Chapter 1

Early afternoon, Alana Duke glared at the dashboard clock and maneuvered her Hyundai in front of a cab stopped at the curb in front of the arrival section of the Philadelphia International Airport. She turned off the motor, took a deep breath, then got out of the car. She barely noticed the snowflakes drifting down and the light covering already on the ground.

"Rush hour," she muttered. *Whoever came up with that name for snail-pace traffic had a mean sense of humor.* She took a deep breath. *Yvette has to get her luggage, so she won't be ready yet, anyway.* Alana sighed as a security guard approached her. "I'll only be a couple of minutes, I swear," she explained to him. "I'm just going inside the door."

She pulled out her driver's license to show him who she was and hoped that would persuade him to let her leave her car. He stared at the license, back to her, scanned her face, then moved his attention back to the license. *Much longer, and Yvette will be out here and I won't have to beg him.*

"I'm a reporter." She glanced inside the building once more before pulling out her newspaper ID. "Maybe this will help. A few minutes, that's all I need." He stared at the ID for a while longer and then back at her before he spoke.

"That's all I can give you." He pointed a good distance away to the sign marking the beginning of Terminal B.

"When I come back this way, if you're still here, I'll have to ticket you." He shrugged. "I still might get into trouble for this."

"Thanks," Alana flung over her shoulder as she hurried to the doors that swished open. She started into the terminal, then went back to the car. Snowflakes, no longer timid, marched down before finding a place to land. It was becoming harder for them to find a space not already taken. Alana barely noticed.

She unlocked the car door, grabbed her jacket from the passenger side, and ran back to the terminal, ignoring the white drops accumulating on the ground.

Once inside, she eased between groups standing as if waiting for something to begin, and scanned the crowd for her sister. *Had every plane decided to arrive at the same time?*

Finally she found a small clearing, stood on tiptoes, and slowly looked around again.

"Yvette." She waved at what seemed to be a familiar figure, hiked her purse back up on her shoulder, shifted the jacket to her other arm, and ran toward Baggage Carousel A. Suddenly she hit a puddle and slid as if on a surfboard. She tried to keep her purse in place, the jacket from falling into the water, and herself upright.

Just as she resigned herself to a sprained wrist, scraped knees, and being covered with the dirty, cold water pooled around her, a pair of strong hands grabbed her.

"Careful," a deep voice said in her ear as she was pulled toward a chest that felt like a wall—a comforting, living wall—before his hands released her.

"Sorry, I . . ."

"Alana. Hey, big sis." Alana turned and smiled as Yvette stopped a few feet in front of her. In spite of the puddles, Yvette let her luggage drop to the floor. The two young women closed the space between them and wrapped their arms around each other. Finally they allowed space between them again. "I saw your antics. Some people will go to extremes to make some space around them." She frowned. "You are all right, aren't you?"

"Yeah." Alana smiled and turned around. "Thanks. You saved . . ." Her words faded as her gaze met an empty space. She looked around and frowned. "Where did he go?"

Yvette looked around also. "If he weren't already wearing street clothes, I'd say to find a phone booth so he could change clothes." She shrugged and looked back at Alana. "What happened anyway?"

"I discovered that cars aren't the only things that can hydroplane." She looked around again. "You didn't see where he went, did you? I didn't have a chance to thank him."

"All I saw was a glimpse of his back." Yvette wiggled her eyebrows. "A broad, solid-looking back." She released an exaggerated sigh. "Made me wish I had seen him from the front. As Mama says, 'Mercy.' Did his face live up to my expectations?"

"You haven't changed a bit."

"Thank you."

"That wasn't a compliment."

"Sure it was. Did it?"

"Did what?"

"How did he look?"

"I don't know. I didn't see his face."

"How could you not see his face?"

"I was busy trying not to embarrass myself and add to my dry cleaning bill. I felt him hold me and then you came over."

"That's right. Blame me for your missed opportunity." Alana glanced around as Yvette continued. "I'm sure he realizes that you appreciate not having filthy water all over your suit." She sighed. "It's just as well he's gone. Sisters fighting over a man would not be a pretty sight. You would *be* a story instead of writing one." She frowned. "Where's your coat? Don't you know it's winter?"

"Not officially for another few days. Come on." Alana hurried through the crowd.

"Tell that to the temperature." Yvette looked outside. "It's snowing. Great." The door swished open as somebody came in. Yvette grabbed the jacket that Alana handed to her and scrambled into it.

"Yes, but we don't expect much accumulation." Alana took the handle of one of the suitcases and Yvette got the other. They eased around a large group holding a family reunion in the middle of the terminal.

Finally they reached the doors and Alana led her sister through them. "I'm parked down here. At least I hope I still am." She looked for the tennis ball on her antenna, but a van was blocking her view. "To answer your question, I didn't want to wear a coat over my suit jacket. Too bulky." She hurried down the sidewalk.

"I'm gonna tell Mom." Yvette rushed to keep up. "You know she'll lecture you about not wearing a coat in the winter and how 'You're gonna catch pneumonia, young lady.'" Yvette's imitation of their mother made Alana laugh, but it didn't slow her down.

"You can't tell her. She and Dad won't get in until tomorrow. By then it will be old news, your mind will be on something else, and I won't have even a hint of the sniffles."

"I'll let slide the inference that I can't hold a thought for long. Why are you dressed up, anyway?"

"I just got back from interviewing two local writers." She smiled. "They're sisters and they write romance novels. One is older than Mom is. When I questioned her about writing about romance, she said 'It takes years of practice to get romance right.' " Her smile widened. "When I grow up, I want to be just like her." She laughed. "This will get me a byline. The story is going to be on the front page of the lifestyle section. The paper even sent a photographer with me." Her smile widened. "My first byline. Isn't it great? Down there." She pointed to the right. "There's my car." She released the car alarm and opened the trunk. The amount of luggage Yvette had finally registered. "Are you planning to move back here?"

"I couldn't make up my mind about what to bring." She lifted the suitcases into the trunk. "I can't move back. Florida would miss me too much."

"Of course, you wouldn't miss Florida, especially not the year-round sunshine and heat." Alana closed the trunk. "Go ahead and get in."

"Thank you." Shivering, Yvette pulled the jacket tighter and wrapped her arms around herself. "It does get cold in Florida, you know," she said before she scooted inside.

"One day a year in the middle of the night," Alana chimed in as she dusted the snow from the windshield.

"We had six days below freezing last year." Yvette fastened her seatbelt.

"Poor you." Alana started the car and eased around another double-parked in front of her. "Either I wasn't gone as long as I thought, or the security guard had a touch of the holiday spirit."

"'Tis the season." Yvette looked out the window. "I hope we get a lot of snow."

"Spoken like a visitor."

They laughed as Alana left the airport and headed for the Platt Bridge.

"Speaking of being a visitor, the last time you were here, you said something about moving back."

"At the time it was the end of May and the beautiful

weather made me lose my mind. I found it before I left."
She turned to face Alana. "I'm surprised you remember that."

"You know I don't forget stuff."

"Anyway, I can't move back. Dave's Computer Software Technology couldn't get along without me." She laughed. "I keep trying to convince Dave of that."

The conversation turned to Yvette's flight from Orlando and what Alana and she were going to do while she was in Philadelphia.


Keith Henderson stared at the door long after the two women exited the terminal. Rather, he stared at one of the women; the one who made a physical impression on him. *If I close my eyes, I can still feel her pressed against me.* He frowned. *I should have at least gotten her name.* He thought about her long, sexy, full legs that took her away from him. *Full legs.* He smiled. *Not matchsticks. Legs the color of raw honey.* He shook his head slowly. *I do appreciate skirts that barely skim the knees. Slacks cover too much.*

His thoughts returned to the way she felt pressed against his chest. *Solid. Substantial.* He frowned. *You're losing it, man. There was a time when you would be sharing a cup of coffee with her by now. You're mighty slow this morning.* He shrugged. *I can't blame it on jet lag, since I only came from Boston.*

He frowned and shook his head with regret as the thought of the missed opportunity rippled through him. *You saw her once. And touched her once. And that was only for a few seconds.* He stared at the door, even though she had been gone too long to still be outside. *Then how come the memory of how she felt against my chest is so strong?*

People jostled past him going in both directions, but

his gaze held on the doors, as though waiting for her to push through the crowd exiting and come back to him.

Finally he turned from the door and his logical mind returned. *If I never meet her, then I can't hurt her.*

With regret tagging along, he went to Baggage Carousel B to get his suitcase.

# Chapter 2

Keith adjusted his carry-on bag on his shoulder and leaned against the wall in the baggage-claim area. He allowed his mind to drift back to his recent pleasant, though brief, encounter, rather than to more troubling thoughts. He watched people crowding and grabbing as if there were a penalty for the last suitcase left. He shook his head and waited, letting his mind go back yet again to the mystery woman.

He had seen her face only from a distance, but she was beautiful. Lines from an ancient song about a stranger across a crowded room came to him. He knew what the songwriter meant. He felt as if opportunity had knocked and he was too slow in answering, so it moved on. He frowned. *What's wrong with me?* He shook his head. *I don't need this. I'm meant to be a loner.* His frown deepened. *Must be the holidays.*

Finally, when only a few pieces of luggage continued to ride the circle of the baggage carousel, he lifted his suitcase off. *No hurry,* he thought as he made his way to the terminal door. *Nobody special is waiting for me.*

The line in front of the security guard, who was at the exit checking claim tickets against luggage tags, was down to a few people. *Do enough people try to get away with somebody else's luggage to make this worth the time and salary?* He shrugged. It wasn't his call and he was glad. Even with something as simple as that, things could go wrong. *What would the guard do if somebody did try to make off with somebody else's luggage?* He glanced at the gun strapped to the guard's side. *Would he really use it, with all of these people around? Was it worth somebody's life, the thief's or one of these people milling around, to get back a suitcase?* He shook his head. *What was worth a life?* He shrugged. *Not your call,* he reminded himself.

He glanced out the window at the snow falling. Large flakes floated slowly but steadily to the ground. Only small patches of pavement peeped through the growing white blanket. He shrugged. *After four months in Boston, Philadelphia weather will be easy.* He glanced at the dark gray sky. He hoped. He shrugged again. It didn't matter. Mount Airy wasn't that far from here and he had driven in worse.

He let the guard check his honesty, then left the terminal. There was no line at the car-rental agency and soon he was driving the Saturn on the Schuylkill Expressway.

Some drivers acted as if they had just wandered onto the road and weren't sure why they were there, and others drove as if the roads were dry and they had all three lanes to themselves. These two groups made up for the lack of volume.

Keith took the ramp leading to Lincoln Drive and noticed that the road had recently been repaved and salt had already been spread. He shook his head as a driver swerved around him near a curve and passed on the wrong side driving at double the twenty-five mile per hour speed limit. Then he smiled. Some things never change.

He rode to the end of the drive and made a right at Allen's Lane. He passed his old elementary school looking down on the street from its hill. It was good to be home. He refused to remember some of the things he had experienced since those innocent days.

He turned left at the next corner and then right, then he drove three blocks before pulling into the driveway that had been paved since he was here last.

A smile softened his face as he noticed the freshly painted white trim around the windows and the eaves. *Tara does keep things up.* Candles stood in each window of the large stone house. He knew Tara followed the ritual their mother had started and lit each one as soon as it got dark, as if the light were needed to guide somebody home. He blinked hard. *If it were only that easy.*

A Nativity scene took up a large portion of the yard near the porch. He smiled at the old familiar figures. His mother had gotten the set from Grandmom Jones. Starting from when they were young and until they left home, he and Tara had helped set it up each year. He laughed as he remembered the year baby Jesus was missing and they found Him in a doll crib in Tara's room. "It was too cold for Baby Jesus out there," the four-year-old had explained. Their mother had to let Tara wrap the figure in a blanket before she took Him back outside.

Keith shook his head. *Young and so innocent.* That's what he had been before he learned just how heavy life could get. He shook his head. *No. Not now.* He forced his mind to leave the past and stay in the now. His smile came back. It grew stronger as he walked onto the porch. Before he could ring the bell, the door was flung open.

"I don't know why you insist on not letting anybody know when your flight is due in." Tara Henderson grabbed her brother and, in spite of the cold clinging to him and the snow covering his shoulders, held him close.

"Sure you do." Keith kissed her cheek and winked

down at her. "If I told you that, you'd be calling the airport and who knows who else every two minutes if I wasn't at your door one minute after the plane landed." He shook his head. "Tell me you haven't been waiting at this door for . . ." He frowned. "How long *have* you been waiting here for me?"

"I'm not that bad." She grabbed his arm and pulled. "As Daddy used to say, 'Come on in and quit heating the outside.'" She closed the door. "I came downstairs just this minute."

"Uh-huh. I will show the Christmas spirit by not reminding you of three years ago." Keith set his luggage on the hallway floor. "Neither will I ask you if you called the airport to find out the arrival time of every flight from Boston."

"I refuse to answer." She tried to erase the guilty look on her face that told Keith that he was right. "I also don't know why you insist on renting a car. You know you can feel free to use mine while you're here."

"It's too complicated trying to juggle one car."

"You're still getting up during the night and going driving?"

"It's no big deal for me to rent a car."

"Still having trouble sleeping?"

"Not as bad as it once was." He moved to the doorway leading into the living room. "I see you've got the tree up already."

A large tan angel, her arms open as if waiting to welcome anybody who needed rescuing, perched on the top. Keith chewed his jaw. *What a nice bit of fallacy.*

"I always put it up the week after Thanksgiving." Tara's voice dragged him back to this house where he had grown up, and away from unsettling thoughts. "You know that."

"Just like Mom did." He wrestled a smile away from

the heaviness determined to cloud the moment. "And you used the spot that Mom always used."

"I always do that, too." Her voice softened. "It's been a long time since you've been here."

Keith shrugged. "You know how it is."

"Yeah, I know." She stared at him. "The dreams will go away in their own time."

"Yeah. That's what they tell me. Got any coffee?"

Tara stared at him before she answered. "I knew you were coming, so I made a pot."

"Let me take my things upstairs. I assume I have the same room?"

"You know I wouldn't dare change it. Come on out to the kitchen when you come back down."

Keith grabbed his suitcase and went to the dark oak stairs. He smiled, as seeing the banister brought back memories of him and his brother, Dave, sliding down and jumping off just before they hit the end. He touched the top of the newel post. That was back when he had no idea of what was waiting for him in the future. He released a heavy breath and climbed the stairs.

He barely paused to look out the leaded glass window on the landing before he continued to his old room. The snow had slowed, as if already tired. Maybe this snowfall was only a practice for what might come later in the week.

He unpacked his clothes, as he always did as soon as he got to any place where he'd spend more than a day. He had had enough of living out of a suitcase or, if he weren't that lucky, only a bag. He tried not to frown as he put the empty carry-on into the suitcase and put both of them into the closet. He was finished, but he didn't go downstairs. Instead, he sat on the bed.

If, when he had used this room every day, he had had

a clue about what the future held for him, could he have changed it?

He thought about four years ago.

When the opportunity had come for him to join the Special Operation Forces, he had grabbed it right away, afraid it would be snatched from him. He thought he was making a smart decision. And it was for a while. Then he learned that not everybody could handle special assignments. He also found out that he was part of the 'not everybody.'

"Did you fall asleep up here?" Tara peeked in.

"Nope." Keith stood. "I was just thinking." He managed to smile at her. "I'm coming."

"No comment on the guardian angel?" Tara touched the filmy skirt of the figure in the middle of the dresser. This angel looked like a sister to the one on the treetop downstairs.

"I hadn't noticed her."

"I don't think we're supposed to notice them unless we need to."

"Been watching episodes of that show, huh?"

"Don't laugh."

"Hey, I could use a special guardian as well as the next person." He stood. "Let's leave Miss Goodness," he glanced at the angel. "Or is she Mercy?" he shrugged. "It doesn't matter. I could use some of both." He went into the hall and never looked back. "I could use that cup of coffee, Sis."

He went down the stairs leaving Tara standing in his room.


A while later, Keith set his empty coffee mug down and leaned his arms on the kitchen table. "When is Dave coming?"

"This evening." She pretended to glare at him. "He said he'd call so I can pick him up."

"Some people are more dependent than others."

"You know I'm gonna tell him."

"That's okay. I can still take him."

"I'm gonna tell him that, too."

"Some people never outgrow their need to tattle."

"It's a gift." She smiled. "Speaking of which, did you finish your shopping before Thanksgiving as you usually do?"

"Not this year. I've been busy."

"Nothing dangerous?" Her smile disappeared.

"Mostly businesses that want a perfect security system in place, but one that costs only as much as a deadbolt lock."

"So. You have to go shopping."

"I only have to get a couple of things."

"Anybody special in your life?"

"Just you and Dave."

"You know what I mean."

"Nobody." He thought of the woman at the airport. *I wouldn't mind one of those small world incidents while I'm here. It could happen. She obviously lives here; she was picking up somebody.* The memory of the feel of her body against his was as strong as if it were happening now.

"You still with me?" Tara touched his arm.

"I'm here. How about you?"

"I think Mr. Right found another Miss Right, and it's cool." She smiled again. "How's Boston?"

"Cold and snowy."

"It's supposed to be."

"I'm thinking about moving back here."

"You knew it was cold when you moved up there last year."

"It's not that." He shrugged. "I need a change."

"Where to this time?"

"I'm not sure." He stared at her. "When was your last day of school?"

"I'll let you change the subject as long as you are aware that I know what you're doing."

"Thank you." He managed a smile.

"You picked up some bad habits somewhere. You didn't used to be sarcastic. Anyway, last Friday was our last day, but the kids' minds were already on vacation." She laughed. "When they get back after New Year's Day, it will take a week to get them focused again. Right after Thanksgiving, their minds are on what they want for Christmas, and after the holiday their thoughts are on what they got and how soon they can get back home to them." She laughed. "I can imagine how hard it is for the teachers of the first three grades." She stood and grabbed his hand. "Come on. Let's see if there's enough snow to make a decent snowball."

"I'm not dressed for this."

"Sure you are. Besides, if you're as good as you think you are, the only things that will get wet are the bottoms of the boots you left here the last time. Of course, I'll prove you wrong."

"With a challenge like that, you'd better hope there isn't enough snow to put two flakes together."

He followed her into the hall, humoring her into thinking he could pretend, even for a little while, to be a kid again.

# Chapter 3

Alana stood at her living-room window and watched as snowflakes floated down as slowly as soap bubbles. Unlike bubbles, though, they didn't burst when they touched the ground. Instead, they joined with the others trying to cover every speck of bare space. If the weather reports were correct, this was just the beginning of what would eventually be at least a foot of snow. A week from now, if there was enough snow left to anger people who had to travel in it, Alana would complain with the others. Today, however, she smiled. After all, it was only two days until Christmas. *We* should *have snow for Christmas*. Her smile widened.

She stared a while longer, hypnotized by the real Christmas-card scene painting itself in front of her.

"What are you doing, big sis?" Yvette, her bunny slippers whispering across the floor, padded over to Alana. She covered a yawn and looked out the window. "A white Christmas. Cool." She grinned. "I don't suppose you have a sled hidden in some corner?"

"Afraid not." Alana laughed. "I do have a couple of trash-can lids, though." Yvette laughed, too. "Remember the year after I had decided that I was too old to go sled riding and we got a huge snowfall? "

"Yeah, and you had given our sled away."

"What do you mean *our* sled? You gave it to me after you

decided the same thing." Yvette recited her part in the conversation that surfaced whenever they were together and there was a trace of snow.

"I'm not getting into that this morning." Alana smiled at her sister. "We did know how to improvise, didn't we?"

"Dad almost improvised *us* when he saw what we had done to his trash-can lid."

"Not to mention how we dumped his things out of that cardboard box and cut it up so both of us could ride at the same time."

"That was your idea," Yvette said. "Besides, we did not dump his things. We placed them carefully on his work table."

"It still got us a week's punishment."

"Yeah, but it was worth it." Yvette giggled.

"Yeah," Alana shook her head. Then they both sighed. "Do the kids still sled down rat road?"

"Probably." Alana looked at Yvette. "If we had a sled, we could go check it out." Their laughter filled the room.

"What are you two doing?" Sarah Duke came into the living room and gave each of her daughters a hug.

"Reliving past snows."

"Maybe I'd better go hide the trash-can lids." The three laughed. Then their mother shook her head. "I had forgotten how beautiful Mount Airy is when it's covered with new snow." She sighed. "Of course, it's beautiful any time. Sometimes I wonder if we did right in moving away." She frowned. "Then I remember the cold that goes with this beautiful covering and I'm thankful for San Diego temperatures." They all laughed again.

"You guys ready for a cup of coffee?" Alana stepped away from them.

"Whether I want coffee or tea depends. Is the coffee left over from Memorial Day?" Yvette asked.

"I bought it this morning, smarty."

"This morning? You went food shopping while it was snowing?"

"I'm sure it was better than it would have been had I gone yesterday. If folks acted the traditional Philadelphia way, yesterday the supermarkets were packed from the time a weatherperson said the 's' word until the shelves were empty."

Yvette patted Alana's shoulder. "Poor thing. You have to put up with that."

"I'd accept your sympathy if it didn't sound so much like a gloat." She smiled and turned on the coffeemaker.

They sat at the kitchen table and talked about years past.

"I see everybody's up." Dr. Duke came into the kitchen and sat with his family.

"I thought we'd make the traditional southern breakfast, if Alana has the makings." Sarah stood.

"I made sure of it."

"Good. Of course, Alan, you're going to have to hide your doctor hat so we won't hear about the cholesterol."

"I can do that. Besides, if you eat in a healthy way most of the time, pigging out once in a while won't do permanent damage." He smiled. "I hope breakfast includes biscuits with lots of butter, too."

"A southern breakfast." Yvette said. "That means grits instead of home fries. Good."

"Girl, I remember a time when you wouldn't touch a grit," Alana reminded her sister.

"Grits are an acquired taste. A taste which I acquired while I was at Cheyney."

"A plus to your excellent education," Dr. Duke added. "Need any help?"

"We got it covered, Daddy. You just sit there and think about what you're going to do while you're here."

"I've already made plans. I'm going to look up a couple of my buddies. Jason Washington just got back from volunteer service in Africa." He smiled. "We were roommates in med school at Howard a lifetime ago. I'll also make my pilgrimage to the Paul Robeson and Marion Anderson houses, as I always do."

"No sled riding with us?" Yvette laughed, and the others added their laughter to hers.

"It wasn't funny at the time." Dr. Duke laughed.

Soon they were eating and talking about times past. Every so often, someone shared a memory that made them all laugh.

"I guess we can mention our plans now?" Mrs. Duke looked at her husband as she placed her napkin beside her empty plate.

"May as well."

"What plans?" Alana began stacking her dishes.

"I'm leaving the practice."

"Are you retiring?" Yvette stopped gathering the tableware.

"No, I'm not ready for that just yet."

"We're planning to move to South Carolina. Charleston, to be exact." Mrs. Duke added.

"South Carolina?"

"We'll be closer to both of you guys. Dealing with the long plane ride from California and jet lag has gotten to be too tiring. Besides, we don't see you two often enough. The climate in Charleston isn't too cold for too long."

"I've gotten accepted on the board of several hospitals in that area," Dr. Duke added. "They told me to just let them know when I'm available."

"When?"

"It won't be for at least four months. Probably closer to six. I have to make sure that my patients have a smooth transition to other doctors."

"That means if either of you have any plans to visit us on the West Coast, you'd better do it soon." Mrs. Duke said.

"I can't right now," Yvette said. "I'm not sure how much longer DCS Tech will be in business." She looked at their faces as she sat back down.

"What? What are you talking about?" Alana set the dishes on the counter and came back to the table. "When you got here, you didn't say anything about this."

"I decided to wait and tell everyone at the same time." She sighed. "Rumor has it that somebody is leaking company secrets. Several of our software programs were released by a competitor just before we could get them onto the market. Whoever did it had to have access to our source code."

"Couldn't they have been working on the same thing at the same time?"

"Maybe once. Twice would be a stretch. The code is too complicated for two different companies to develop them at the same time." She shrugged. "I also heard that somebody got fired after everybody was subjected to another background check. The leaks seem to have stopped, so maybe that was it. Of course, I'm way down on the totem pole, so I can only go by rumors." She shrugged. "Maybe they're wrong and the person was fired because of something else."

"Weren't the programs copyrighted?"

"It takes forever for a copyright case to work its way through the court system, and then we have to prove that we developed ours first." She sighed. "The cases are still pending."

"Rumors are too often true." Alana thought about how her own situation proved that. Later would be time enough to share her information with her family. It wasn't going to change; bad news seldom did.

"That's right." Yvette nodded. "Anyway, we were planning to go after government contracts, but we'll never get them unless we can be sure the leak is plugged. The last thing we need is for the government to find a reason not to accept our bid."

"Even if the company is in trouble, I know you're not worried about a job. Not with what you can do with a computer." Alana smiled. "You're almost as good as I am."

"Somebody get a tape recorder." Yvette smiled back. "I've got to have a record of this."

"When you girls were young, you had us worried that you'd hack into a government site that would get you into big trouble, and we'd only see you on visiting day." Mrs. Duke shook her head. "Just when we started to breathe easy about Alana, Yvette, you picked up where she left off."

"You know I wasn't copying her, no matter what she said."

"We know," Dr. Duke said. "It was that boy."

"Tom Casey." Yvette sighed. "I had a thing for him and he had a thing for computers." She shrugged. "So I learned about computers. I figured the brain might be another way to a man's heart."

"I never did understand why him," Alana said.

"He was so smart. I swear he knew more than our teachers did, but he never bragged nor showed off." She smiled. "He wasn't bad to look at, either." She shook her head. "In fact, he was one fine young man."

"You never told us why you broke up with him."

"I didn't tell because it was an ego thing for me. Here I was, a good-looking young lady."

"Um-hmm."

Yvette glared at Alana. "Other guys were looking at me and trying to get next to me, and the only thing Tom wanted to get next to was a computer. He was so deep I couldn't get through on any other level. I doubt if he even realized when we stopped seeing each other." Her smile widened. "He probably still doesn't know that there is more to life than computers. " She shrugged. "Anyway, I made a discovery of my own. I discovered that I was hooked on computers, so I stayed with them."

"I don't want your feelings to get hurt, Sis, but I heard that Tom is married and has three kids."

"Thanks. That's really good for my ego."

"You'll find somebody else."

"I'm not looking. If I trip over him or he trips over me, okay. If not, still okay." Yvette stood. "I'm changing the subject. Do you think the stores will be open today in spite of the snow?"

"You want to go shopping?"

"Only to Cheltenham Square. A couple of the stores have African clothes and art, and Liguorius Books carries Afrocentric titles that I can't find at home."

"We can call and see. I'll go with you, but you know I'm not into shopping."

"I know, but I don't understand it. You must have a defective gene. Let's finish in here so we can go." She turned to her mother. "Want to come?"

"Maybe another day. I told you this jet lag is something. Right now I'm going to sit on your window seat, admire your beautiful Christmas tree, and watch the falling snow. I'm not the doctor in the family, but I believe it's as soothing as watching fish in a tank."

Alana and Yvette finished in the kitchen and left with their mother's "drive carefully" riding with them.


The temperatures kept the snow in place over the next two days, but no new flakes joined them. From time to time Alana's thoughts stole to the man at the airport, but she managed to push them away.

# Chapter 4

Weak rays of the sun had barely begun to announce Christmas day when Alana slipped out of bed. She stifled a yawn and moved quietly through the sleeping house. Twenty minutes later she pulled the turkey from the refrigerator as the coffeemaker gave its last groans.

"So early?" Yvette covered a yawn and stretched.

"The bird refused to prepare itself again this year." Alana looked at Yvette. "Since you're up, you're elected to help."

"You think it's big enough?" Yvette stared at the huge turkey on the counter.

"You know you'll be making a sandwich this evening."

"There's enough for this evening, for three meals tomorrow, next week, next month . . ." she frowned at Alana. "When is Easter next year?"

"Don't be smart. It doesn't look good on you." She smiled. "You have to have a big turkey. Otherwise it will look like a chicken with a wannabe complex." Alana smiled.

"Okay, let's get this done. This poor bird is looking a bit peaked. Maybe a nice tan will help it." Yvette laughed. "I know you already cooked the giblets because I stole the liver last night."

"So what else is new?" Alana took the giblet juice from the refrigerator and got out the rest of the ingredients.

As they worked, they talked about the Philadelphia they grew up in, school days, and classmates. Then the conversation turned to Cheyney University and what changes had been made since Yvette graduated.

"If this weather breaks and the roads are clear, let's take a ride out there this week," Yvette said as Alana slid the roaster into the oven a little after seven.

"It's closed for Christmas break."

"I know, but I want to walk around the quad and the rest of the campus."

"I'm game if the weather cooperates."

As they worked, Alana gave Yvette an update on a few of their old friends. Then she brought up other little bits of news. What she did not talk about was her job as a reporter for the *Philadelphia Chronicle.*

"Let's go stare at the tree like we always do," Yvette said after she patted the final kente cloth napkin into place on the table.

"It doesn't take much to make a tradition for you, does it?"

"I do what I can." Yvette went into the living room and got comfortable on the couch. "I see the bubble lights still work. Not bad for antiques, huh?"

"You'd better not let Mom hear you call them that. She said 'Anything that I remember as a child cannot be an antique.'" Alana laughed. "I guess we'll just have to call them old." Yvette laughed, too. Then they sat staring at the colors bubbling.

"Okay," Yvette said about fifteen minutes later. She pointed to the pile of gifts spilling from under the tree. "Something under there is calling my name, and I need to answer it right now. I'm seriously considering waking Mom and Dad. I never did like the tradition of waiting until after breakfast to open the presents."

"We're already awake. Dare I ask how long you two

have been up?" Sarah Duke set her coffee mug on the table and sat on the couch. She tucked her batik print caftan around her. "My nose tells me the answer is long enough for the turkey to announce its presence."

"Your elder daughter got up before the crack of dawn, as usual."

"You haven't outgrown your tattling," Alana said. "Mom, didn't that get on your nerves when we were young?"

"A mother always wants to know what her children are doing."

"Always?"

"Almost always." She laughed.

"Merry Christmas, everybody." Alan Duke kissed his wife's cheek and squeezed each of his daughter's shoulders. "Anybody ready for breakfast?"

"Dad's waffles and sausage on Christmas morning. That tradition I like." Yvette hugged her father as she passed him on the way to the kitchen. The others followed.

Warm feelings settled over the kitchen table as the family talked about nothing important. The company was what mattered, not the conversation.

"Everybody finished?" Yvette stood and stacked the plates. Then she set the dirty dishes into the sink and gathered the silverware. "I'm cleaning up." She set them in the dishpan and hurried back to the table for the glasses.

"In record time, too," Alana said.

"My poor baby never was good at waiting." Sarah stood. "She was even born two weeks earlier than the doctor expected."

"Enough about me." Yvette set the empty platter on the counter. "Come on. I want you guys to see what I bought you." She led the others into the living room, with their laughter trailing behind them. Then she put in a CD of Christmas music.

"You give your gifts first, Alana. It's your home."

"How gracious of you, baby sis." She pulled a large flat package from against the wall beside the tree. "I thought you might like this," she said as she handed it to her parents.

Her mother slipped a finger under the tape holding the paper in the middle and the wrapping fell away.

"Oh, my." Sarah touched the edge of the carved gilt frame. An enlarged photo of her and Alan on their wedding day stared back at her.

"We were so young." Alan covered Sarah's hand with one of his and touched the frame with the other.

"And so in love." Alana smiled at them. "That is so obvious from the looks on your faces.

"And so scared," her father said.

"You are right about that. I was fresh out of college and going from my parents' house to live with a husband. I still remember how my stomach felt, as if a parade of bass drums were marching through it." She touched her husband's shoulder, leaned over and kissed him. "I have not regretted one moment of the last thirty-five years."

After a few seconds of savoring the moment, Alana spoke. "Now that I know you'll be moving, I'm not sure it was the right gift for you. It's just one more thing you'll have to pack."

"We're not going to talk about that now. It's a long way off," her mother said. "Let's enjoy the moment."

"I guess we should have broken our vows of silence about telling about our gifts." Yvette pulled a similar flat package from the side of the tree near her and handed it to her parents.

"You didn't," Alana said.

"Not quite." Yvette watched their parents unwrap her gift. A collage of family pictures, beginning with Alana's first Christmas and ending with last year, filled a frame. "This goes with it." She handed them a bulky package. "Open it." Her father pulled out a thick album. "The same pictures plus others are there."

"Great minds travel the same path," Alan smiled at his daughters.

"When did you take these pictures from the house?" Sarah asked.

"The last time we came out there. I knew you'd never miss them from that glorified shoe box."

"Let's open the other gifts before I start crying."

"If you think of how you're going to have to manage these on the plane, it will probably keep the tears away." Yvette laughed.

Alana opened a Palm Pilot from her parents and a leather bag from Yvette that Alana had raved over the last time they were together.

"You didn't buy one, did you?"

"No, but it has been nudging me every so often. Your turn." Alana handed her a package.

Yvette unwrapped a figure of a black woman with her hands on her ample hips and attitude screaming from her pose.

"It reminded me of you," Alana shrugged. She noticed Yvette's glare and laughed. "You know it does."

"Well, sometimes a little attitude is necessary."

They opened the other gifts. When the space under the tree was empty, their father handed each of them an envelope. "Open tickets for round trips to visit us. Come when you can fit it into your schedule."

Hugs were exchanged. Then Alana's clear alto picked up the Christmas song coming from the CD. One by one the others joined in. The Christmas spirit was not only alive, it was also strong as the family enjoyed each other's company. It was still present when they ate an early dinner.

Small talk tinged with family love stayed with them through the meal. That sense of love was still there when they took their dessert back to the living room.

"What language are you studying now?" Yvette asked Alana.

"Swahili. I finally found a teacher last spring at the International House on Penn's campus. I want to learn other African languages, too."

"How many languages have you learned so far?"

"I went through Spanish, Italian, and Portuguese. Those vocabularies are a lot alike. Then French, which was completely different."

"I know you showed a knack for learning languages when they taught Spanish in grade school, but all of those others." Her mother shook her head. "Don't you get them mixed up?"

"Sometimes." Alana laughed. "Especially when I'm reaching for a word in the new language. Then the word comes out in the last one I studied."

"Not a split personality, a fractured one."

"Thanks, Sis."

"Do you ever think you'll get a chance to use any of them?"

"I use Spanish a lot. Part of my assignment is to write stories concerning the local Hispanic communities, in addition to those with an African-American slant. A lot of Hispanics aren't comfortable with English." She grinned. "I've gotten quite good at it. They understand me. In fact, sometimes somebody will ask me where I'm from." She laughed. "I guess my Philadelphia accent isn't one they've heard before." She took a deep breath. "Maybe some of the others languages will be useful." She stared at each one in turn, then took a deep breath. "When I get a new job they might come in handy."

"A new job? You're leaving the *Chronicle?*"

"More like the *Chronicle* is leaving me."

"What? It's folding? After so many years?"

"We'd heard rumors for a while that the paper might close." She shrugged. "They made it official last week."

"So close to Christmas? Is one of the owners named Scrooge?"

"I guess they didn't want anybody to spend a lot of money or max out their credit cards when they might be out of a job for a while."

"What are you going to do?"

"I'm not sure. Some of the people are taking jobs with other local papers." She shrugged. "The pay won't be as much, but at least they won't have to relocate their families. A few are going to New York." She shrugged again. "I could go there, but probably not. The *Chronicle* offered us a generous severance package, especially since I've only been there for five years. I'm looking at this as my great opportunity. You know, I'm making lemonade with the lemons that life has given me."

"If you need anything from us, just let us know," her father said.

"Are you considering using your computer major to get into that field?" her mother asked.

"I'm afraid I'd lose the rest of my mind if I had to deal with computers all day every day." She shook her head. "Nope. My mind isn't as stable as Yvette's. I'm staying with journalism. I'm going to follow my dream." Three heads nodded in approval as Alana went on. "I want to get the kind of stories that my idol, Ed Bradley, does. After all, we have a lot in common." She smiled. "We both graduated from Cheyney and we're both journalists." She stared at Yvette. "Ever since you mentioned it, I've been thinking that maybe I'll look into the problem at DCS. Who knows? Maybe I can solve it."

"What?" The question came at her in stereo-plus-one.

"What do you mean?" Yvette got her question completed first.

"At one time I considered joining the CIA." She stared at each face in turn. "Well, I did. Did you know they put ads up at colleges just like normal businesses do?"

"The CIA? I know you didn't. Not for a second." Her mother frowned and put her hands on her hips. She shook her head. "I know I did not hear what I think I heard."

"I only thought about it for a little while."

"Lord," Sarah looked up. "I don't know if this is because of my hope for a strong independent daughter or my mother's 'I hope you have a daughter just like you some day' being fulfilled, but this child scares me with her notions sometimes. I thank you for the common sense that you mixed in with everything else in her." She stared back at Alana and she shook her head. "Now you're talking about going to DCS?"

"Mom, I know how to do investigative reporting. I've done it a few times before."

"I know you can do your job, baby, but this isn't a story about local health clubs or roofing rip-offs. This could be dangerous. Really dangerous." Sarah stared at her daughter.

"I know the stories that I've investigated weren't as big as this, but I know how to do this. You have to start small and I did. I'm sure Ed Bradley did, too. Like he did, I think I'm ready to move up."

The room was silent, as if the others were waiting for the last few minutes to disappear so they could start over. Finally her mother quit waiting.

"Promise me you'll think about this."

"I have thought about it."

"Then think about it some more. Please," her father added.

"I will." She smiled at him. "Enough about me. Tell me what you have planned for tomorrow."

She listened as her father spoke, but part of her attention was back on the last conversation. She would keep her promise to think about it, but she knew that her thinking would center on how best to put her plan into operation, not on changing it.

During the rest of the family's time together, Alana's idea never came up again and she was glad. The passing of time only strengthened her resolve.

By the time she took her parents to the airport to go home a few days later, she thought she had forgotten all about her almost accident when she had come to pick up Yvette, but the memory of it came charging back as if it had taken a vacation and was eager to get attention now that she was back at the scene. It didn't matter that this was a departure terminal. It didn't matter that she had never seen her mystery man's face, that he had said exactly one word to her. She shook her head. *I don't even know him. I wouldn't know him if he came right up to me.* She frowned. *Yes, I would.* Especially if he held me or said anything in that deep, sexy rumble.

She savored that idea for a few seconds before shaking it away. *This is ridiculous,* she thought as she walked her parents to the door. Still, she scanned the entire area.

"What's the matter?" her father asked.

"Nothing, Dad." She pulled her attention back to her mother and father.

"You've seemed preoccupied since you pulled up to the curb." Her mother smiled at her. "Don't worry about your job, baby. You're an intelligent person who is great at what you do. You'll get another position without any problem." She wrapped her arm through Alana's. "You might even decide to move to Charleston. You could get a head start. You know we'd love to have you closer to us."

"I'm not worried. Really." She smiled back. *How can I tell them that I'm looking for a man that I wouldn't recognize if he were standing next to me?* She glanced to each side of her. Then she shook her head. *Not unless he held me close like before.*

She tried not to remember how his arms felt around her. She sighed. This felt like something from a movie or a romance novel. Regret crept in as she shook her head. *Nothing ever comes of people meeting like that. Even fate would give a person more to work with.*

She gave each parent a final hug, then watched as they went through the doors. She saw them show their tickets and picture identification to the uniformed guard at the beginning of the line.

She glanced around once more, both inside and outside the building, to see if she saw anyone who looked as if he had strong arms, a solid chest, and a deep voice that would have stayed in her memory for so long. Then she left.

The same lack of concentration affected her when she took Yvette to catch her flight home a week later.

"Okay, Sis. I have tried to ignore it, but I can't." Yvette turned to her before she went inside. "You don't really think you'll see him, do you?"

"What are you talking about?"

"You don't even know what he looks like." Yvette held up her hand when Alana started to speak. "Don't try to deny it. I know you. You're looking for that guy who caught you." She shook her head. "It looks like you're still caught."

Alana stared for a few seconds. Then she shrugged. "I know it's silly, but I can't help but think that I'll see him, that something is supposed to happen between us."

"I will not explore that 'something.' I will remind you that Mom always said that you had an oversized imagination. I see you never got rid of it." She touched Alana's arm and leaned close. "Forget it. Look for a real man instead of the Phantom Rescuer." She winked. "The real deal will be a lot more fun."

"I know. I gotta get him off my mind." She sighed. "I'm not really looking for anyone. I just . . ." She shrugged. "I don't know. There was something about him." She shook her head again. "Okay, I'm making a belated New Year's resolution: Forget about him."

"Good idea." Yvette hugged her. "Well, this is it. Keep me posted on what you intend to do. I'm glad you decided to come to Orlando, and I'm looking forward to having you close, but you should get a normal job. I know you're hanging on to your crazy idea, but maybe the world is not ready for a female Ed Bradley."

"There are no normal reporting jobs."

"Some jobs are closer to normal than others." Yvette frowned. "What you're thinking about isn't really a job, anyway. What you're planning to do is freelance."

"Some of the best stories come from freelancing."

"I sure hope something else gets your attention before you leave the *Chronicle*."

"Maybe so." Alana kissed her cheek. "You'd better go before you miss your plane."

"Let me know as soon as you decide when you're coming."

"You know I will."

Alana gave her a last hug, then watched her pull her luggage through the door. After Yvette had moved on, Alana went back to her car. As she slipped into the driver's seat, she tried not to see if anyone fit the memory rooted deeply in her mind.

# Chapter 5

A month after Christmas, Keith stood in front of the door to the airport. It was already afternoon, but the weather hadn't softened. It didn't matter to him; he was oblivious to the raw January wind and rain. He would have been unaware even if a blizzard were doing its thing.

This was his second visit to the airport since a few days before Christmas, and he acted now just as he had then. When he had picked up Dave, Dave had noticed his preoccupation and had questioned him about it. His brother had been kind not to question his excuse about expecting to see a friend, even though they both knew that was lame. He shook his head. *I know I won't see her.* Still, he scanned the crowd looking for the woman who would have fallen if he hadn't caught her. *Irrational. And stupid. That was arrivals. This is departures.* He frowned. Calling himself names didn't stop him from looking. Or thinking about her, as he had been doing too much ever since that day.

He shook his head. *Why am I looking for her? Why her?* Even as he asked himself, he could almost feel her against his body, her hands against his chest. *Stop it before your body lets everybody know what you're thinking about.*

He released a long, slow breath. Just one more thing about himself that he didn't understand.

After he checked his luggage, and again after he went

through the upstairs security checkpoint, he allowed his gaze to touch each face around him, lingering for a second on any female remotely resembling his woman. *What am I doing?* When *looking for my woman* formed in his head, he frowned. *My woman? She's not* my *anything.* He shook his head at the illogical disappointment that flew though him. *Get a life.* He frowned. *Why does it seem as if she's meant to be part of this one?*

He sat in the waiting area and picked up the copy of the *Chronicle* that somebody had left on the seat beside him. Headlines screamed in heavy black letters. He shook his head. *Another newspaper folding. Don't people read anymore?*

He glanced through the pages until his row was called to board, but his mind was as far away from the newspaper as it could get. *It's a good thing I don't have to answer questions about what I just read.* He set the paper back on the seat. *Maybe somebody else will get something from it.*

Soon he was walking into the Orlando Terminal from the ramp. *At least I won't waste my time looking for her here.*

He tried to adjust to the change of weather as he picked up his car. Work hours were over, but he drove to Dave's office as they had planned. In spite of there being no similarities between here and Philadelphia, part of his mind was still back, a little over a month ago, to that city. Back to the woman who took up too much space in his thoughts. *I've got to get these daydreams under control,* he thought as he saw Dave in the lobby. *And now.*

He greeted his brother; then they got on the elevator. As soon as they reached the offices, Dave handed him a folder.

"So. What do you think?" Dave asked a few minutes later. "Is everything good to go?" He paced in front of the floor-to-ceiling window beside his desk, but he didn't look out.

"Listen, little brother, wearing a hole in this carpet

won't make a bit of difference." Keith closed the folder in front of him and shifted in his chair. "I'm still not sure. I know you want to know yesterday, but it ain't gonna happen. Remember the tortoise in that fable? I don't intend to move that slowly, but I do plan to be thorough." His stare intensified. "And I plan to succeed."

"But we haven't had a problem since I fired that programmer, Marge." He stopped moving and stared at Keith. "Our new software game had the Christmas market to itself. Nothing else came out before or since that resembled it or anything else of ours, even remotely. We must have caught her before she could pass the information on."

"Who says you only had one problem?" Keith watched realization replace the puzzled expression on Dave's face.

"You think—"

"I think I need to look into it some more. What I did before Christmas was just preliminary, using your paperwork. You want to make sure before you bid for government contracts, right? With them, one strike and you're out forever. Especially now." His face softened. "Give me a little more time." He frowned. "DCS isn't in serious financial trouble, is it?"

"Not yet." Dave cracked a knuckle.

"But close, if you're punishing your knuckles." Keith stood. "I'll find out if you still have anything to worry about. If something is there, I promise I'll find it. If not, I'll find that out, too."

"Okay. Sorry I'm so impatient. We can wait for a while." He sighed. "Not long, though."

"Good. You know I'll work as quickly as I can. Now, first you hire me."

"Hire you?"

"As of now, I'm not your brother. I'm your new project

supervisor, manager, whatever is needed so I have freedom to nose around without it being obvious. If somebody is dirty, we don't want to give him time to clean up and cover his"—he stared at Dave—"or *her* tracks."

"You got it." Dave frowned. "Let's say a headhunter recruited you in anticipation of our expansion into government contracts."

"Works for me." Keith smiled. "Unless I come up with something better. If so, I'll let you know." The two laughed together. "Also, any contact we have like this will be after hours. From now on I'm Keith Rankin."

"Rankin? As in that little town outside Pittsburgh where Grandmom Waddy grew up?"

"That's the one. The less you and I can be connected, the better."

"You always were thorough."

"I don't like unsolved puzzles." His face looked as if the laugh had never happened. "I learned that they can hurt you if you overlook them." He stared at Dave. "And I haven't always been thorough."

"Everybody makes mistakes."

"Yeah. Some are more costly than others."

Dave looked as if he were going to say something more, but then changed his mind. He went to a file cabinet in a corner. "Let me give you background info on the company and its workings." He began pulling out files. "You also need to know what we're working on right now."

"And information on what was stolen." Keith chewed on his bottom lip. "I need as many specifics as you can give me."

"Will do." Dave added to the pile. "Let me give these to Jamila to copy and I'll get them to you tomorrow."

"Is that copier operational?" Keith pointed to the machine against the far wall. "The fewer people who know what we're looking at, the better."

"You suspect Jamila? She's been with me since the beginning."

"I suspect everybody, little brother." Keith managed a slight smile. "Everybody except you." He stared at him. "And we have to make sure you haven't done anything to make the company vulnerable." He looked at Dave's shocked expression. "Just making it real. I doubt you've done anything to help your spy. These things usually don't involve the top." His smile widened. "You folks up there usually don't know as much of the details as you think you do." His smile widened. "Especially when it's my brother we're talking about."

Dave frowned. "I'd object, but I think you might be right." His frown deepened. "I hope I didn't make things easier for them." He stared at the papers in his hand, added them to the pile, and then began copying.

As Dave worked, they discussed the details of Keith starting work at DCS, but part of Keith's mind was already on his next move.

Hours later he left, avoiding the security guard. Keith had a ream of papers crammed into his briefcase. He shook his head. A suitcase would have been better, but it would have attracted too much attention. His success depended upon his ability to blend in.

He went to the executive suite he had rented for the time he'd be in Orlando. Long term, he was sure, regardless of what Dave hoped. He set the papers on the desk, made a pot of decaf in the efficiency kitchen, and began looking through the papers for anything that might help him.

From time to time, a full face surfaced from his memories even though he hadn't had more than a few minutes to look at it. In spite of the crush of people who had been crowding that too-small airport space, she had grabbed his attention from the second she had rushed into the terminal like a tan whirlwind. Her face had been left exposed by the sophisticated knot of hair that had been pinned at the back of her head. If she was trying to look older, it hadn't worked. She looked like a young woman trying to look grown-up.

His imagination took his memory and ran with it. Just the image of her no-nonsense hairdo made him wish he had pulled out the pins and let her thick black hair sift through his fingers. Regardless of the consequences, it would have been worth it. Did her hair curl when it was loose? Or just lie against her shoulders?

Whenever her image appeared, as it did now, he allowed her to stay for a short while. He shook his head. *I only saw her for a few minutes, but it was long enough for me to know that she had a dimple in her honey-brown cheek.* He smiled. Her full lips had been curved up in a smile before she slipped. *How would her lips have felt against mine? What if it had been me she was coming to meet?* He closed his eyes and remembered the feel of her against him. Then he shook her away and got back to the papers in front of him.


He worked for hours until he gave in to hunger. He shrugged. *I have to go food shopping anyway. May as well get that over with now.* He left the papers, but his mind was still turning over the information he had read so far. Then it slid to his mystery woman again. *Who is she? And why do I care?*

He stopped at the superstore on Route 192 to buy a paper shredder. He opted for the more expensive one that made confetti instead of one that just cut strips that could be put back together if somebody wanted to badly enough.

Anybody who looked at him while he shopped would have thought he was angry at the machines. They wouldn't know about the unanswered questions that had nothing to do with business or machines but that were nagging him. Questions about a beautiful woman.

His frown that had been evident since he left his place was still settled in when he stopped to get a take-out meal from Johnson's Diner on Robinson Street. Dave had recommended it, and as fussy as he was, it must be worth the trip.

Keith went back and worked as he ate. Dave had declared the food to be the best in the country, but Keith would have to taste it another time to find out for himself. He was too engrossed for the taste to register. In fact, in alternating between the pen he was using to take notes, and the fork, more than once the wrong tool found its way to his mouth. When that happened, he stared at the pen, switched to the fork, and continued.

Finally, at midnight Keith looked at the shredder basket. It looked as if it were waiting for a parade. Keith reached in and tumbled the pieces even more. He picked up a handful and stared at it before letting it sift through his fingers. *Enough.* He stood, stretched his shoulders, and then got ready for bed.

The same face that had plagued his concentration off and on all evening danced back strong, as if determined to make up for the time it had been shoved away. This time Keith let it stay.

*I wonder who she was? She must live in Philly since she was picking somebody up. Somebody named Yvette. He frowned. Sister? Cousin? Friend? At least it was another female.* His face softened. *What if her smile had been for me? What if things were different and she had been meeting me?* He shook his head. *She didn't even see me, not until I stepped from the side and caught her.* He shook his head again. *She hadn't even really seen me then.* He blinked. *That's my fault, all my fault. I could have introduced myself. I could have started a conversation. I could have invited her to have a cup of coffee.* He released a heavy breath. *It's better this way. It doesn't cause any damage to think about her. If she were in my life, I would end up hurting her.*

He crawled into bed still thinking about her despite his efforts to reason with himself. He sighed. *Maybe she'll stay with me through the night. Nobody would get hurt and it might help me sleep.* He drifted off, clutching that thought as a hope.

"Captain, it's falling apart. Everything is falling apart."

"We can do this," Keith answered in a whisper that matched Sawyer's. "We only need a few more minutes. We won't get a second chance at this. This mission is important. HQ needs that info. A lot of lives depend on it. Just a little longer."

"But Captain . . ."

A spray of gunfire cut off Sawyer's sentence and he stopped talking forever. The rest of the team returned fire. Somebody groaned, but Keith concentrated on the file cabinet drawer he had just popped open. His fingers rifled through the folders before he grabbed one.

He snapped quick pictures as he shifted each sheet of paper to the front, then slipped the file back into place.

"We're outta here." He didn't allow himself to hesitate or to stare too long at what used to be Sawyer.

Rassan took Sawyer's position at point and Keith slung Sawyer over his shoulder and followed Rassan and the others into the woods surrounding the hut. Jackson fired a round behind them, and nobody fired back any more.

The only sound for the next fifteen minutes was the soft shuffle of their feet as they made a path over decaying leaves to the boat hidden in the brush beside the river, waiting to take them to the rendezvous point. *"Captain? We're here, Captain. You can put him down now."*

Keith looked at Rassan. Then he looked around. How long had he been standing there? He laid Sawyer carefully on the ground and stared at his once brown shirt. Red covered it, the same red that was probably the reason for the stickiness on the back of his own shirt. Nobody could leak that much blood and live. Still, as Keith watched, Sawyer's mouth opened.

*"Captain, we should . . ."* His words stopped, but his eyes accused Keith. *"We . . ."* A slow trickle made its way down the side of his mouth.

*"We had to do this. They need this info. You know that."* Keith begged him to understand, as if understanding would reverse the flow of life from him. *"You see what it's like going in with the wrong info or with no info at all."*

*"How many. . . ?"* Sawyer didn't finish that question. Nor did he ask any others ever again.

Keith sat up and tried to shake away the nightmare, which was one of several that visited him regularly. Sawyer's words, Sawyer himself, and the others faded with the forest. Keith knew they hadn't disappeared. They had just retreated deeper into his mind to wait for their next chance.

Later he had finished Sawyer's question about 'How many?' He knew Sawyer's next words would have been 'have to die.' The answer was: none. That had been his last mission, his last assignment, almost the last time he had worn the uniform. In spite of reassurances from the others on the mission and HQ, in spite of hearing of how much good the info did and how many lives it saved, he had left the service.

He sat in bed and waited as his heartbeat fell back to

normal. He wasn't sorry about leaving the service, only sorry that he hadn't left one mission sooner.

He pulled off his sweat-drenched T-shirt and wiped his forehead with it. Then he got up, pulled on a pair of shorts and a fresh T-shirt, and slipped into the predawn darkness.

The street of single houses a block away from his building was as quiet as it should have been. Most people were probably turning over to grab another couple hours of sleep. Keith jogged to the end of the block and turned onto a side street. Would he ever be one of "most people"?

The vision of a beautiful, peaceful face stayed with him through the miles he used up while trying to leave his failure behind. He welcomed her, allowed himself to imagine that she was in his life and that his life was as normal as anybody else's was.

The sun had just started to share its light as Keith jogged home slowly. Again, his demons had retreated for a while. He knew it wasn't forever, but he'd use whatever time they gave him.

He stretched his legs on the curb outside his building. Another jogger emerged from further down in the complex. Keith looked at the man as they nodded at each other. He allowed himself to envy the well-rested look on the man's face. Then he went inside to face the day.

# Chapter 6

Before Keith could speak as he entered the offices of DCS, Jamila greeted him.

"Good morning. May I help you?" She wore a corporate receptionist's smile.

"I'm Keith Rankin." Keith smiled back.

"Dave told me to expect you. I'll let him know you're here." She spoke on the intercom, then looked back at him. "He'll be right out. May I get you a cup of coffee?"

Keith declined the offer. He had enough trouble sleeping without adding caffeine to his system.

Dave came out a few minutes later, and Keith followed him as he worked his way through the cubicles and offices, stopping at each and introducing Keith to the workers. Keith smiled at the appropriate times, but his focus was on each face and the reaction to the news that he was going to be involved in the projects. Surprise showed on some, apprehension on others. Only normal when a new person was hired, especially somebody not starting at the bottom of the ranks. There was no such thing as job security nowadays. If anybody's reaction was from more than that, he'd find out.

By the time they finished the tour, Keith had made mental notes about each employee, but he was far from forming any conclusions. He hadn't expected to. It was way too early.

He followed Dave back to his office.

"What do you think?" Dave asked as soon as he closed the door.

"I saw the size of the offices before, but I didn't realize how many people it takes to keep your company running."

"What did you expect? Two nerd types peering at computer screens in a room that looks like a science lab?"

"No." Keith smiled. "At least three." He shrugged. "I didn't realize how many facets there are to bringing a computer game to market."

"Ours is a small company. You should take a look at the bottom line of the big guys. Kids control a lot of money in this country." Dave smiled. "Our games are geared to kids, but it's not just kids who like them. Adults hold tournaments throughout the country. Some companies specialize in games slanted just to adults, but we don't. Nevertheless, computer games are big business. I mean big."

"I think I need to read up on the industry itself so I can get the whole picture."

"Here." Dave took two books from a shelf. "Start with these." He smiled. "There are plenty more where those came from." His smile left. "Do we need to do anything else right now?"

"No." Keith shook his head. "I'll settle into my office. It should be cleared out by now." He stared at Dave. "Of course, Harry might be waiting for me, wielding a keyboard." He shrugged. "I can't blame him for being mad. I'd feel the same way if I had to leave a plush office so the new guy could have it."

"He'll get over it. It was time for him to make an attitude adjustment. He's good at what he does. The problem is he knows it, and makes sure everybody else knows it, too." He smiled. "I'll give him back his office after you finish. See you for dinner?"

"Maybe."

"As the guys in the commercial say, 'Ya gotta eat.' Much as I would like for you to, you can't do it all in one day."

"Give me a call before you leave and I'll let you know."

He went to the office Dave had given him. A disgruntled Harry was moving the last of his things to the office at the end of the cluster and against the far wall. Dave had told Keith that they called it the detention room. The only person who would be happy there would be somebody coming from a cubicle. Not only was it smaller than other offices and away from most daily activities, but, unlike most corner offices, it had no window. Definitely a step down.

Keith shrugged. *The lack of a window wasn't required for Harry: he was far from the type to jump out because he considered this move a negative.* Keith shrugged again. *I, on the other hand, don't need a window.* What he did need was an office in the middle of the action so he could observe the movements of the employees.

He opened the top drawer of the file cabinet. Copies of all of the projects, past, present and future, were arranged neatly as if waiting for his examination. Only he and Dave knew that he had already checked the most recent ones. The others he'd examine later.

He went to the now-clear walnut desk and sat in the chair. The desktop would still be clear no matter how long he was here. Neither photos nor personal items would disturb the surface. He always did travel light and he had never been one to mix business with pleasure. Still, just once, it would be nice to have something of personal importance to clutter his space.

He leaned back. *Where to next? Where will I go when I'm finished here? In which city will my next sparse office be located?*

A now-familiar face insinuated itself into the front of his mind. In spite of himself, he was getting used to her. *How can I find her?* He frowned. *And what would I do if I did?*

He picked up a pen, but the marks he made on the pad in front of him were meaningless. His mind tried to form a plan of action for finding her.

Too long a time later, when he had finished writing, what was on the paper still didn't mean a thing. He forced his mind back to the job he had to do for Dave. He revised his plans in his head, still not putting anything on paper. He was still at it when Dave convinced him to go with him to eat. He didn't refuse. *Maybe she won't haunt me if I'm with somebody.*

Keith followed Dave to Johnson's Diner, and this time, in spite of the woman on his mind, he really tasted the food.

"The best meal I've had since I can't remember when." Keith laid his napkin on the table.

"Told you so." Dave patted his stomach. "I'm surprised you tasted it, though. You looked as if you were somewhere else the whole time we were eating."

"I have things on my mind." Keith stood. "See you tomorrow."

The next day he started digging.


Over the next few weeks Keith methodically examined each aspect of DCS on the surface. Then he began to bore deeper.

He used up January and started on February. He hadn't uncovered much, but he wasn't ready to quit. He hadn't touched some aspects of the company. *Who was in a position to not only know what went into these games, but also have the opportunity and expertise to manipulate things somewhere during the process?*

With those questions in mind, and despite the woman trying to dominate his thoughts, he dug some more.

# Chapter 7

Alana put the crystal paperweight on top of the papers in the box on her desk, or what used to be her desk. She'd sort through the papers when she got home. It was too depressing being alone in what should be a busy newsroom. She sighed. Hopefully most of the papers could be thrown out. She already had a car trunkload to take to Florida with her. She released a big breath. *I should have waited before I shipped that last box of stuff.* She shrugged and took one final look around.

Her bookshelves were as bare as they had been five years ago when she had been assigned this section of the large pressroom. She blinked several times. *Back then my goal had been to get assigned to one of the real offices with four walls of my own.* She stared across the other bare desks and out the windows at the far side of the room.

She couldn't see it or hear it, but she knew Broad Street traffic was moving at a considerable speed down below.

She glanced at the list of names and new addresses and workplace numbers on the top sheet of paper in the box. *How many of the people at the farewell get-together last night would really keep in touch?* She shrugged. *I'll probably be one of those who won't.* She took one last look around to make sure she had everything. Then she picked up the box and went toward the elevator.

Her footsteps clicked across the concrete floor and

echoed off the empty walls as if trying to make the room sound busy. When the elevator came, she stepped inside without looking back. She was already gone.

A slight ripple of sadness moved through her, but she calmed it. *This is progress. I'm moving forward.* She blinked rapidly. *It's just the dust that collects in this old building irritating my eyes.* She closed her eyes and rode down, leaving her old job and a lot of memories twelve floors above.

The elevator doors opened. She balanced the box against the wall, wiped her eyes and stepped out.

"Bye, Mr. Sloan," she said to the security guard standing at the door. He straightened as if trying to make the uniform fit his slight build better. It didn't work.

"You got everything? I don't want to have to be bothered letting you back in the way I had to do for too many of the others." He wore his usual glare. "I'd expect big-time reporters to be organized enough to make sure they had everything. Of course, I'm just a dumb old security guard. My time's not as important as theirs." His glare softened a bit. "At least you always spoke to me. You didn't act as if I'm invisible. Most of those others, they never took the time to even learn my name." He stared at her. "You got yourself another job?"

"Not yet." The question surprised her. She had never gotten more that a mumbled 'morning' or 'bye' from him. "You?"

"The agency will assign me somewhere. With times being like they are, everybody's got a need for security guards."

"Well, you take care, now."

"You, too." He busied his hands with the papers in the clipboard on the desk. "If you get a chance, you can let me know through the agency how you're doing."

"I will."

Alana took a deep breath before she went out into the late February cold. If March acted in its usual way, the cold would carry over through most of it, and maybe into April. She swallowed hard. *If things go according to my plans, I'll be gone before then.* She shivered. *This cold is one thing I won't miss.*

She glanced at the temperature gauge in her car and as soon as it moved slightly from the 'C,' she turned on the heater. Now that she knew she'd be leaving Philly, it was as if her body had already adjusted to Florida temperatures. She turned the heat up as far as it could go and rode home dreading getting out of the car to go even the few feet into her apartment.

Once she reached her place, she dashed from the car as well as she could, juggling the box for the last time. She fumbled with her keys before she slipped inside. Quickly she set the box on the hall table, locked the door behind her, and turned up the thermostat. It wouldn't make the apartment warm up any quicker, but it was comforting to see the dial turned to 80. Then she picked up the box and the phone, moved to the living room, and settled at the end of the couch closest to the radiator.

"This is it," she told Yvette when she answered the phone. "I left the *Chronicle* for the last time today. It was kind of spooky: that big pressroom was never quiet the whole five years I worked there. Today I know I could have heard a pin drop if I had tried it." She dumped the contents of the box beside her onto the couch. "Are you ready for me down there?"

"As ready as I will ever be. Alana . . ." Silence took up the space waiting to be filled. "I'm still not sure this is best for you. You're welcome to stay with me for as long as you want." Her words raced as if trying to catch up with something. "You know that's not a problem. It's just that . . ." Again silence took over until she found more words. "We haven't had any problem with leaks at DCS since I got back after the holidays. Yesterday Dave told us that we're going ahead with plans to obtain the federal contracts. We're talking high-tech sensitive stuff, so Dave must feel that everything is secure now. He even hired a new consultant."

"Uh-huh."

"I'm serious. Why don't you get a job on one of the newspapers down here? We have a lot of them in this area and I'm sure you can find a job on one of them. We have a large, growing Hispanic population, so you could use your knowledge of the language. You can make your lemonade with life's lemons that way." She laughed, but it was weak. "Ed Bradley isn't going anywhere anytime soon, anyway."

"We'll talk when I get there. I'm leaving in a week, give or take a day or two. I already took care of any loose ends here." She glanced around the apartment. "I didn't expect to feel this way, but I'm gonna miss this place."

"I'll gather the information about the area newspapers so you won't have to do that after you get here."

"Okay, but don't spend too much time on it." She hesitated before she continued. "I'm not calling you again before I leave, so this is it until we do a face-to-face. If I don't show up on your doorstep in exactly nine days, which gives me two days to stop over on the drive down, do not, I repeat, do not notify the state or any other kind of police. I have identification. Yours is the first name to contact if something happens to me, so if I *am* laid up in the hospital or they find me in a ditch beside the road, they will notify you. Don't call them."

"Don't joke about something like that."

"Joking never made anything happen. I just want to

make sure you don't fall apart if I don't ring your bell in exactly seven-plus-two days. Okay?"

"Okay. Drive carefully. I don't want any police officers coming to see me."

Alana hung up and began sorting through the pile on the couch. She hoped Yvette wouldn't go through too much trouble getting the information from the newspapers. *I might end up as a reporter for one of the papers, but not until after I check out DCS.*

Exactly one week later as planned, Alana put the last of her things into her trunk and drove away from the curb before seven o'clock in the morning. She had been surprised at her emotions each time she closed the door on some part of her Philadelphia life. If somebody had mentioned her ties to this city, she would have explained that she only stayed here because of her job. Now she knew better. She would miss much more than the soft pretzels and cheesesteaks. *I hope they sell coconut Tastykakes in Orlando.* She sighed. *I'll miss the Eagles. No more home games with men painted green and white.* She swallowed hard. She was going to miss the city itself. The next time she came back here, if there were a next time, she'd be a visitor.

She glanced back once, but that was all. *I'll never find my mystery man now.* The thought crept into her mind. She tried to get rid of feelings of regret, but didn't succeed. *I wonder who he was. Why was he at the airport? Just arriving or waiting for somebody?* She frowned. *Why am I spending so much energy on something that never happened? Something that can never happen?* She shook her head. *You can't always reason with yourself.*

She drove along Stenton Avenue, glad she didn't have to go anywhere near the airport.

She realized that when she stopped for the night, she should be at least as far as Roanoke Rapids, Virginia.

She quelled the fluttering in her stomach and drove toward the Blue Route. By the time rush hour started to get serious, she'd be way down I-95 heading south.

# Chapter 8

The sparse group coming into the glass-walled building early included Keith Rankin. He leaned against the wall opposite the doors, watching the entrance. Unless somebody knew differently, they would think he was waiting for somebody.

He filtered the bits of conversations that came to him. *Nothing of importance.* He shrugged. He hadn't expected anything. This was just a means of checking for habits. No one would notice that he paid a little more attention to the DCS employees who were at the office yesterday. Two women walked by and he recognized them from one of the departments. He shifted his position, but he still overheard snatches of their conversation.

"Last night was the last straw, Marcie. I can't deal with his insecurities anymore. I broke it off."

"After so long?"

"I thought he was gonna change. I shoulda known better. Men don't change unless they think they need to and Steve didn't think he needed to. I had to kick him to the curb. I shoulda done it a long time ago."

They passed Keith and went to the newspaper shop further down the lobby.

*Doesn't she know that some insecurities are well founded?* Keith shook his head slightly. *Not my business.*

He resumed his relaxed stance and focused back on

the entrance. Suddenly he straightened. *That can't be her. I don't deserve to be so lucky.* He watched a young woman step confidently into the lobby. Her French twist and charcoal gray two-piece dress allowed her to blend in with the other women coming to work. *What's she doing here?*

Keith waited for her to pass him and take the elevator. Then he would speak to her, remind her of how they met in the Philadelphia airport before Christmas. He frowned as she casually took a position on the low window ledge on the other side of the door instead. Instantly his mind shifted to work mode. She crossed her legs and opened a newspaper and his mind shifted again.

Although he could have read the headlines, he had no idea what they said. His attention was on the full legs so elegantly crossed. Her skirt barely exposed the top of her knee and teased with a side glimpse of thigh, but that didn't stop him from imagining. Or remembering the brief while that those thighs were pressed against his. *I know that's her.* He smiled. *If I could hold her, I'd have proof.* He shifted away from the wall. *What can I say to her? Remember me? I hope you do because I sure remember you.* He smiled even though his body tightened uncomfortably at the brief memory. *Should I approach her?* He shook his head. *I can't. I'm on a job.* He exhaled. *But I can look at her.* Then his investigative mind took over again and he frowned.

*What* is *she doing here? She lives in Philly. If she's here on business, why is she hanging out in the lobby? Is she waiting for somebody?* He eased his stance and relaxed a bit. Maybe that was it.

He watched her scan each person who came into the building as if searching for somebody. Suddenly, another woman caught Keith's attention, another familiar face. He straightened. It was the second woman from the airport, the one the first had called Yvette. He focused his attention on *her* now. He expected the two women to greet each other as they had at the airport. They didn't.

The second woman saw the first, stopped suddenly, and frowned. The first shook her head slightly. If Keith hadn't given her his full attention, he wouldn't have noticed it. He frowned as the second woman hesitated, then went to the elevators. From the look on her face, she was not happy about this. *Does she work for DCS? She wasn't in the office yesterday. I would have remembered her if she had been. What's going on?*

The woman, whose image had visited him regularly since a few days before Christmas, glanced around. She let her glance slip right past him.

Keith tried not to be disappointed. After all, she hadn't seen his face. She had been too busy trying not to fall. At the time he had regretted the fact that she didn't notice what he looked like. Now he saw it as a good thing. He leaned back and waited to see what she would do next.

Alana stared at her newspaper, but she wasn't reading. She steadied her hands and took a deep breath. *Part one is over and Yvette hasn't blown it for me, at least not yet.*

Yvette had taken yesterday off and spent the entire day trying to get Alana to change her mind. She may as well have gone to work. Alana frowned. She hadn't told her that she was coming here today. She hadn't wanted the hassle. She watched Yvette glare at her once more before she got into an elevator. Alana sighed. She still wasn't sure Yvette wouldn't mess things up later.

She glanced over the top of the paper as another group of people came into the lobby. Two men went to the travel agency and unlocked the door. Soon after a woman opened the flower shop. Alana knew it was too early for the cleaning staff, but she still wanted to see everybody. If she could have waited in the DCS offices, it would have made things simpler. She would know which of these corporate people were going there. She turned the newspaper page and shrugged. *I'll bet Ed Bradley's stories don't come easily, either.*

While she glanced at everybody who came into the building, she formulated alternate plans to present to Yvette just in case. One of them had to work. She couldn't have come all this way for nothing.

She watched for the uniform of a janitorial service. *If I had asked Yvette the name of the company that cleans DCS offices, this would be easier.* She frowned. *If Yvette had told me. Which she probably wouldn't.* Her frown deepened. *Sometimes that girl can be so stubborn.*

Alana kept watch, hoping for a break. She was not going to consider that there might be a service entrance that the cleaning help used.

Fifteen long minutes later, she saw a woman in dark blue pants and a light blue shirt. Alana couldn't read the logo on the shirt from here, but she knew this woman wasn't dressed for a higher-up job. She smiled, but her smile changed to a frown when another woman called to the first. She wore a uniform, too, but hers was tan. Alana's frown deepened. *Which one cleans DCS?* She sighed. *How many different janitorial services work in this building?* She shook her head. *I'll have to ask Yvette the name of the company after all, and hope she tells me.* She took a deep breath and released it slowly. *I still have to convince her that I can do this without being in any danger.* She chewed on her lip. That would be the hard part since there was some element of danger. She shrugged. No matter how simple it seemed, every story has the potential for danger. She nodded. *Maybe that argument will work on Yvette.* She shrugged. *I hadn't planned to talk to the cleaning woman today, anyway. I can't approach the woman dressed corporate, but looking for a jan-*

*itorial job.* She shook her head. *At least I learned that they use the main entrance.*

Alana noted that both women wore their hair pulled back into ponytails and both had clear faces. Nothing fancy and no makeup except, maybe, a pale lipstick. They also looked Latino. She checked her watch. Almost eleven. She would assume that this was the usual time for the cleaning people to come. *I'll be here tomorrow. If I have to, I'll talk to both of them and make up a story about wanting to clean the DCS offices.*

The crowd slowed to a few people every now and then. Then there were large gaps of time between people coming into the building, and many of them were in a rush. Alana glanced around the lobby. Her gaze rested on the man sitting on the ledge at an angle to her. She frowned as it registered. *He's been there for a while. What is he doing here? Is he making connections with his contact from DCS? Is he involved with the problem? Will it be that easy?*

She made her gaze move on, but her mind stayed on the man. He was sitting, but he looked tall. He looked as if he would fit in with the running backs in the football games that held her attention every Sunday. She frowned. *It won't be the Eagles any more unless they're playing a Florida team.* She shook her head. *Focus, Alana.*

She stared at the security guard's desk blocking the elevators. He seemed to take a quick glance at the ID tags pinned on those who went past him and onto an elevator. Anybody who didn't wear one signed the book on the counter. *Yet another reason why I had to hang out down here.* She stared at the guard for a short while, but she could still see the mystery man out the corner of her eye.

*If he works here, why isn't he at work? If he has an appointment, why doesn't he go? Have I stumbled onto something already?* She frowned again. *I hope not. He is one fine man.*

She allowed her stare to stay on him. *Superfine with a capital S.* She sighed. *Focus, Ms. Investigative Reporter. Focus.*

She continued turning pages of the newspaper, but her gaze found the door every few seconds. Maybe another cleaning service worked in the building, too.

The number of people entering the building slowed to almost none. Then a few came from the elevators. Alana glanced at her watch. *Lunchtime.* She smiled as she folded her paper and stood. She still didn't know which service was used by DCS, but she was satisfied with today. Things had gone better than she had expected.

She left the building, planning to come back the next day, but not as early. She glanced at her watch. She would need every one of the hours left until Yvette came home to think of a way to calm her.

"What were you doing there?" As soon as Yvette walked in her house, she skipped the 'hello' preliminaries and cut right to the chase. "Why did you come to the building today?" She set her briefcase on the white wrought-iron table in the hall.

"I wanted to check out the situation."

"I thought you were going to get a job with a newspaper." She slipped off her shoes and slid her feet into the slippers that she kept under the hall table, just as her sister had at her own home. "I know you asked all those questions about the company, but I thought that was just your reporter curiosity."

"I never said I was going to look for a newspaper job. You just assumed." Alana watched as Yvette put her hands on her hips and opened her mouth. "Okay, okay." She held up her hands as if to prevent Yvette's words from coming. "I know before I got here I said I'd consider that possibility and I did, but if I can nail this story,

I'll have a better chance of getting a full-time job with a byline without waiting twenty years."

"If you get into something that you can't handle, you won't have twenty years."

"Thanks for your trust in my ability."

"I'm just trying to be realistic and pass it on to you."

"I made your favorite dinner. Come eat."

"Don't change the subject." Yvette sniffed. "You're trying to appease me."

"Yep. Is it working?"

"Alana, fried chicken, not even your milk-soaked, secret-herb-recipe fried chicken, will change the situation. It's dangerous." She went into the kitchen. "You don't know what's going on."

"You said nothing is going on any more."

"I know that." She stared at Alana, but didn't sit. "If there *is* something still wrong, DCS doesn't even know it and we've got more information than you do."

"I know all that." Alana moved behind her, pulled out a chair then moved aside. "Sit. Eat. I'll fix you a plate."

Yvette glared at her, but she sat. "This isn't going to make a bit of difference, you know." She bowed her head for grace after Alana set a filled plate in front of her.

"Just hear me out." Alana sat across from her. "I have a plan."

"Is it better than a trash-can lid?"

"I was a kid back then." It was Alana's turn to glare. "Listen to me." She pointed to Yvette's plate. "How are the greens? Don't you think the gravy turned out perfect?"

"Everything is delicious, as you know. It still doesn't have anything to do with what you plan to do." She took a bite of chicken and tried to keep from reacting, but an 'umm' escaped from her anyway. "Look. The problem is gone. Dave told us today that he's definitely going ahead with his plans to bid on government contracts. If the leak wasn't fixed, he wouldn't do that."

"Maybe he only thinks it's fixed. I still want in."

"You watch too much spy stuff."

"I need you to tell me the name of the company that cleans the offices."

"The cleaning company? I don't know. Why?"

"I'm planning to get a job. What color are their uniforms?" Yvette frowned. "I'll make it easy for you: blue or brown?"

Yvette hesitated for what seemed like forever.

"Blue," she finally answered. "You're planning to get a job cleaning offices?"

"Only at DCS."

"Why cleaning offices?"

"Because I can be invisible. Nobody notices the cleaning people."

"Some people do." Yvette frowned. "A janitor? My college-educated janitor sister." She shook her head.

"It's a way in. Are they cleaning while you're at work? I saw a couple in the lobby this morning."

"Mom and Dad will be so proud of the way you plan to use your college education."

"They'll never know. Stay with me here. The cleaning people?"

Yvette hesitated and stared at her long enough for Alana to figure that she'd need a Plan B. Then Yvette sighed. Then she answered.

"They come in at twelve to empty the wastebaskets, so I guess they start before noon."

"When you guys are at lunch. Great."

"Not great. Everybody doesn't go out for lunch."

"That's okay. Tell me more." Yvette hesitated. Alana held her breath. It would be much easier if Yvette helped. But she'd find a way to do this without her if she had to. She released her breath when Yvette continued.

"They come back and clean around four. I don't know what they do between those hours. I don't see them." She glared at Alana. "It's none of my business. My office is cleaned. That's my concern." She frowned. "They're still working when we leave." She stared at Alana. "I repeat: you're planning to get a job cleaning offices? Why not work *in* the office? I'm sure I can get Dave to hire you as a receptionist if nothing else."

"I have to be able to move about the offices freely. A cleaning person can do that. Besides, nobody notices service people. Haven't you noticed that hitmen or hit-women and spies pose as uniformed personnel? It's like they're invisible."

"I notice them. I always speak to Corina."

"Corina." Alana nodded. "Good. Now I have a name." She stared at her sister. "You're the exception. Most people ignore them." Her face lit up. "I can ask her how she got the job."

"I'm still not convinced that this is a good idea."

"You don't have to be. I'm the reporter, remember?"

"I'm not sure you know what you're doing."

"I'm not asking for an endorsement. I just want a little information." She pointed to Yvette's empty plate. "Want seconds?"

"No, I'm stuffed."

"You have to have room for a piece of my coconut cake." Alana set the cake plate on the table.

"Homemade coconut cake." Yvette shook her head. "Freshly shredded coconut?"

"Absolutely."

"You really want this, huh?"

"More than I've wanted anything in a long time." She leaned forward. "I can do this." She shrugged. "I can get the information myself, but it would be easier if you just looked for the logo on the uniform."

Yvette hesitated again. "It's Squeaky Clean Services." She stared at Alana and shrugged. "I was trying to discourage you." She shrugged. "We laughed at the name when we first saw it."

"They don't clean the whole building, right? I saw women wearing two different colored uniforms."

"Each office hires their own service. Squeaky Clean might clean other offices in our building. If they hire you, they might send you some place else." She stared at Alana. "Which might not be such a bad thing."

Alana glared at her, but ignored Yvette's last remark. "If I have to deal with that, I will when the time comes. I have to think of a reason for needing to work in the DCS offices. Is Corina the only cleaning person you've seen?"

Yvette hesitated before she answered. "She is right now." She shrugged. "There was a second person, but I haven't seen her for a while." She hesitated again. "You'll have a chance to use your Spanish; she once told me that she doesn't speak much English." She stared at Alana. "When do you intend to start this?"

"Tomorrow."

"Tomorrow? So soon?"

"Why not?"

"I thought you might want to take a little more time to think this through."

"No sense wasting time, and I have thought it through."

"I still think wasting time is exactly what you'll be doing if you go through with this."

"If I'm wasting time, it means that there is no danger. If there is, then—"

"Then you could get hurt."

"I hate it when you finish my sentences. I know how to be careful. I'm just going to investigate. I'm not going to interfere with their plans. In fact, they won't even know what I'm doing."

"In theory, they won't know. In fact, if they are smart enough to steal plans, they won't have trouble uncovering an amateur investigator."

"You worry too much, sis. First, you tell me nothing is going on, then you tell me how much danger I'll be in. Since you gave me so much information, I won't even go into that 'amateur' label."

"I hate it when you go logical on me." Yvette slipped a bite of cake onto her fork, but didn't eat it.

"So we each have idiosyncracies that the other doesn't like." Alana pointed to the cake. "Eat. I didn't slave over a hot grater for you to let my cake go to waste."

"Are you sure you want to do this?" Yvette stared at Alana.

"I know there's a story there. I just have to dig it out."

"How long are you going to do this?"

"As long as it takes."

"I hope it doesn't take long for you to find out that there's nothing to find."

"Don't worry about me. I know what I'm doing. This will be a piece of cake." She touched the edge of Yvette's dessert plate. "Speaking of cake, if you don't eat that, you'll hurt my feelings."

She watched as Yvette held her fork but still didn't taste the cake. She knew her sister was still trying to think of something to make Alana change her mind. Alana also knew exactly when Yvette realized that it wasn't going to happen. She nodded as Yvette finally tasted the cake.

"This is good."

"Good? Is that the best you can do? Good?"

"Okay. It is so delicious that bakeries all over the country would offer you more money than the government has for your recipe."

"The country?"

"All right, all right. The world." She chewed another bite and swallowed. "This is really good."

"Thank you, it's just some old ingredients that I threw together." She stared at Yvette, who stared back. Then they both laughed. When they finished, Alana announced, "I'm changing the subject. Any promising young men at DCS?"

"I told you, I am content with my singleness."

"Nobody, huh? What about Dave?"

She shook her head. "Please. Dave is like a brother. There's no one there that I'd want to get serious about." She frowned.

"There's a lot of that going around."

"Yeah. And it's okay. At least I don't have to wrestle anybody for the remote control."

"Good point. Speaking of the remote, anything good on tonight?"

"Probably not, but I'm sure we can find something to waste our time with. We can check later."

The conversation turned to television, but Alana was only halfway paying attention to what Yvette was saying. The rest of her thoughts were on the next day.

# Chapter 9

Tuesday morning, Alana woke before daybreak. She didn't get up, but she knew she wasn't going back to sleep. Her mind was racing past her plans, not only for this morning, but two, three, a dozen steps ahead. They seemed perfect. She sighed. *Plans usually give that impression until you put them into operation.* She shook her head and sat on the edge of the bed. *Not this plan. Nothing is going to go wrong. I've worked out every possibility.* She sat there a while longer, going over her plans yet again.

Finally she got up and put on a pair of running shorts and a T-shirt. *Just once it would be nice to start an assignment in a calm way, instead of having adrenaline set every muscle on alert.*

She slipped into the kitchen, grabbed an apple, and eased out the door. The perfect Florida morning was wasted on her. She had other things on her mind. As she stretched on the porch, she tried not to remind herself that the only assignment she had was one of her own making. After all, if things went as she hoped, it would lead to big things.

She was still trying to calm down as she broke into a jog.

An hour later she was back. Already the temperature was close to complaining level, but the jog had put her in a mellow mood. Her energy level was down, but she knew from experience that, in a few minutes, it would come back, but to a more manageable level. She glanced at her watch. *Still too early to do anything.* She found some patience deep inside and went into the kitchen.

"Did you think about this some more?" Yvette, still in her robe, came in, poured a cup of coffee and added a few drops of cream.

"Sure."

"And you're still going to do this?"

"Yep. I've got it all planned out."

Yvette stared at her for a long time before picking up her cup. "Since you insist on going through with this crazy idea, do you want a ride?"

"I can't go this early. I might attract attention if I hang around until Corina gets there. The way I'll be dressed today I won't blend in." She smiled. "Thanks for the offer, though."

"This comes under the 'If you can't change her mind, offer to help' column." She shook her head as she set her cup down. "I gotta get dressed. You'll probably be in the shower when I leave." She hugged Alana. "See you this evening. Think about this some more on your way in, okay? It's not too late to change your mind."

"Don't worry about me. You just concentrate on the latest Kelley to the Rescue computer game."

Alana alternated between sitting at the table and pacing a path across Yvette's floor. If wishes worked, time would have jumped ahead. She grabbed the notepad beside the phone and began writing. She didn't need to write it down since it was carved in her mind, but she outlined her plan anyway.

She glanced at her watch. *What to do with over two hours?* She headed to her bathroom to use up some of the time with a shower.

After she finished, she pulled on a denim skirt and a dark blue T-shirt. Then she pulled her hair back into a ponytail. She frowned at her image in the dresser mirror and was tempted to put on makeup, but she resisted.

By ten o'clock, after checking her watch every five minutes for the past hour, Alana left to find her story.

At ten thirty-five she took a spot far enough away from the door inside the lobby that she shouldn't attract too much attention, but close enough to see everybody who came in.

She shifted positions when, fifteen minutes later, she saw a familiar form coming from the elevators. *We must stop meeting like this.* The line from an ancient movie popped into her head. *Who was he and why was he back here?* She frowned and turned slightly away from him. *Don't worry. He didn't notice you. Even if he did, he wouldn't recognize you from yesterday.* She smiled and released a deep breath. Her transformation from corporate to casual was enough to fool anyone, or at least anyone who wasn't looking for her. She held her breath when he glanced at her, but released it when his gaze moved on.

*What is she up to? Why the dressing down? Who is she waiting for? She didn't talk to anybody yesterday. Why is she back today?* He shrugged. *Whatever her reason, I'm grateful for this second chance.*

Keith kept moving out of the building, but took a spot against the wall of the building across the street. His little voice wasn't so little now; it was practically shouting at him. He had learned the hard way to listen to it. He focused his attention on the large windows of the building where Miss Mystery was waiting. *For what? Or for whom? Is she a contact? A carrier?* He shifted to the right so he had a better view of her in the lobby.

He didn't have long to wait. At five minutes to eleven he watched as she approached a young woman wearing the blue uniform of a janitorial service, the same service he had seen cleaning the DCS offices.

Keith didn't move. *The cleaning woman is involved?* He watched his mystery woman write something in a notebook, then tuck it into her purse. A few seconds later she left the building and walked to the corner. He crossed back to her side and was a few feet behind when she went into the multilevel parking lot. He frowned. *I can't take a chance on her noticing that I'm following her.* He positioned himself at the building around the corner from the exit ramp.

His interest in her now was strictly business. He leaned back against the wall, back into the shadows, and waited, thankful that there was only one way out of the lot.

She paused before easing into the flow of traffic, and he allowed a slight smile of satisfaction to form as he wrote down her license number. When she was half a block away, he got his car. He knew he couldn't follow her without taking a chance of her noticing him, but with a little help from a friend he could find out who she was and, hopefully, where she was living.

He drove to the Orlando Police Station, gave his name, and asked for Lieutenant Ben Harris. A few minutes later, Keith held out his hand to his old military buddy and explained what he needed. He handed Ben the license number he had copied, glad that the two of them didn't need to spend a lot of time on preliminaries before they got to the purpose of his visit.

"We have a problem with security at a company doing sensitive business here in Orlando. I could use your help."

"You got it." Harris glanced at the number. Then he went over to a computer and punched in the information. Soon a sheet of paper was sliding from the printer.

"Thanks, Ben. I appreciate it," Keith said as he took the information. "Alana Duke. Residence: Philadelphia."

He nodded. *I was right about her living there.* He folded the paper. "I hope this doesn't get you into trouble."

"Man, I know if you asked for this info, it's needed." Ben's rugged face softened. "If I trusted you with my life, I can trust you with license and social security numbers. Let me know how you make out." His stare hardened. "I thought there'd be no need for these skills after we got back home."

"We still don't need all of them." Keith met his stare. "I know you're just as thankful for that as I am." He slipped the paper into his pants pocket. "Thanks again. I'll keep you posted."

He got into his car, but he didn't start it. He pulled out the paper and looked at it again. *This is only a start. What's her local connection? And for whom is she working?* He frowned. *Her address in Philly is only a few blocks from Tara's house. Mount Airy: hiding place for a mole?* Even to his suspicious mind that seemed ridiculous. He shrugged. He had no proof that she was mixed up in anything that wasn't legal. Just because it looked like a duck didn't mean it quacked.

He started the car and hoped this was one of those times when his little voice was wrong. He also knew that hope didn't have anything to do with reality. He sighed. *I have to put my laptop to some serious work.*

As he went back to his place, he tried to ignore the way his feelings were jumbled together. He was attracted to her. She was a stranger, but that didn't change his pull toward her. She could also be involved in stealing secrets; at the least, corporate secrets. He didn't want to think about the government contracts that were pending at Dave's company. He didn't want to think about any of that, but wants never ruled his thoughts before, so he wasn't surprised when they were ignored now. He shook his head slightly.

Even dressed in a T-shirt and denim skirt, she was beautiful. The fact that she hadn't worn any makeup hadn't detracted from her beauty. In fact, it gave her face more of a look of innocence. He frowned as he went inside his apartment. *I'll live with whatever comes from this. I'm living with worse now.*

He booted up the computer. He knew from experience that looks could be deceiving and, in the business he was involved with, that was part of the plan. Still, her face lingered in his memory. *What would it be like to be on the receiving end of a smile from her? How would it feel to hold her on purpose? What if we . . .* He shook his head. *Stop. Just stop it.* He made his thoughts leave the not-distant-enough past and concentrate on what he was doing.

Soon he reached the proper computer site and went to work. *It shouldn't take long to find out all there is to know about Miss Alana Duke, including the brand of toothpaste she uses.* He tamped down his regret that he had to learn her identity in this way. Then he dug some more.

He shook his head. If citizens knew how easy it was to get into their business, there would be a revolution the likes of which the country had never seen. The Boston Tea Party would seem like just that: a tea party.

He dug deeper still, entered different sites and took notes. *Why did she leave Philly? Where was she staying in Orlando? Was she in Orlando or Kissimmee or some other nearby city?*

Her beautiful face and sexy lips were almost forgotten as he worked. Once, hope that she wasn't involved with anything illegal tried to surface, but he controlled it just as he had learned to control most aspects of his life. If she was, she was. Nothing had developed between them. *Not yet.* He frowned.

*Most likely, not ever.* He kept working the keyboard, not letting regret interfere with his work.

In a short while he leaned back and stared at the words coming up on the screen. *Why is a reporter from Philadelphia in Orlando talking to a cleaning woman at a company with a security problem?*

# Chapter 10

Alana parked across from the pizza shop in a section of town that tourists never saw. It was hard to believe that these shops had ever been new. They had not aged well. She took a deep breath and left her car. Then she turned back twice to make sure she had locked it.

She passed the laundromat, which was *lavandería* in this neighborhood. The young woman and man sitting in the folding chairs in front of the window were too busy talking to more than glance at Alana, who kept moving. She smiled to herself and shook her head as her mind translated the Spanish conversation. Men tried to impress women in all cultures and the smart women were able to recognize a line whether it was in English or some other language.

She had to step into the parking lot to get around the three small children chasing each other on the sidewalk outside the thrift shop next door.

The nerves in her stomach quivered faster as she continued past the narrow shops. *How could anybody call these butterflies?* At the least, a flock of crows was a more accurate description.

Finally she read the name on the door of the office at the end of the row, took a deep breath, which had no effect on the crows, and went inside.

"Yeah?" The man behind the desk looked at her as if

she had interrupted a top-level conference instead of his newspaper reading.

Alana swallowed hard, then purposely ignored the rules of Spanish grammar that had been drilled into her head. *Mr. Ortiz would take back the As he gave me if he heard me,* she thought, as she asked the man about a job.

"Where you from? Not from the island."

"Sí." She nodded. "San Juan."

"No. Where are you from? ¿De dónde está?" he asked again.

Alana took a deep breath before she answered. "San Miguel." She hoped this man had never been there. She knew her accent was nothing like the one the woman whom she met when she vacationed in that area of Mexico two years ago had.

"Where's your green card?"

"I-I forgot it." Her nervousness had nothing to do with him thinking she was an illegal.

"Yeah?" he stared at her. "You sure you got it? Why you don't have it with you? You know you need it for a job."

"I-I maybe lost it. I-I got it. At home."

He stared at her a few seconds longer. "I give you a job, I'm taking a chance. They find out, I'm in big trouble."

"Corina say you need somebody to clean."

"You know Corina?"

"Yes." She nodded, hoping those were the magic words.

"I can't pay you what Corina gets. She got a card. I'm taking a chance with you."

"Sí." Again she nodded.

"I let you help Corina. You learn from her. I can't pay you for the three days while you learning. Comprende?"

"Sí."

"She tell you she's gonna be leaving in two weeks?"

"No."

"She just told me this yesterday. They don't never stay in a job. Then they wonder how come they don't ever have no money. You do good, you got her job."

"Gracias."

He named a salary well below the legal minimum wage. "Okay?" he asked.

"Sí." Alana made herself smile and act grateful. *He should be ashamed.*

"Wait here."

He got two uniforms from the closet to the side. "I take out for this from your first paycheck." He told her how much.

Alana took the obviously not-new clothes from him. She worked at still acting grateful, thanked him again, and left.

She browsed through the thrift shop instead of going back to her car in case he was watching. She didn't want to have to explain to him how she could afford a car.

Finally she made one more stop before she went home.

She parked on the street outside the trailer park that Corina had told her about. Then she walked under the faded "Happy Living" sign at the entrance and past a long row of trailers almost touching each other.

*Accent or not?* She asked herself as she made her way through the kids playing in the narrow road as if it were their playground. The mixture of Spanish and English coming from them helped her decide.

"Corina said you might have a trailer for rent," Alana said to the tired-looking woman sitting behind the desk in the tiny trailer serving as an office.

"You know Corina?"

"I'm going to be working with her."

"Humph. You make sure that Miguel pays you what you're worth." She stared at Alana. "The only place I got right now is small. You alone?"

"Sí, it's just me."

"Good. Two would be bumping into each other inside, but it's fine for one." She took a key from the rack behind the desk. "That Josie moved out and didn't tell nobody." She shrugged. "I treated her nice, too." She shrugged again and stood. "It wasn't the first time that happened. I'm Mrs. Banto." She didn't hold out her hand and neither did Alana. "Come with me." She led Alana outside, then locked the door behind her. It's just down there," she pointed down a narrow cross street, "but I don't like to take chances leaving the door unlocked. It's safe here," she added hastily, "but you know how kids get into things."

Alana followed her past more trailers jammed together. Many residents had taken the time to plant flowers in front of their homes. They had crammed as many plants as they could in the space not more than a few feet deep that was allotted to each trailer before the road took over.

They stopped at a small unit at the end of the row. "I cleaned it up good." She shook her head. "That Josie, she left it such a mess." She gestured to Alana. "Go on in and look around. It's cozy, but it's got everything you need. You'll see."

Alana took three steps inside the trailer and stopped at the small table between two built-in benches. A three-burner stove touched the side of the two built-in closets. Using a real oven was not an option here. A double bed spanned the back end of the trailer.

"Look here." Mrs. Banto opened a folding door next to the counter. "You got your own bathroom." Alana peeped in. A toilet, a small corner sink, and the smallest shower she had ever seen filled the room. "This is a newer unit. Some of the older ones don't have this. They only have the community bathroom at the other end of the row." She nodded. "You're lucky." She opened the overhead cupboards and the narrow closet that provided the only place for hanging clothes. "There's all this space and you have these." She pointed to the drawers under the bed and the benches that gave them a boxed-in look. "You got plenty of space here." She looked at Alana. "That air conditioner in the window looks small, but it cools this place off real good. It's almost new." She closed the door to the cabinet under the stove so she could get past. "What you think?" She quoted her a price. "You can't find a better deal nowhere else."

"Yes." Alana nodded. "This is what I need." *How can Corina afford the rent on the small salary she gets? How many others have to stretch their little money such a long way? They have to run out of money before the end of the month.* The term "working poor" came to mind.

"Good. We go back to the office and talk. I need a deposit. If you don't have the full month's rent, you can give me part now so I know to hold it for you. The rest you give me when you get paid. I do that because you know Corina. I got people coming in here every day looking for a place, but I like you. I wouldn't want to see you miss out."

Alana followed her back to the office, giving thanks that she'd only be here for a short time.

She gave Mrs. Banto half a month's rent and left the trailer park, glad to have enough space to take a deep breath again. *Get used to it,* she reminded herself. *Until you finish your investigation, you'll be here every day starting tomorrow.*

In spite of the changes coming in her lifestyle, she drove home full of excitement. *I know I can get a story from doing this.*

As soon as she got home, Alana began sorting her things into two groups: those to take and those to ask Yvette to keep for her. *I'm going to miss being with her. It's gonna be weird seeing her every day and acting as if I don't know her.* She took a deep breath. *I can do this.*

By the time Yvette came home, Alana's excitement over the story had made every other emotion disappear.

"I did it." Alana grabbed Yvette as soon as she walked into the house. "I got the job, found a place to live—"

"Place to live? What's wrong with here?"

"I can't take a chance on somebody finding out that I live here. What's a cleaning woman doing living in a place like this? On what they'll pay me, the only way I could afford this is if I had a live-in job working for you."

"Where will you live?"

"I found a place."

"Where?"

"The same place where Corina lives."

"Where? What kind of place is it? What can you afford on your new salary? You said it's not much."

"Don't worry. I'll be fine. It's only temporary."

"How long is 'temporary'? How much time do you intend to give this?"

"I don't know. I haven't even started yet and already you want me to set a deadline."

"I think you need to set a date by which you'll quit whether you find a story or not."

"I will as soon as I get an idea of what's going on."

"I told you, there's nothing going on. Not anymore." Yvette frowned. "Does this mean that I won't see you until you're through chasing the pot of gold?"

"I don't see why I can't visit you on the weekend." She shrugged. "Maybe I can come on Friday and stay until Sunday." She grinned. "How does that sound? I'll be here so much you'll get tired of me."

"What I'm worried about is what you'll get into when you're not here."

"I was in Philadelphia all those years without you and I survived."

"You weren't trying to replace Ed Bradley then."

"Look, sis, if you're right," she stared at her, "then there's nothing to worry about. The worst that could happen is that I'd get fired. Right?"

"Don't be so logical." She frowned. "What if you're right?"

"Aha. You admit something might be wrong."

"I'm not admitting anything. I just said what if."

"Quit worrying and come eat. I fixed a going-away dinner, even though I'm the one going away."

Yvette went into the dining room as if, if she took long enough, she could make Alana change her mind.

During the meal, Alana had to talk enough so it would seem as if Yvette were taking part in the conversation.

Finally they were finished. Yvette's plate was almost as full as when she filled it. Alana stared at it but didn't allow herself to comment. She just cleared the table.

"I left a lot of my things in the room. If they're in your way, I can move them."

"How can they be in the way? Nobody will be using that room now that you're going to chase wild geese."

"Okay." *I refuse to go through that again.* "Hang on to these for me?" She handed her keys to Yvette, who stared at them instead of taking them. "I can't take my car. How could I explain owning a late-model car?"

Yvette stared at the keys a few seconds, and then she took them.

"Bye, sis. See you on Friday. If I'm not coming, I'll call you." She opened the door, then picked up her two suitcases.

"At least let me drop you off close to where you're going."

"I don't know."

"Nobody's watching you. You don't even work there yet."

"Okay. I'd appreciate it."

The only sound in the car was the hum of the engine until Alana turned on the radio and tried to ignore the lack of conversation.

She directed Yvette from time to time and finally had her pull over at a bus stop. "This is good."

"Are we close?" Yvette looked around at the motels lining the highway.

"It's a straight run from here so I'll take the bus the rest of the way."

"You're not going to let me see where you live?"

"Thanks, sis." Alana kissed her sister's cheek. "If you'll pop the trunk, I'll get my bags."

"Take care, Alana." She hugged Alana. "Don't you do anything stupid." She frowned. "I mean it. Don't you get hurt."

"Love ya." Alana slipped from the car, grabbed her bags, and moved to the shelter of the bus stop. She let out a heavy breath and gave silent thanks when she saw the bus a block away.

"Bye." She waved. "Bye," she repeated when Yvette didn't move the car. She nodded when Yvette finally eased the car back into traffic, leaving her behind. Again, fluttering built in her stomach. Again, her determination forced it to stop. *This is it. Step one over, on to step two.*

She watched Yvette's car until the bus stopped. Then she turned her back on her old life, picked up her suitcases, and walked toward her new, but temporary, life.

Twenty minutes later she got off the bus and started down a side street. In the middle of the block she set the luggage down, hoping that her decision to do this was smarter than her decision to bring so much stuff.

She frowned, flexed her hands, and then picked up the suitcases again. *I only have to do this one way. When I leave, it will be by car.*

She set the bags down once more when she got to the corner. Then she picked them up, turned down another little street, and walked to her new home halfway down the next block.

# Chapter 11

Alana unpacked her things in the dim light inside the dark trailer. She made a mental note: *Buy 60-watt lightbulbs tomorrow; these 40-watt ones are not going to work.* She thought about her mystery man. *I wouldn't mind being in the dark with him.* She shook her head. *Evidently my libido thrives in this southern climate.* She shook her head again. *I haven't fixated on a man that I haven't met since what's-his-name burst on the music scene a few years ago.* She frowned. *I'm way too old to worship from afar. It might be safe, but it certainly isn't satisfying.* Her imagination formed a picture of what would be satisfying. Then she eased it away with regret and made herself concentrate on storing her things in the little space she had.

As she put her things away, she tried to ignore the outside noises that were as loud as if there were only cardboard walls separating her from them. She sighed. *Maybe that's because that's all there is: cardboard and a thin sheet of metal. I have to find Corina,* she thought, as a loud group of boys, with rap music blasting even louder than their voices, strolled past. *The sooner I get things going, the sooner I can finish and the sooner I can leave here.* She didn't let herself think about the ones who were stuck in this place for a whole lot longer that she would be.

She stored the suitcases on one of the benches. Then she left the trailer and stepped into her new community.

*I know my Spanish is good enough to make myself understood. I only hope it's good enough so that I can understand others.*

"Hola, Corina." Alana smiled when the familiar face showed itself at the trailer three doors down. She relaxed. *I don't have to ask for directions to get to her trailer.*

"You get the job?"

"Sí. Yo—"

"English, please. I like to use it when I can. I'm trying to get better."

"Okay." *Now all I have to do is keep it simple. How could I explain using fluent English?* She sighed. "I start with you tomorrow. I'll take the bus in with you."

"How many free days is Miguel getting from you?"

"Three."

Corina shook her head. Then she told Alana when to meet her at the bus stop in the morning. "You go food shopping yet?"

"Not yet."

"You need a loan until payday?"

Alana's face softened. She shook her head. "I got some money from my last job. Thanks anyway."

"De nada." Corina frowned. "I mean, it's nothing."

After the woman left, Alana went to the small store on the corner. *The working poor catch it everywhere, don't they,* she thought as she bought just enough food for dinner and breakfast, but paid twice as much as she would have elsewhere. *It will mean an extra stop on the way home tomorrow, but I'm going to the Wal-Mart Superstore for my other groceries,* she promised herself as she returned to her trailer.

She turned on the small television while she ate her microwaved meal, but nothing short of a war could have gotten her attention. Her mind was already on tomorrow.

\* \* \*

Alana awoke early the next day, but it wasn't because of any noise. She smiled. Last night the park had quieted down about 10:30 as if somebody had sounded curfew and everybody thought it meant no noise at all.

*I can do this,* she thought as she got up. *How hard can it be? I've been cleaning since Mom made me start cleaning my room when I was little. If I could meet her tough standards, an office should be easy.* She smiled. *I won't even have any clothes to put away as part of the cleaning.*

Until it was time for her to go to work, she busied herself moving things around, trying to make more space where there was none.

As she walked to meet Corina at the bus stop, she spoke or waved to her new neighbors. The friendly faces made her feel at ease. Her only concern now was whether or not she would be wasting her time on a non-story. She hummed as she went on her way. *Maybe I can find a lead on something else, if this one doesn't pan out.*

By the time six o'clock in the evening came, Alana had discovered exactly how hard cleaning offices could be. There were set procedures for everything and she was having trouble following them. She couldn't just empty the trash; she had to separate the soft drink cans from the rest, first, for recycling. The paper that had found its way to the general trash had to be pulled as well.

"Why can't they put these in the right container?" Alana asked in the hall as she removed yet another can from the big container where she had dumped it before checking.

"Some of them forget," Corina answered. "Others feel that's what we get paid for." She stared at Alana. "And they are right." She pulled a can from the wastebasket she had taken from one of the offices. "This is why I wear plastic gloves. We got to buy our own, but I think it is worth it. You don't know what's in them." She pointed to the wastebasket and moved to the next cubicle. "It is easier if you remember before you empty the small cans," she said gently as Alana started to dump the next wastebasket.

"We do this twice a day?"

"Sí." She shook her head. "Yes. When we first come in and then before we leave at seven."

"Why don't they give them bigger wastebaskets?"

"There is no space. Look how crowded it is." Corina pointed around. "Besides, you want they should cut your hours?"

"No." Alana sighed. "There's just more to this than I thought."

"Some people think this job is what they call a no-brainer."

"Yes, I know." Alana pushed the large wheeled container to the next room. *I used to be one of those people. I can't wait to see how much trouble I'll have with that monster floor-cleaning machine later.*

"Let me show you again." After the offices were empty, Corina eased the floor machine from Alana, who frowned. *Who knew there were so many steps to something as simple as cleaning a floor?* She paid closer attention as she watched Corina buff the newly washed and waxed floor. "You have to do this every week, more often if it looks like it needs it, like after a hard rain. Other days, you mop it with plain water. Make sure you get the corners and edges even when you just mop, or it will be very hard to get them clean when you use the machine."

Slowly she pulled the machine along the wall, then turned it off. "That's it." She pushed it toward Alana. "You do the next section. The next time the floors must be done, it will be your job alone, sí?"

"Yes." Alana took a deep breath, grabbed the handle, and turned on the machine.

"Slowly, amiga. You control the machine. Don't let it control you." She watched as Alana tightened her hold on the machine and slowed it down. "Bueno." She nodded. "That is very good. Nobody could find fault with your floors." She smiled at Alana and they moved on.

When seven o'clock came, Alana felt as if she had been to a gym for a full workout, especially so with her arms.

She was glad she hadn't started on a Monday. She wouldn't have survived a full week at the start.

She tried not to groan as she got her things from the closet, but reaching for her purse from the shelf was her undoing.

"You will get used to it," Corina said with a smile. "I did. I am not going right home, so I will see you tomorrow."

"Okay." Alana followed Corina down the hall, trying to ignore her protesting muscles.

As Alana rode the bus, she thought over her day. *This will work out.* A few of the office workers spoke, but most acted as if she and Corina weren't there. She smiled. That was what she was counting on.

She did as much food shopping as her cupboards and small refrigerator would hold, then caught the bus home. Home. She shook her head. It was strange to think of that small place as home after her large apartment in Philly.

The next morning she groaned as she turned over. Muscles that she never knew she had, ached, from her feet to her neck, but her arms most of all, just as she had been afraid of. She rubbed her upper arms and got up slowly. Her back wasn't in much better condition. Hopefully her body would get used to the work soon.

At ten, she and Corina rode the bus to work together.

"Miguel said you're leaving, but he didn't say where you're going." Alana settled in the seat beside Corina.

"I gave him two weeks' notice, but he called and told me that he won't need me after Monday." She stared at Alana. "He said you will do my job." She shrugged. "It is all right. I got a job at a motel as head of housekeeping. I know they will let me start early because they need somebody now." She named a little independent motel about six blocks up the highway from the trailer park. She shrugged again. "It's not much, but it's a little more money than I make now, a little less to do, and no evening work." She smiled. "I can walk there, so I can save bus fare, too." Her smile widened. "With my new hours, I can go to night school and get my GED. Then I can get a better job."

"It's good to have plans."

"You have your diploma?" She stared at Alana.

"Yes."

"Then maybe soon you will look for a better job, too."

"Maybe."

"I got plans for my future." Corina nodded.

"That's a good thing."

They rode the rest of the way with each woman thinking about her own future.

Alana was grateful when seven o'clock came on Friday evening. She went directly to Yvette's from work. *I sure hope Yvette doesn't have plans for the rest of the night. I plan to take over her tub until my muscles decide to forgive me and go back to normal.*

She shifted in her bus seat and managed not to groan as her body protested. *Maybe I'll camp out in her tub all night.*

Yvette opened the door as soon as Alana put her key in the lock. "How did it go? Nobody suspected, did they? You weren't in any danger, were you?"

"Tell me you haven't been worrying since I moved out. You saw me at work." Alana stepped inside and closed the door against any insects wanting in.

"I won't answer since you know how much Mama and

Daddy frown on lying." She grinned. "Go on out to the kitchen. I fixed dinner."

"Good. I'm starving." Alana urged her body to move by mentally promising it relief in a little while.

"Why are you walking like that?" Yvette frowned at her.

"Because muscles that I didn't know I had are protesting because I'm disturbing them after working them all day." She eased into a chair at the table. The sigh that escaped was beyond her control.

"From cleaning offices?"

"If you only knew." Alana chuckled. Then she groaned as she shifted. "I hope you never have to find out."

"*You* didn't have to find out." Yvette set a full plate in front of her.

"Yes, I did." Alana said a quick grace before attacking the food.

"I'd ask how you like that, but you're eating too fast to taste it." Yvette put her own plate down and sat across from Alana.

"Not so." Alana stopped long enough to take a sip of water. "It's delicious."

"I think you would say that about a plate of dry toast."

"Maybe." She ate a forkful of baked chicken. "But this is good."

"So. How did it go? I was afraid to talk to you at work. I didn't want to blow it for you."

"I appreciate that. As for the job, it went." She swallowed a mouthful of food. "Do you know that cleaning is hard work?"

"I know." Yvette nodded. "I have cleaned a time or two myself, you know."

"I'm talking about cleaning offices. It's a completely different process."

"Does that mean that maybe you've changed your mind?"

"No, it does not. What it *does* mean is that, when I finish eating this awesome dinner prepared by my sister's loving hands, I intend to soak in a hot bath until the water feels as if it came from the refrigerator."

"Oh. I thought maybe . . ." A shrug replaced the rest of Yvette's words.

"I'll be fine. I told you, after they get used to me taking Corina's place, nobody will notice me."

"You won't start digging right away."

"Absolutely not." She patted Yvette's hand. "Stop worrying. I'll be all right." Alana moved her plate aside and put the slice of pound cake in front of her.

"Homemade?"

"Not unless somebody lives in the bakery department of Food Lion." She shook her head. "The way you're eating, it wouldn't matter, anyway."

"True." Alana got a glass of milk and went back to the table. Yvette had just started her dessert when Alana stood, took her dishes to the sink, and started to wash them.

"I'll do that. You go soak."

"I appreciate it. Tomorrow is my turn. I'll even fix dinner. If I can move, that is." She tried to walk normally as she went into the bedroom to get her things, but she knew it wasn't happening.

The rest of the weekend flew past and soon Sunday night came. *I'm glad Yvette gave up trying to talk me out of going on with my plan,* Alana thought as she lifted the small canvas bag holding a few more of her things.

"I'll drive you back."

"Thanks, but that's not necessary. I'll take the bus," Alana said.

"You're sure?"

"I don't have anything to carry but this, so it will be

easy." She hugged her. "See you next Friday. I'll call you if things change.

"Change? Like what? What might make you change your plans?"

"Nothing." *Sometimes you just don't know when to stop, do you?* "I'll be here."

"You'd better be." She stared at Alana. "I mean it. You better show up here on Friday." Her stare pulled into a frown. "And I better see you cleaning every day until then."

"Yes, boss."

"You know I didn't mean it that way."

"I know." Alana gave her a quick hug. "See you."

"Take care. I mean, take really good care." Yvette squeezed her again, then let her go.

"I always do." Alana did not look back to see how long Yvette stood in the doorway watching her leave.

She caught the bus at the corner and tried not to look ahead to a full week just like the end of the one past.


When Corina left at the end of Monday, Alana felt panic try to fill her. She controlled it. *I can do this.*


By the end of the week, she felt competent to do the job. It hadn't become second nature yet, but nobody complained. She even felt capable of waxing and buffing the floors the week after next and that was the hardest, most complicated part of the job. She had also decided that cleaning people didn't get nearly as much money as they deserved for what they did. Maybe there's a story in that. She frowned as she pulled a folded newspaper from a wastebasket. *I can do this.* She had to do this.

Her walk was easier when she went to Yvette's on Friday;

this weekend she didn't have to camp out in a tub of hot water.

At the end of the second week on the job, she felt confident that no complaints would reach Miguel about her. She had even gotten better at not snapping back at the few who took their problems out on her. Even Nelson, the company security guard, gave her attitude, and he was way down the chain of commands.

"You got to wear that badge all the time," he had snapped when he asked her for it on Monday and she had to fumble in her pocket to find it. "That's part of the job."

"Okay."

"If you can't do the job right, you shouldn't have taken it."

"All right."

"Put it on now." He watched as she slipped the chain holding the ID over her head. "I got enough to do without waiting for you to find something you should have on. One day you're going to show up here without it and then you'll have to go back home for it."

"Okay." Alana's tongue was sore from biting it as she walked away. *Little fish trying to be a shark.*

She was still fuming when she got the equipment from the cleaning closet and went to the first office.

Keith stood in the doorway of his office. *What is she doing here?* For the past two weeks Keith had been asking himself that question as he had watched the new cleaning woman go through her duties. He would know that she was new at this even if he hadn't dug into her background. He frowned. But he had dug. He frowned again. *Even the way she empties the wastebaskets tells me that she isn't used to this.* If the situation hadn't been serious, he would have smiled at the tentative way she fished aluminum cans from the trash. She tried to control herself, but her nose still crinkled when she had to do that task. *It's a cute nose to crinkle; smooth honey tan skin. . . .*

He shoved that thought away. *Business. This is business, and she's part of it.* He almost got back to a neutral attitude. Almost. He watched as she pulled a newspaper from an office basket after shaking it off. He couldn't help it; he smiled. *I can imagine her cleaning the bathrooms.* He shook his head and went back to the papers in front of him.

"Hello." He got his first up-close look at the woman who had been occupying too much of his thoughts since he landed in Philadelphia.

"Hello." Alana hesitated at the door. "I came for the trash." Her eyes widened, and then they quickly went back to normal.

*She must have seen me in the lobby that day,* Keith thought. *She has no idea how many times I've seen her.*

"Okay." He tried to make his stare casual. He tried to look away from her and back to his desk. He tried to listen to the voice that said she was part of a case, but the vision in front of his eyes made all of his trying fail.

"I will get the can now." She glanced quickly at him, then at the desk, but she stayed in the doorway as if she had no idea where the basket was.

"It's right there." Keith pointed to the can beside the desk. Something in his voice changed and pried her loose. She grabbed the basket, dumped it, and put it back. Keith noticed that she hadn't taken the can from the top of the trash before she emptied it. He refused to think of how her nose would crinkle when she had to do it later. *Where did that accent come from?* She left and he didn't watch her move down the hall.

That evening he watched as Alana maneuvered the awkward floor machine down the hall. At first, when she saw him, she hesitated for a few seconds before she continued.

He watched as she worked her way down the hall, but a security leak was not on his mind. He was too busy watching the way her light blue uniform shirt hugged her back and her dark blue slacks skimmed her backside and hips. He watched how they swayed with her movements as she moved the floor-shampooing machine from one side to the other almost as if she were dancing with it. Dancing. How would she feel in his arms, moving slowly to soft music? How would she feel pressed against his body, her softness pliant against his hardness? Forget the music. How would she feel, taste, and smell if he held her close and she held him back, and they made sweet love until the world disappeared? He sighed. Why do the floors get washed and waxed only once a week?

Keith shifted as he tried again to find a neutral groove, one safe enough to allow his body to ease back to normal without acting on his fantasy. He didn't even pretend to be on the job as he continued to watch her.

Neither the shirt nor the dark blue slacks were tight, but that only let his imagination go to work. When she bent over to pick up a piece of paper that somebody had dropped, he forgot why he was there. He forgot everything except to imagine how she would feel if he were allowed as close to her as her clothes were. He frowned as his body reacted to his imaginings again. *I guess men can have a thing for uniforms, too, especially when they contain someone as luscious as Miss Alana Duke.*

Not until she had turned the corner did he enter the office next door to his so he could really go to work. The staff meeting that Dave had called at lunchtime had given him time to do a preliminary check of some of the computers. Now that everybody else was gone, he could check more thoroughly.

He moved quickly into the program manager's office

and entered a password. Immediately he typed in a code. Files that were supposed to be secure appeared on the screen. Soon he was lost in his search.

Fifteen minutes later he had backed out of the third computer he had checked and was in the hall. *Dave can't hold them in his meeting much longer.* Keith shook his head. *It's a good thing he's the boss. He'd have a hard time explaining why the new guy wasn't at the first staff meeting.*

He took a detour past the staff room on his way out. His work was over until tonight.

Close to midnight Keith turned off the computer and rolled his shoulders. He wouldn't sleep well, but it was time to go home.

"What are you doing here?"

"I work here." Keith stared at the security guard who was staring back. *I should have heard her coming.* He frowned. *I'm slipping.*

"I need to see some identification, sir," she said. Her hand held her gun as if she intended to use it. "I haven't seen you here before."

Her stare stayed on his hand as it moved, but her gun remained pointed at his chest.

"Here it is." Slowly Keith drew out his identification badge and held it out to her. Not much was scarier than a nervous person with a gun. "I'm a consultant." He waited patiently. He'd do this her way.

She stared at the identification as if expecting the words to change. Then she handed it back. "I'm just doing my job. I fill in for Nelson a lot. He couldn't come in until later." She shrugged. "Nobody is usually here this late. Will you be working late many nights?"

"Depends. If you see me, you know I'm working late."

"Yes, sir. Of course. I-I just wanted to know so I won't be surprised. They told me that everybody has to have an ID."

"And I do." When she didn't move he added, "Dave will be pleased to hear how diligent you are."

"Yes, sir." She managed a hint of a smile. "Have a nice evening, sir. I go off duty in a few minutes." She nodded, looked around once more, then left the office.

*You're slipping, man. You didn't even hear her coming.*

When he left the office a few minutes later, she was still in the hall, as if she was waiting for him. He glanced at her, held her stare for a second, then continued walking away from the room, but he could feel her staring at his back as he went. He shrugged. *At least no stranger will get past her.*

He shook his head as he got on the elevator. *It's not strangers that we're worried about.*

His frown stayed in place as he drove home, but it wasn't because of the hours he had just used up. *Tonight was not a waste of time,* he reminded himself. *If nothing else, I uncovered the vulnerability of DCS.* He shook his head. *One thing Dave's going to have to do is revamp his computer-security procedure. Any password can be determined if somebody wants to badly enough, but there's no sense in making it easy for them.*

His thoughts drifted to Alana. *Does Little Miss Chameleon have anything to do with this problem?* He frowned. *I hope not.* His frown intensified at how strong his hope was. His self-imposed rule had always been *Don't get personally involved.* This was the first time he needed to remind himself of that, but he was having trouble obeying his own rule. He forced his thoughts to what he'd do next to find the leak.

# Chapter 12

A day later Alana was putting in late hours, too, but she wasn't doing what she had been paid to do. She turned from the computer in one of the offices and knocked a messy pile of papers off the desk. *I am not cut out for this spy stuff,* she thought as her glance flew to the door. She tensed as her mind scrambled for a plausible explanation. She relaxed when no reaction came from the hall. *Girl, you've got to be more careful.*

Still watching the door, she took a deep breath and bent to pick up the papers. She straightened them carefully and set them back on the desk, hoping they were still in the same order and showed the same degree of messiness. Then she picked up the wastebasket and went into the hall to empty it. She doubted if anybody was there, but no sense in being even clumsier or in not looking as if she were working. *If anybody asks me why I'm late, I'll tell whoever it is that I'm making up for time I took off earlier. Nobody will question anybody working extra time.* She frowned. *Will they?* She tried to relax. *If somebody had been out there, they would have come to check when I got noisy.* She frowned. *Spies can't afford to make mistakes, not even the good ones.*

Slowly she glanced up and down the hall. *Nothing.* She allowed a smile. *Sometimes nothing was good.* Satisfied that she was still undetected, she went back to the computer. She shook her head. *They have some serious problems here.*

She hadn't done this for years, but already she was in the supposedly secure site. An average junior-high computer nut could do this. She frowned. *I hope they correct this before they get any government contracts. I'm only as safe as the government is. What kind of government contracts wouldn't need tight security?* Her frown deepened. *None. Everything in the government is linked together. What am I going to do about this?* She exhaled, as if that would allow room for an answer to emerge. *I can't go to somebody and tell them how weak the security is. How could I rationalize how I found out? Few people like for you to rub their noses in their weaknesses.*

She shook her head as she easily hacked into yet another site from this same computer. Maybe Yvette could find a way to suggest to her boss that he examine their procedures. She frowned. *What would Ed Bradley do in a case like this?*

She looked at the screen. Mr. Willis spent a lot of time at the Date & Mate Web site. *I hope there isn't a Mrs. Willis at home who thinks her marriage is solid.* Alana shook her head.

"What are you doing?"

Alana whirled around, knocking down another pile of papers. Her biggest concern wasn't getting them back in order.

"I-I this computer was on and I was trying to figure out how to turn it off." She hoped her surprise made her fumbling Spanish seem more authentic. *Would a cleaning woman who spoke mostly Spanish use the words "figure out" or was there a better Spanish phrase?*

"Nice try." Keith stared at Alana. He tried not to notice that she was every bit as attractive up close as he had thought. "Who are you?"

"Yo soy—"

"Uh-uh. That might have worked if I hadn't heard you

speak English." He fixed her with a stare. "Perfectly, I might add."

Alana frowned. *When did he hear me talk?*

"Who are *you?*" Nothing like a good offense when you have no defense.

"I'm asking the questions. The uniform is a nice touch. What are you really doing here?"

Alana took a deep breath. What else did he know about her? It didn't matter. Unless he was the spy, she could explain her way out of this. "I was—"

A door opened somewhere around the corner. Alana and Keith reached to close the door at the same time. She stared at him, but she didn't say a word. *So. He shouldn't be here, either.* She swallowed hard. That did not make her feel any safer. If he wasn't the spy, why was he being so secretive?

The footsteps they were waiting for never came.

"Back out of that program, Alana."

Alana's eyes opened wide. "How do you know my name?"

"You'd be surprised at how much I know about you." He tried to prevent the next thought. *You'd really be surprised at how much I want to know even more about you.* He frowned at the direction his mind was taking him.

Alana, unaware of his internal battle, stared at him for a few seconds. Then she shrugged and did as he had ordered. She couldn't do any more tonight, anyway. She turned off the computer, wishing it would take more time to shut down so she could try to figure a way out of this.

"We have some talking to do."

"I have to finish cleaning or I'll lose my job."

"I don't think that's your biggest worry right now." He wrapped his fingers around her arm.

"Where-where are you taking me?"

"We have to talk." He checked the hall before he led her from the office.

"Let's call the police." *I'd rather explain to them. At least I know they'll give me a* chance *to explain.*

"First we talk."

Alana hesitated. Then she stopped resisting. That security guard must be around somewhere. Who else would have opened the door? Mean and suspicious seemed a plus right now.

"Don't make a sound."

She nodded. *Not unless I see somebody who can help me.*

Neither spoke a word as they walked to what Alana was sure was her doom. She wouldn't even be around for her mother's "I told you so."

They turned the corner and the blue-white light spilling a few doors ahead from what could only be a computer screen into the hall made them both stop at the same time. Keith motioned for her to wait. Then he slipped against the wall and quietly made his way toward the light.

Alana stayed against the wall, never questioning herself as to why she didn't leave. Why didn't she take this opportunity to turn and run for the back exit, or at least call out for help?

*Why am I trusting this man, whom I don't even know?*

The man came back to her as quietly as he had left. Still not speaking, he motioned for her to go back the way they had come. The sound of a chair sliding across the floor stopped them both before they reached the corner.

"In here," he whispered as he pulled her into the open cubicle beside them.

"What—"

His arms wrapped around her as his mouth met hers. Several emotions raced through her, tripping over each other, trying to be in command. She stood within his embrace passively, even as he backed her against the wall, pressing the whole length of his body against hers.

For a few seconds, shock was in charge. Then anger took over as she pushed against his solid body. *How dare he.* Then recognition made shock return, stronger than before. *This couldn't be the same man from the airport.*

She shifted positions and he shifted with her. *He feels the same.* He withdrew his mouth a fraction. She frowned as her mind worked on how the man from the airport in Philadelphia could be here. He pressed his mouth back to hers and her mind quit working completely. She tried not to be aware of just how perfect his body felt glued to hers.

Then it was time for a stronger emotion to lead. His mouth coaxed her lips apart and her mouth softened beneath his. Her arms found a path around his neck. Her body, ignoring the fact that it was almost impossible, tried to get closer still. His kiss deepened as she allowed him to sample her mouth, as she tasted his.

"What's going on here?"

Alana's eyes flew open and her stare targeted Nelson, standing just inside the doorway. She tried to jump away from Keith, but his body held hers in place.

"Isn't it obvious?" His words were low, slow, and sexy. If Alana weren't able to see the warning in his eyes, she might have believed that his voice indicated his feelings. He eased away from her and turned to the guard, but he kept a tight grip on her waist. "Just looking for a private place. I thought we had found it."

Nelson's usual mean look was missing, but a threatened one had replaced it. *Why? We're the ones caught. Was he the one using the computer a few minutes ago? What was he doing?* Alana frowned and watched as conflict played across his face, but his hand had no problem. It stayed on his gun.

"How long have you been here?"

"Just finishing up." Keith chuckled. Alana felt heat flood her face, but she didn't deny it.

Nelson stared at them for what seemed to Alana to be forever. "You two better learn to get it on in a different place." He stared at Alana. "And on your own time." He continued to stare. Then he eased his hand away from his gun and to his side. An oily look covered his face. Alana liked the mean one better. Nelson nodded. "I thought there was more to her than what it looked like." He laughed as if he was the only one who got an inside joke. "I guess you found out what it is, huh?"

Keith shrugged. "You know how it is."

"Yeah." Nelson hesitated a few seconds. "You better leave the floor. It's late and Miss Thing has to work tomorrow." He stared at her. "I mean her usual job. Or is this her usual job?"

"You—"

Keith smothered Alana's next words with a kiss. The warning was back in his eyes when he released her and spoke. "We were just leaving."

He wrapped his arm around her shoulders and led her from the room. His arm stayed in place as they went down the hall and onto the elevator that was waiting.

Anger grew in Alana as they rode down to the first floor, but she didn't say anything until they left the elevator.

"How dare you." She jerked away. "You—you—"

"Let's get out of here." He pulled her toward the door.

"I'm not going anywhere with you."

"We still have to talk and we can't do it here." His jaw tightened. "As they say, 'Your place or mine?'" When she didn't answer, he continued. "Look, I know you're a reporter for a now-defunct Philadelphia newspaper." Alana's gasp didn't stop him.

"I also know you have a sister who works here." He

frowned. "I just don't know what you're doing working as part of the cleaning staff." He stared at her. "Well?"

"Well what?"

"Look, Alana, I need more information from you about you."

"What? Your trusty computer snooping didn't tell you everything you need to know?"

"No." *There's a whole lot more that I want to know, and a lot of it doesn't have a thing to do with this situation.* He shook his head, then glanced at his watch. "I don't know of any place open this time of night where we could talk uninterrupted. We can go to your place, if you would be more comfortable there." He hesitated. "Something is going on at DCS and I think you're involved somehow."

"What does it have to do with you?"

"Come with me and we'll talk about it."

Now it was Alana's turn to hesitate. "I don't think it's a good idea to go to my place." She didn't know, but she doubted if many cleaning people living in trailer parks had visitors who drove expensive cars. She frowned. She didn't know *what* he drove, but she was sure it wasn't something somebody in her circumstances would drive.

"Do you want to follow me to mine?"

"If you know so much about me, how come you don't know that I don't have a car?"

"Because I don't know your new name. I *do* know that Alana Duke *does* have a car." He stared at her. "Look. It's not getting any earlier. Are you coming with me, or do I go to Dave with what I know about you? From what I know so far, you might be stealing plans for another company. It wouldn't be the first time it happened."

"I am not. I'm working for myself."

"Selling to the highest bidder? What does you sister have to do with this?"

"No, I'm not. At least not until . . ." She stopped and

drew in a deep breath. "Yvette doesn't have anything to do with what I'm doing."

"Until what? Finish your sentence."

Conflict tumbled through Alana. Then she shrugged. She wouldn't be able to do anything more here, now, anyway. "Okay." She sighed. "I'll go with you. What's your name?" It was Keith's turn to hesitate. "No name, I don't go."

"Keith Henderson."

"Well, Keith Henderson, I have to make a call."

"A call?"

"I need a phone booth."

"Who are you calling?"

"My sister. No way am I going off with some stranger without telling somebody where I am." She frowned. "I want to see some ID, too."

He stared at her, then showed her his driver's license.

She looked at it closely, then straightened, but she didn't move. An impatient driver on the street outside the parking lot let another driver know how he felt. He whizzed past them before Alana made a decision. "I still need to find a phone."

He handed her his cell phone. "Use this."

Alana wasted some more time. *How stupid does he think I am?* It would be easy for him to get Yvette's number from his phone if she used it. *I can't put her in jeopardy like that.* "There's a telephone at the next corner. I'll use that."

"Suit yourself." Keith shrugged. *I don't need to know whom she's calling. I have her.*

He followed her, trying not to think of another way he would like to "have her." He made that thought disappear. Regardless of whether or not she was part of the problem, he would be glad when it was all over. The sooner this situation was cleared up, the sooner he could move on. He tried to concentrate on the moving-on part, but the slight wiggle in her walk was making it all but impossible.

*It's been a long time, Keith. That's your problem with her. You need to find yourself a no-strings-attached woman. That will clean Alana out of your system and you can. . . . What? Drift to another city? Another job?*

As they walked to the corner, neither noticed the figure standing within the shadows cast by the building, watching everything that went on between the two of them. Looking at the uncharacteristic behavior from two people supposed to be lovers.

# Chapter 13

As Alana waited for Yvette to answer, her thoughts tried to re-organize, but it was hard. She had no plan B. She shook her head. *You should always have a back-up plan.* She shifted from one foot to the other, which was hard to do in a phone booth. Finally the answering machine kicked in.

"Hi." She hesitated and stared at Keith.

"Her name is Yvette."

Alana shouldn't have been surprised at his comment. He said that he knew she had a sister working at DCS. Learning Yvette's name would have been the easy part.

"I'm going to discuss the problems at DCS with Keith Henderson. He *says* he works there." She glared at Keith. "That's Henderson. H-E-N-D-E-R-S-O-N. I'll call you tomorrow." She hesitated. "If I don't, you call me."

She hung up. She had mixed feelings about reaching the answering machine instead of her sister. *On the one hand, if Yvette had answered, she would have asked a whole lot of questions, and I don't have any answers.* Alana sighed. *On the other hand, she might have been able to talk me out of this.* She glanced at Keith.

Alana shook her head. That wasn't true. Yvette had never been able to talk her out of any scheme she had ever had. It would be unrealistic to think she could have done so now.

"Ready?" Keith's voice poked at her from outside the booth.

*Am I?* Was she ready to go with this stranger on the chance that she might get a story out of it? She frowned. *I trusted him inside when I could have gotten away easily; Nelson had a gun and could have helped me. Keith didn't have one.* She felt her face flush as she remembered how she knew this. The only way he could have held her closer than he had while they were kissing was if they had been. . . . She shook her head. *Please don't go there,* she begged herself, even as an image of two people, close enough to make one, formed in her mind. She and Keith.

"It's not getting any earlier." Keith glanced at his watch. "Or I should say it *is* getting earlier. Are you coming?"

She moved away from the phone without saying a word and followed him back to the parking lot.

"Back here." He led her to a black Camry parked in the far corner. Nothing fancy. Maybe nobody would have questioned it if she had a visitor at the trailer park who drove this, even though it was new. She shrugged. It didn't matter now. *I'm already committed.* She released a deep breath. *Or maybe I should be committed.*

Keith opened the front passenger door and she got in. *Even the upholstery is dark gray,* she thought as she slid into place. The term "no distinguishing characteristics," came to mind. She didn't even glance at him when he slipped behind the wheel and started the car. She was still going over her situation, as if she could change the past fifteen minutes.

As Keith left the lot, Alana questioned her wisdom again, but she kept quiet. Her frown was the only indication of her feelings. *Please don't let it be a deserted spot with a place to hide a body so even the alligators can't find me. Please don't let that be where he's taking me.*

\* \* \*

Keith never glanced at Alana, so he didn't see that her frown matched his own. *What does she have to do with what's going on at DCS?* He kept asking himself that question, but he still hadn't discovered an answer. *If the answer is nothing, why is she here at this time of night? Her shift at her janitor's job was over a long time ago.* He frowned. She has a college degree. *What is she doing working a janitor's job, anyway? There is no reason. At least not an innocent one. Why here?* He never had believed in coincidences.

He glared at the road as if it had done something to him. He didn't believe in getting emotionally involved in his work. He'd been there before and was still trying to deal with the results of that. Still, he hoped she had a good explanation, one that would satisfy him. His frown deepened as desire settled below his waist. *Don't put Alana and satisfy in the same thought.* He shifted positions, hoping that his professional side would be back in charge by the time they reached his place.

When Keith stopped the car twenty minutes later, Alana looked out the window. She relaxed a little as she recognized the name on the sign as a national chain used by transferred executives waiting for permanent housing. Bright lights made the parking lot almost as bright as daylight. She sighed. So far, no place to hide a body. *Her* body. This time she didn't hesitate when he told her to follow him.

In the elevator she stared at the floor numbers as they lit up as if she expected to see a new sequence. When it got to six, the door slid open. The hall was as deserted and quiet as it should be in the early morning hours, but that didn't make her feel any better. *Nobody knows I'm here,* she thought, as again she followed him to what she hoped was not her doom. Should she take a chance and use his cell phone to call Yvette and tell her where she was? She vetoed that idea right away. *If I'm in danger, Yvette will be, too.*

Keith stopped suddenly outside number 610, and she almost crashed into him. He didn't seem to notice. *Good sign or bad? Maybe he's planning how to get rid of my body.* She hesitated before she followed him inside.

"Okay. Talk." Keith had barely locked the apartment door behind them when he turned to her. "You can sit over there if you want to," he pointed to a blue chair next to a matching couch, "or anywhere else, but let's hear it. First of all, what name are you going by?"

He crossed his arms across his chest and Alana felt as if she were facing a twelve-foot high-fence with a locked gate.

"Why is it any of your business?"

"I'm a loyal employee."

"Then why didn't you just turn me in?"

"Is that what you want?"

"No." She frowned. "You were as anxious as I was not to be discovered at the computer. Why?"

"This is my party. I get to ask the questions."

"Inquisition is more like it."

His stare hardened. He ignored her comment. "What last name are you using?"

Alana chewed on her lip. Then she shrugged. "Cortez."

"What were you looking for?"

Alana took a deep breath. *May as well talk. I won't be able to continue at DCS now, anyway.* She took another deep breath. "You know I'm a reporter." She stared at him, but not a word escaped from him. She took a deep breath and went on. "Yvette told me there was a security problem at DCS." She shrugged. "When my paper folded, I thought I might be able to get a story out of the problem and launch a new phase of my career." *Please don't let* him *be the problem.* She stared at him. "How long have *you* been working there?" She hadn't realized she was holding her breath until after he finished answering. *I wish I had had time to question Yvette about him.*

Keith stared at her. "I got there after the problem surfaced." His stare continued. "Dave and I go way back. I offered to help him."

"Have you found anything?"

"Nice try." His lips curved up, but it wasn't a smile. "You first. Did you?"

Alana met his stare with her own. "Nothing to do with security. A few people spend a lot of Internet time on something besides company business, but that's probably the case everywhere."

"How do you know what they do? How did you get access to secure sites? How did you get past the firewalls?"

"First, let me make one thing clear." She held up her hand. "Yvette doesn't have anything to do with my being here. In fact, she's still nagging me to forget about this. She mentioned the problem casually when my family was together during the holidays."

"In Philadelphia."

This time Alana wasn't as surprised at what he knew about her as she had been the last time. She went on. "This is all my doing."

"Exactly what are you confessing to?"

"I'm not confessing to anything. I don't have anything to confess to." Her voice lifted. She forced it back down. Sometimes stress management worked. Maybe this would be one of those times. She took several deep breaths. "I'm just explaining that my sister is not involved. She even tried to talk me out of coming to Florida. Not that she isn't happy to spend time with me," she added hurriedly. "All I'm trying to do here is get a breakthrough story."

"You didn't answer my questions about how you got into the sites. How did you get the passwords?"

She shrugged. "I don't know."

"Do I need to tell you that's not good enough?"

"Look." She glared at him. "I don't know how I do it. I've always had a knack for getting into computer sites. My mother used to worry about it." She shrugged. "Some people make it easier than others. Like the staff here." She stared at him. "Your turn. How do you get in?"

"Do you know the potential risks here?"

"As much as you do. You didn't answer my question."

"I don't think you do know how dangerous this is. This isn't a cutesy spy movie where the beautiful woman solves the problem and saves the day. This is not a plot for Charlie's Angels minus two."

"Beautiful woman? Cutesy spy movie?" Stress management techniques faded. Her voice rose. "Cutesy spy movie?" Forget the part about her being the beautiful woman. She stood and placed a hand on her hip and shifted her weight. It was that or shove past him and leave.

He shook his head and held up his hand. "Calm down and think about this. Once the government is involved, it's a whole new ball game. Whoever is dirty"—his stare intensified—"if anybody is, they have a lot to lose. They will try their best not to be discovered. Right now, they're probably covering their tracks. People in that kind of business won't let an amateur detective get in their way."

"I'll let the insults slide this time. Especially since it's coming from somebody who is only a consultant. That is what you are, right?" When he didn't answer, she continued. "Besides, if I got in, I know the government, with its sophisticated equipment, won't have any problem." She frowned. "The government isn't involved." Her frown deepened. "Is it? The company still has a chance at the contracts, doesn't it?" She thought about how much Yvette enjoyed working for the company.

"If DCS is to survive, Dave has to find out if he still has a problem." He shrugged. "It could be that the programmer who left was all there was. Or there could be more." He pinned her with a stare. "The government isn't involved. At least not yet. I'm trying to make sure that all of the problem employees have been weeded out so DCS will be secure enough to pass the government screening."

"Are they?"

"I don't know yet. Why don't you sit back down?" He sat in the chair opposite the one she had been sitting in. "Exactly what have you discovered so far?"

She sat. "I want an exclusive after you finish."

"You haven't uncovered anything that I can't, and I'll be able to continue digging."

"Why duplicate work?" She leaned forward. "I know DCS is in a hurry to bid on those government contracts because it needs them. Whether or not the company survives depends on its security." His stare still held her. "Look, two heads are better than one and stuff like that. We can split the duties. I can work at night after everybody is gone. A consultant can only be there so much after hours before somebody starts to wonder."

"You mean everybody is gone except the guard."

Alana's thoughts flew to earlier. *To Keith's hard body against hers, to his mouth on hers, persuading her to let him in to taste her. To the way his body grew harder the longer he held her against him.* She shook her head slightly. *The way they held each other. How far would they have gone if Nelson hadn't—?*

"What about the guard? How do you intend to get around him? Or her?"

Alana almost thanked him for yanking her mind away from where it had no business going. She shook her head again. "I'll be more careful the next time."

"You weren't successful tonight."

"Neither were you." Her stare held his. "Do you think Nelson was the one on the computer in that closed room?"

"Do you know how dangerous this could be?"

"I know. I won't get sloppy again."

Keith continued to stare at her, but she refused to blink. She could almost see the gears in his mind working. She felt some of her tension leave when he finally talked.

"Let's set some ground rules." He leaned back and began speaking.

For the following half hour, the conversation jumped back and forth between them as if they were opponents negotiating a groundbreaking contract. Finally he sat back. "I'm still not comfortable about your involvement."

"Chauvinistic, are we?"

"Realistic. You're inexperienced at this. You said so yourself. You don't know where this might lead."

"And you do?" She leaned her head to the side. "How can a consultant know more about how to proceed than an investigative reporter? And why are you so sure that you do?" Suspicion filled her face.

"I've done this before."

"Yeah? When and where?"

"Never mind. That's not important here."

She stared for a few seconds, then decided not to push it, at least not now. She sighed. "Maybe we're both wasting time. Maybe we're not finding anything because there isn't anything to find. Maybe the only problem was the programmer who left." She shook her head. "I still don't understand how she could destroy her career like that."

"Family ties can be strong. She felt her brother had gotten a rotten deal when Dave prosecuted him for stealing."

"I know, but . . ." She shrugged. "How will we know when to stop looking?"

"I'll know." He stood. "We should meet next weekend.

I need your phone number in case I need to get in touch with you before then."

Alana didn't argue that he'd see her every weekday until then. She gave the number to him without hesitating. He had found out so much about her already. A phone number would be easy.

"I'll take you home. We both have a long day ahead of us." For the first time he smiled. Alana had trouble following his words. "Although my day will start before yours." *He should smile more often.* She frowned. *Don't even think about going there. You still don't know him and his only interest in you is related to this case. If it is a case.*

"Ready? Or do you intend to spend the night?"

*Don't go there, either.* Both minds formed the same thought. Alana's reaction was to avoid eye contact and hope the heightened color in her face didn't show. Keith's response to his thought was to try to shake it off. They stood at the same time.

This time, Keith didn't touch her shoulder or her arm. In fact, he left enough space between them for two other people to fit comfortably.

She followed him to the elevator, trying not to notice how well his slacks fit over his behind. She also tried not to notice how wide his shoulders were and how his shirt fit across them as if made for him. She didn't want to, but she remembered how those shoulders felt under her hands while they were kissing. She frowned. *There should be a better word for what went on between us. Kissing is so inadequate.*

Just as she failed to hear him coming at DCS, she failed to control her thoughts. If she were lucky, this case would only take a few weeks.

She didn't look at him when they got into the waiting elevator, or during the ride down. Maybe only one week. Why wasn't she happy about only having to see him for another week or so?

# Chapter 14

"Where do you want me to take you?"

"You don't know my new last name. Now you don't know where I live, either? Maybe you should review your own spy network. I guess a handsome face doesn't make you an expert, huh?" Alana glared at him, regretting the "handsome face" part of her remark as soon as she said it. Just because she thought he was handsome didn't mean she had to let him know.

"Why are you so snippy? You have what you want. You'll get your story."

"I would have gotten my story anyway. And I don't like being manipulated." She glared at him. "I don't like insults, either."

"Insults? You mean the 'cutesy amateur detective' thing I said?" He frowned. "You can't possibly mean the beautiful woman comment?"

"I mean both."

Keith stared at her. "How can you object to being referred to as a beautiful woman?"

"For one thing, it was the way you used it."

"I'll give you that. And another thing?"

"Nobody ever accused me of being beautiful before."

"Maybe they were afraid you would snap at them if they did." He suddenly remembered to watch the road. "Look. I apologize for the 'cutesy amateur detective' comment." He glanced at her again. "As for the 'beautiful woman' remark, I will not apologize for telling the truth." He glanced at her and then back to the road. "I never heard of referring to a woman as beautiful being an accusation." He continued to stare ahead, but a smile showed in his voice. "Now about your 'handsome face' comment, what about that?"

"I'll let you know where you can let me off when we get closer. I live off 192."

"You're right. We should save that discussion for a more appropriate time."

*There will never be an appropriate time,* she thought. *I don't even want to* think *about what made me say that out loud.* But for once she had enough sense to be quiet.

During the drive to drop Alana off, Keith had time to rethink the whole plan. *It could be dangerous. If it wasn't for the fact that I truly believed that DCS is okay as far as security is concerned, I'd never agree to let her get involved.* He shook his head. *If I do find something, she's out of there; I don't care how beautiful she is.*

He fought the urge to stare at her to make sure that his opinion of her was based on fact and not some sudden quirk in his mind. After all, he had seen her enough times and even watched her closely, and the way he had reacted each time he saw her proved his point. His thoughts backtracked to earlier tonight. He had seen her really up close. Of course, his eyes had been closed most of the time. He frowned. What had gotten into him? *I could have found another way out of that situation without going that far.* His frown deepened. It was bad enough to have his body remembering how she felt after that brief encounter in the airport. How was he going to control its reaction to memories of her after that kiss? He commanded his breathing to slow and take in what should have been deep cooling breaths, but he had expected too much. *That kiss.*

What had started out as a cover had quickly grown to an 'I finally get to satisfy my curiosity' kiss. It didn't work; his curiosity had magnified. The kiss had only made him want to delve deeper into her. As deep as a man can go into a woman. He shifted to try to ease the tightness of his lower body.

He shifted again and made his mind find another track before he had some awkward explaining to do. *I should never have agreed to let her get involved at all. I should have had Dave get her fired. I don't need this.* He sighed heavily. Now all he had to do was convince his body of that when it was telling him that was exactly what he needed. His no personal involvement rule was so far away that it might as well have not existed. Then the reason for it gave him strength. *She'll get hurt if I let her get close. She's the kind of woman who wants forever and I just want to solve this situation and move on. Again,* his mind added.

"You crossed 192 a block back." Alana's voice cut in.

"Why didn't you say something at the time?" Keith pulled into the parking lot of the small shopping center ahead and turned around.

"You're the driver. I thought you would be familiar with this road since you live down here. When you get back to it, turn left. I'll get off at the nearest corner."

"It's late. I'm not leaving you out here."

"Nobody made you my guardian. I'll be all right."

"Sure you will because I'm taking you home." He turned onto 192. "Tell me where."

"You have to go to work before I do. You're the one who won't get much sleep."

"I'm used to operating on little sleep. Where do you live, Alana Cortez?"

Alana tried to think of a reason that would make him drop her off before the trailer park. They were less than a block away and she still hadn't thought of anything. *What the heck.* "Turn right at the next corner and go half a block."

Keith stopped after he followed her directions. "Here? You live here?"

"There's nothing wrong with living in a trailer park. Some nice people live here." She opened the car door.

"I don't doubt that. How far do you have to walk once you get inside the park?"

"Not far." She faced him, trying not to notice his face. She was right. He wasn't pretty, but he definitely was handsome. His full mouth reminded her of the kiss. She shook her head slightly. If anybody ever rewrote the definition for making love, his kiss would be at the top of the list for consideration. It had started sweet but had moved to strong in less than a second. It had been sexy and full of promises that she had wanted him to keep. Still wanted him to keep. Just remembering it made heat seep through her body and settle where his kiss promised that he would . . .

"Did you change your mind?"

"No." Heat flooded her face. She had to get away from him before she tried to find out if another kiss would be as potent. "Thanks for the ride."

"I'm not sure about this." He put his hand on her arm, just barely touching, but it was almost too much for her.

"You don't have to be." She made herself concentrate on the conversation they were having with words, not the one she wanted to have with his body. She had to get away. She had to find where her common sense was hiding and bring it back. "Nothing can happen in the park without everybody else hearing it. Besides, people will be sitting on their steps talking." Quickly, before she

```
          B O R D E R S   E X P R E S S


EMPLOYEE    1722   102   9632   09-24-05
SALE        REL 7.8/1.07  08  17:37:16

START GROUP DISCOUNT
01 1583145389     *             6.99
02 1583145370     *             6.99
03 1583143734     *             6.99
04 0060512180                  14.95
05 0060579218                  11.99
06 0060564067     *            23.95
END GROUP -- SUBTOTAL          71.86
DISCOUNT 36      33% OFF        23.71-
                 SUBTOTAL       48.15
                 NO TAX
                 TOTAL          48.15
XXXXXXXXXXXX8407 M C            48.15
              PV# 0029632


      BOOKS MAKE THE GREATEST GIFTS


===========CUSTOMER RECEIPT===========
```

changed her mind, she got out and walked through the entrance, never looking back.

*I'm not sure about this,* she thought. *There must be another way of getting a story without working with him. He stirs feelings in me that I don't want.* She frowned. *Why couldn't he be ugly and obnoxious?*

She stopped, looked around, saw the trailer three spots ahead of hers beside her, then went back to her own trailer.

The blinking light on her answering machine was glaring when she opened the door. She played it back, but she already knew who it was.

"You'd better call me as soon as you get in. None of that 'tomorrow' stuff," Yvette's voice demanded. Alana glanced at her watch. One o'clock. She shook her head, but she didn't hesitate. She quickly punched in the numbers.

Yvette bypassed a greeting and went right to fussing. "What was that message about? Have you lost your mind? And *you* accused *me* of doing something stupid? How could you go off with some strange man in the middle of the night? Do you know how worried I've been?"

"I can explain, if you give me a chance." Alana settled onto the built-in couch. "I wasn't really in any danger."

"That's not how you sounded. You sounded a little mad and a lot scared. Who is this man?"

"He works at DCS and—"

"That doesn't mean anything. There are people who work there that *I* wouldn't trust and I've been there longer than you have. You never should have started this. I think you should back off. Now. Maybe I should go to Dave and—"

"No. If you will listen, I can explain. Okay?"

"It had better be better than good."

When Alana finished, Yvette was still not happy, but she no longer threatened to go to Dave. "Don't you ever leave a message like that and then make me wait forever to hear from you. Another ten minutes and I was going to call the police. I mean it. Promise."

"Okay, okay, I promise." Alana's voice gentled. "Go to bed, sis. You have to get up soon." She hesitated. "I'm sorry I made you worry. Thanks for waiting to hear from me."

"You know I have to find this Keith Henderson tomorrow, don't you? I have to see what kind of man made you lose what little common sense you have left."

"I won't tell you not to, because I know you won't listen to me."

"That seems to run in the family, doesn't it?"

"Good night. See you tomorrow night."

Alana hung up. Since Keith knew they were sisters, there was no harm in Yvette talking to him.

She got ready for bed with Keith on her mind. Did he sleep in pajamas? She shook her head. *Girl, you are in deep water and going in deeper still.* She turned off the light. *I have to rethink the statement I made to my family about not looking for somebody.* She shook her head. *No, I don't. I'm not looking, but it sure feels like I found somebody anyway.*

On Monday, Alana almost bumped into Keith when she turned to empty a wastebasket. He stared at her and she at him. They looked as if somebody had ordered them to stay right there and not move. Then he broke the connection. "We have to stop meeting like this," he growled before he moved down the hall.

"You got that right," she muttered as she stared at his back, his broad back that made her hands want to stroke across it, go down past his waist, and settle at his hips. She tore her gaze from his shoulders and looked lower. Mistake. His tan slacks hugged his hips and molded his behind. *I never realized that I have a thing for behinds.* She frowned. *Cut it out.* The feel of him against her and the image of his strong body stayed with her even after he disappeared into a cubicle. Still she stared as if she didn't have work to do. It was bad when your own mind wouldn't obey you.

*Is he married? Just because he doesn't wear a wedding band doesn't mean he's not. A lot of men don't wear one.* She frowned. *He must at least have a girlfriend, a significant other. No way could a man who looks and feels like that be unattached.*

She felt her face flush as she remembered again exactly how his body had felt against hers all the way down her entire front—her breasts crushed against his hard chest, her lower body pressed against his, his groin nudging her softness. She tried to prevent the way her body was preparing for him even though he was not there. *He must belong to somebody.* She frowned. *Then how could he kiss me like that?* She shook her head. *Does the word player come to mind? Maybe he's just a dog, just a player.* She didn't like that idea, but it stayed with her anyway.

Thursday came, but, since they had just talked, Alana didn't meet with Keith. She tried not to be disappointed. She also tried not to be sorry when she didn't see him during the day.

On Friday, Alana went to Yvette's knowing it wouldn't be a smooth visit.

"I saw your Keith person today." Yvette didn't even give Alana a chance to come inside before she started talking. "He looks familiar, but he just started working there. He's a stranger."

"Hello, little sister. And how are you?" Alana tried to walk casually into the living room, but it was hard because she knew what was coming.

"Don't try to change the subject. *I* don't know anything about him and I work the same hours that he does. Dave was kind of vague when he introduced him at a staff meeting." She paced across the area rug. "I think you should back off."

"I'll be all right. Really."

"That's probably what the fly said as it walked into the spider's web." She glared at Alana. "The last time it was seen alive, I might add." Worry lines formed across her forehead. "I really think you need to change your mind about this."

"Do you have any ice cream? And maybe a couple of those chocolate chip macadamia nut cookies?"

"How can you think about dessert?" She stopped in front of Alana and glared at her again. "Your life might be in danger."

"Yvette, don't worry. We worked out a plan. He's looking for the same thing I am." *At least as far as uncovering the problem is concerned. I wouldn't mind having something else in common.* Her thoughts flew back to the kiss as if they didn't have anything else to center on. "Do you or do you not have any of my favorite cookies?"

"If I thought it would work, I'd make you promise to leave DCS before I brought out my stash." She glared at her for a second longer, then went into the kitchen. "I'm not through with the subject," she warned as she handed the bag to Alana.

"Thank you."

Alana spent at least the next hour trying to reassure Yvette that the plan was still a safe one. When they stopped to go to bed, she still had not convinced her sister. *I guess tomorrow we'll battle round two,* she thought as she slipped into bed. *I am not going to think about Keith,* she promised herself even as his image planted itself in her thoughts, ready to inhabit her dreams.

\* \* \*

The next week Alana had to make herself concentrate on doing her work instead of on Keith. She checked a few more computers without getting caught, but found nothing to keep DCS from getting government contracts. She tried not to think ahead to when they would meet, but Keith's image kept popping up. *Who was he, really? What did he do in real life? More importantly, why do I care?*

Thursday night finally came. She was closing the supply closet door when she turned to see a female security guard. *I never heard her coming.* She frowned. *Maybe I'm not cut out for this after all.*

"Finished?"

"Sí."

"You took a long time tonight."

"I didn't see you."

"I saw you."

"You're new."

The guard's stare was like a cinderblock wall. "I used to take Nelson's place when he wasn't here. He got another job. I'll be here from now on." No hand came out in greeting.

"All right." Alana checked the name tag and reminded herself to pull out her accent. "Miss Harper." *Does training to be a security guard include lessons in hostility?*

She reached back into the closet and got her purse. Then she shut the door, checked to make sure it locked, and faced the guard again. "I'm going now."

"What took you so long in the offices?"

Miss Harper had stepped close enough for Alana to step back. The hair on the back of Alana's neck stood up. *What's this all about?* She toned down her intuition that was screaming a warning. But she stayed alert.

"I spilled a trash can in one of the offices and had to clean it up. Then I had to wipe up the coffee that spilled out of it and onto the floor." She forced a smile. "I am glad there is no carpet. That is hard to clean."

"Be more careful. You shouldn't be here this late." Miss Harper's stare held. "I'll let you out." She didn't move for a few seconds and Alana was very much aware of the gun on the guard's hip. Finally she spoke again. "Go ahead."

Alana forced herself not to look back as she walked to the door. The guard didn't say a word when she opened it. Alana didn't mind that. She felt lucky to get out. It felt as if she was escaping from some danger. The old term "bad vibes" popped into her head.

*Silly.* She shook her head. *You're jumpy over nothing.* Still, she didn't relax until she got to the bus stop.

She took the bus to Keith's place. *This is business, only business,* she told herself as she looked forward to meeting with him.

The bus let her off at the corner and she was so busy reminding herself that the meeting was strictly business, that she didn't notice the car that had followed the bus until she got off.

Now it eased to the curb outside the parking lot. She never noticed how the driver watched her enter Keith's building. Her attention was focused on seeing Keith again.

# Chapter 15

Alana was nervous, but for a different reason this time. She knew that she was in no danger. She was glad when Keith opened the door right away, before she had a chance to admit the reason why.

A hint of musk aftershave greeted her as she walked past him. *I am here to discuss the story. Nothing else.* She hadn't seen him all day. Not even passed him in the hall. She swallowed hard. *It would be so easy to imagine that I'm here for a different reason.* A quick frown flitted across her face. *Quit it.* She took a deep breath and fastened a blank look on her face. *The only danger is from myself.*

"I got takeout from Johnson's Diner," Keith said, as if he didn't have a clue as to the feelings he had activated in her over the little time they had known each other. "I wasn't sure what you like to eat, but I figured that everybody with an ounce of soul likes soul food. We can talk as we eat. Come on."

He led her to the small table just inside the kitchen. It wasn't far, but by the time she sat, she was ready to discuss business.

Keith opened the containers in the middle of the table and then sat across from her. His knees grazed hers before he adjusted into the seat. *Business,* she reminded herself. "I didn't know what you like, so I ordered several different things."

"You bought enough food for at least six people." Alana frowned at the four large takeout containers, each of which was heaped with enough food for a complete meal.

"Don't worry. Whatever we don't eat, I'll have for tomorrow."

"Probably for the next couple of tomorrows." Alana stared at the table and shook her head.

"Better too much than not get something you like." He shrugged. "So. What do you like?"

"If it's soul food, I'll probably like it." She stared at him. "Except for chitterlings, or chitlins as they were called before everybody got so sophisticated. I can't deal with them."

"What's wrong with chitlins?"

"I have to admit that I don't know how they taste. I can't get them past my nose." She wrinkled her nose. "I can't deal with pig feet, either. I keep thinking about them walking around in the smelly sty all day."

She looked in each container, then picked the one with fried catfish, candied sweet potatoes, and greens and began to put some of the food onto her plate.

Keith chuckled. "I didn't get either of those, but I think you're only masquerading as an eater of soul food if you rule out both of those culture classics." He smiled at her. "Your status in The Group of Soul might be in jeopardy."

He looked at the untouched three remaining meals. If he continued to look at her, he was in danger of forgetting things he should remember. He gave himself a mental shake before he slid the container with the smothered pork chops in front of himself. Then he lifted a healthy serving onto his plate.

They stared at each other for a few seconds longer, as if waiting for something to happen; then they both began to eat.

As they ate, the only discussion was about food. In the back of their minds, though, struggling to reach the front, were thoughts of each other.

Finally Alana looked at the rest of the food in the container. "Looks like I have tomorrow's dinner, too. I'm stuffed."

"No room for sweet-potato pie?"

"Not even a sliver." She smiled at him. "Do you have take-out service for the take-out service?"

"For you, I think I can manage." He smiled back. *She should smile more.*

She stared at him. *He should smile more.*

Keith found his senses first.

"Did you uncover anything?"

"What?"

"At DCS. Have you found anything?"

"Not really."

"What do you mean 'not really'?"

"I revisited a couple of the sites, and what I had found before was gone. There was no trace left."

"Maybe somebody just cleaned house."

She shook her head. "I don't think so; at least, I don't understand why they would go to all of that trouble just to get rid of harmless files. A lot of other junk is still there."

"Do you remember what kind of things were erased?"

"From what I can remember, old e-mails that had forwarded attachments. It was a little difficult, but I got into them before. Now it's as if they never existed."

"What were they about?"

"Nothing specific, really. I couldn't make any sense out of them. It was as if somebody had too much time on their hands and so they forwarded all kinds of stuff. Most of the files looked as if somebody had let a young child loose and told him to go play in computer traffic: a child who hadn't yet learned to write." She frowned. "You know, people usually forward the same type of things. It's like a signature: one person might be known to send inspirational stories to everybody on their list. Somebody else might just do jokes. Others seem stuck on sharing rumors." She shook her head. "The stuff I'm talking about . . ." She shook her head again. "It was about nothing. Some of the so-called sentences didn't even make sense. A lot of it wasn't even words."

"Did you print any of them?"

"No, I was afraid to use the printer. You know how loud it can be." She smiled. "But I did forward a couple to myself yesterday." Her smile widened with smugness. "They're still on my laptop."

"I need to see them."

"I can forward them to you." Her eyes widened. "Do you think they mean something?"

"I won't know until I look at them."

Alana leaned back. "A computer specialist masquerading as a business consultant."

Keith turned his head to one side. "A reporter masquerading as a cleaning woman."

Alana shrugged. "I'm working on a story, so that explains me. You already know that. You, on the other hand, are supposed to be just a business consultant."

"This has to do with business."

"Have *you* found anything?"

He stared at her for so long that she wondered if he was going to answer. Then he gave a little shrug. "I meet with Dave tomorrow to try to clear up some glitches."

"Glitches?"

"Some of the paper files in his cabinet were out of order and not quite neat. Dave is a stickler about things like that, but he hadn't been in that particular drawer in a few weeks, so he didn't notice. Also, his computer was used on Tuesday. He was out of the office all day."

"His secretary?"

Keith shook his head. "I don't think so. It was done after six, and Jamila was gone by then. Nobody but the two of them should be in his office at any time."

"I know." Alana nodded. "The cleaning staff has orders to make sure we clean in there before Jamila and Dave leave. Jamila was late leaving one day because I almost forgot to clean, and she refused to leave me there. What files were messed up?"

"Plans for the engine for a new software program that's still in the development stage."

"So. It hasn't stopped."

"We don't have enough to determine if this is part of the same problem. We might have a new player on the scene. This kind of thing happens more often in businesses than we like to think. There's a fortune to be made from a new piece of software if it's good enough, and a few young companies are around as proof of that." He stared at her. "What do you think of the guard?"

"The guard? Which one? Miss Harper said she's taking Nelson's place, but they both have a need to make sure you know who's in charge. I think it's called a Napoleon complex." She frowned. "Why?"

He shook his head several times. "Just a feeling. Probably nothing."

"For a few seconds the other day, I got an uncomfortable feeling around Miss Harper." She stared at him. "Do they often turn out to be nothing? Those feelings of yours, I mean?"

Instead of answering, Keith stared at the table. "Even though Nelson's not there any longer, I'm in the process of digging further into both of their backgrounds." He frowned. "Nelson didn't give any notice. He just didn't show up one day. Dave contacted the security company, and they don't know where he is. He never picked up his last paycheck."

"Miss Harper told me that he got a job somewhere else. Did anybody check to make sure?"

"Somebody stopped by his place, but there was no answer."

"Maybe something's the matter with him?"

"Dave said this isn't the first time he was a no-show. Maybe that's why the security company replaced him." He pushed his chair back. "That's not our problem. I guess we're finished here." He didn't stand. It was as if he didn't believe his own words.

Alana didn't move, either. She didn't want to leave him yet, and she didn't want to think about why. She only knew that when she used the word "feeling" it had stirred something inside her that was still churning, something as uncomfortable as a new pair of shoes. Her self-preservation told her to back off. Her heart told her to go on.

"I have to ask you something that doesn't have anything to do with any of this. What were you doing in Philly? That was you at the airport wasn't it?"

"Why?"

"Just curious. You know a lot about me, but I don't know anything about you."

He shrugged. "Yes. It's no secret. I grew up there. My sister still lives in the old house. I was visiting her. We try to get together several times during the year for holidays. She lives near where you used to live."

"No fooling? You grew up there, you go to Philly every Christmas, and we've never run into each other before?" She smiled. "I don't mean that literally, although that's what happened." The memory of the way it felt to have him against her, not once but twice, made her feel as if somebody had suddenly switched from air-conditioning to heat. She leaned back in her chair, when what she wanted to do was lean forward. "I know Philly is big and Mount Airy itself isn't small, but still." She shook her head. "We probably know some of the same people. You know, six degrees of separation and such." She shook her head again. "You go there several times a year, huh?" She folded her arms on the table to keep her hands from reaching to him.

"I don't always make the get-togethers." He let his gaze slide to the floor. "This year was my first in a long time."

Alana noticed the pain in his eyes before he blinked it away. *Something is hurting him bad.* She didn't know how to help. Nor did she know why she felt a need to. *Should I try to get him to talk or not?* "I guess business keeps you away, huh?"

"Yeah. Something like that." His look softened a bit as he turned the conversation from himself. She let him. "How could you pick up and move like that? You'd lived in Philly most of your life."

*He's good at changing the subject. He must have had a lot of practice.* She shrugged. "Easy. No job there, no family, no ties." She frowned. "Not as easy as I thought it would be, though. I miss that city." She smiled. "I haven't had a decent hoagie or cheesesteak since I got here. We won't talk about Tastykakes or about soft pretzels with mustard."

"No significant other back there?" He held up his hand as soon as the words left him, as if trying to stop them from reaching her. "Never mind. I shouldn't have asked that. It's none of my business and it has nothing to do with what we're working on."

"I don't mind answering." *Why did he want to know? Maybe he feels the attraction, too?* She felt a bubble of hope form inside her and wondered how she could help it grow. *What were they working on besides the problem at DCS?* "No.

Nobody." She stared at him. He had opened that door and she walked in. "How about you? Are you involved?"

"No, I don't have anybody." He frowned. "I'm sorry I took the conversation away from business. That's all that's going on here between us: business." He stood.

"I'm not sorry." She stood within reaching distance, but the only thing that she let touch him was her stare. She took a deep breath to steel herself from his rejection, which she expected to come. "You can deny it if you want to, but you feel something between us, too."

"Nothing could never come of it," he said, even as he took a step into the space between them.

"Why not?" A hint of aftershave wafted to her, curled around her, and drew her closer until only a scant foot separated them. "We're both unattached."

"There's more to it besides that." His sigh was full of regret. "It couldn't work out." His hand brushed down the side of her face as if it hadn't heard his words. "You'd only get hurt." His other hand rested on her shoulder.

"I'm a big girl." She moved forward until mere inches separated them now. Then she eased her hand up to touch the side of his face. "I don't think you'd hurt me."

"Alana, you just don't know." Keith's words ended in a groan as he brought her against him.

Alana felt as if she had found a place where she belonged. In spite of Keith's warning, she felt safe.

His mouth found hers and she pressed closer. Her arms made a path around his neck as his hands drew her against his hardness. His kiss was full of promise and regret.

He pulled away and stared down at her. She could see the heat and desire in his eyes. Then she closed her eyes and couldn't see at all, only feel.

His mouth returned to hers and she welcomed him back as if he had been gone for years rather than mere seconds. Desperation met desperation, need met need, as they tried to make up for all the time they hadn't known each other.

Keith widened his stance so that Alana stood cradled within his legs. His hardness probed against her softness and she pressed closer still. His hand found its way to her breast and his fingers brushed across the tip. Alana moaned and Keith swallowed her moan. This kiss made the last one seem pristine, as if it were only a preliminary to the real thing.

His fingers freed the buttons from the holes of her uniform shirt and stroked across her skin until they found the tip of her breast again, hard and waiting. Only the lace barrier of her bra was keeping him from touching the skin of the swollen tip, but it was one barrier too much.

The kiss deepened more as if, if they tried hard enough, the two of them could learn all about each other from this one kiss.

Slowly, as if hoping that something would change his mind, Keith eased his mouth from hers. He rested his chin on the top of her head, trying not to notice how natural it felt to hold her like this. His low rumble touched Alana. "I—We can't do this." Still, he held her, as if waiting for something to change his opinion.

"Why not?"

"I can't have a long-term commitment."

"I didn't ask for that." She brushed her hands up and down his arms. "I didn't you ask for anything."

"You're a nice woman."

"That word 'nice' has been used to signal the kiss of death to many a relationship, even some that were never given a chance to begin."

"You deserve better than me."

"What if I think that *you* are the best for me?"

He eased away from her, but his hands still cradled her shoulders, still refused to let her go. "You don't know me."

"Then tell me what I should know. Help me to know you."

Keith's only answer was a shake of the head. Alana continued, feeling his rejection growing, searching for a way to stop it.

"I know enough. I know how I feel. I know that if we back off now we'll both regret it for the rest of our lives." She removed her hands from his arms and stepped back. "I know we need to give what's between us a chance." She widened the space. She had to swallow hard to make room for her words to leave her. "I also know that you aren't ready to accept any of this." She turned from him so he couldn't see the tears trying to show themselves.

"Alana—"

"I'm leaving now. I'm going home."

She took her purse from beside her chair and slipped the strap over her shoulder, glad for something for her hands to do, but knowing that the strap was a poor substitute for Keith's hands touching her shoulders. She dug deep inside herself and found enough courage to let her walk away from him.

"I'll—I'll take you home."

"Whatever." She opened the door and left his apartment, hoping that the sorrow filling her would ease the further away she got from what almost happened.

Keith followed her to the car. She stood silently while he opened the door, working hard not to try to change his mind.

The car was full of heavy silence as he drove the distance that seemed twice as long as it really was.

"Alana," Keith put his hand on her arm before she could get out, "this is for the best. We need to stop it before it begins."

Alana moved to the door and tried not to feel the loss when his hand left her arm. *Didn't he know it had already begun?* "Good-bye, Keith. Thank you for the ride."

She walked into the park with her head held high. She didn't have to let him know about the tears streaming down her face. *Stupid. Be glad he said something before you got in too deep.* She wiped her face and took a deep breath. *It's already too late. I was caught before I even saw his face.* She shook her head. *I've heard of love at first sight, but this, this is ridiculous.* She heard his car start up but didn't look back. What for?

She unlocked her door, still thinking about what had just happened. And what could have happened. *Move on. You're a survivor.*

She set her purse on the table and frowned. The napkin holder was empty. She always filled it right away. She stared at it, trying to remember when she had emptied it. She gasped as the answer came to her. *I didn't.*

She peeked into the small wastebasket against the closet door. The only thing inside was her used napkin from this morning. *Where were the rest?*

Now she allowed her stare to slowly touch each thing in the room. Everything else seemed all right. She shook her head. The book that she had left at the very end of the couch now left enough space at the end for somebody to sit.

She stood still and listened as if waiting for an explanation.

Something else needed explaining. A thin scent of roses hung in the air. She had never liked the smell of roses. *I should leave. I should call the police.* She shook her head. *Why? What reason do I have? I think somebody broke in and stole my napkins and moved some of my things around? Somebody left the smell of roses in my house?*

Then, because she refused to think of a reason not to,

she went to the bedroom door, opened it, and stopped just inside the door. *You're supposed to be an investigative reporter. So investigate.*

She stepped further into the room and stopped again. *Something isn't right here.* She glanced around. The little tray that held her hair elastics was closer to the middle of the dresser than the side where it belonged. She frowned. It had been in the same place since she had moved in. *Until now.*

She let her gaze pan the room. The strap of her overnight bag poked out from the drawer under the bed. *I know I didn't do that. I haven't touched that bag since I brought my stuff from Yvette's.*

Several other things had been shifted slightly, but nothing seemed to be missing. She wouldn't know until she checked everything. An uneasy feeling crept up her spine. *I have to get out of here.*

She opened the door, went back and grabbed her purse, rushed out, and almost bumped into Mrs. Banto.

"Were you surprised to see him? He didn't leave already, did he?"

"Who?"

"Your cousin."

"My cousin?"

"Sí. He said he just got to town and he wanted to surprise you. I told him he could wait for you in my office, but he said he'd wait at your door; he said he didn't want to miss you in case you came another way." She smiled. "I told him there *was* no other way, but he wouldn't listen, so I let him go." She sighed. "He had a beautiful bouquet of roses for you. Nobody ever gave me flowers like that." She shook her head. "Nobody ever gave me flowers at all since I left the island." She frowned. "He didn't have an accent, your cousin. He didn't look Hispanic, either. Was he born here?"

"Yes, ma'am." If she told her landlady that she didn't have a cousin down here, that she hadn't seen her only male cousin in the last two years, there would be more questions, and she didn't have time for that. She needed to call Keith. She forced a smile for Mrs. Banto, hoping that would make her leave. It didn't.

The woman leaned against the railing. "How could he leave so soon when he waited for so long to see you? What did he do with the roses?" She looked around at the spindly shrubs beside the porch and then at the porches across the road. "Why would he take them with him?"

"How long was he here?"

"Fifteen minutes. No more than twenty. I didn't see him leave. I don't understand why he didn't wait."

"Don't worry. He does stuff like that."

"His friend seemed anxious to see, you, too."

"Friend?"

"Sí. He said you went to school together. Did they leave a note so you know how to reach them?"

"No, ma'am." Alana made her voice steady. "He'll probably be back soon." She kept her voice steady instead of letting in panic at that thought. "Please excuse me. I have to make a call."

"I don't see how he could have left. I was—" Somebody called Mrs. Banto, interrupting her words. "I have to go. I promised Lilia I would talk to her. She wants to move to a bigger place, and I got one."

The woman was barely out of earshot when Alana took out her cell phone. She knew there was no place for anybody to hide in the trailer; still, she wasn't going back inside alone to use the other phone.

After punching in the wrong first three digits twice, she succeeded in entering Keith's number. Static filled the air. She moved away from the trailer in an effort to escape from the interference, but it didn't lessen. *As soon as I get over the breakdown I'm going to have, I'm calling my phone company. They charge too much for me to have to put up with this.*

"Somebody was at my place," she said as soon as Keith answered. Her voice wasn't as steady as she wanted and she had skipped the hello part of the conversation.

"Where are you? There's a lot of interference on the line."

"I know. You think I can't hear it? I'm at home."

"Did you say you're home? I can barely understand you. Did you say somebody was there? Who?"

"Not any more and I don't know who."

"You're not inside, are you?"

"No. I'm outside calling from my cell phone. I usually get the good reception that the company brags about. I don't know what's the matter with the phone now." She moved it from her ear and shook it, as if that could fix the problem.

"Alana. Are you still there?"

"Yeah. I thought that maybe shaking the phone could fix things. I think there were two of them."

"Did you see them?"

"No, but my landlady did. He told Mrs. Banto . . ." She stopped and swallowed the panic that was starting. "He said he was my cousin. He brought a bunch of roses."

"And you don't have a cousin."

"Not one that I've seen in the last two years and he doesn't even know I moved down here. Look, I can barely make out what you're saying. I'll go back inside and use the phone in there."

"No." His voice kept her from moving. "Stay put. In fact, go wait at your landlady's office. I'm on the way."

Alana didn't question Keith's direction. She glanced

at the door, but didn't touch the handle. *What's going on?* She took a deep breath and left.

If she walked any faster, she would be running. She should have felt silly, but she didn't. She was glad for each foot she put between her trailer and herself.

# Chapter 16

Alana stood at Mrs. Banto's office, but with her back to it. Her glance scanned her surroundings as if it were a lighthouse signal looking for danger instead of warning ships.

There were so many places to hide: behind trailers, dumpsters, and cars. She looked hard at each potential hiding place as if she had Superman's X-ray vision. Then she looked again. Not another person was in sight. She swallowed hard. *If anybody were waiting here for me, would they care if somebody saw them?* She shuddered. *Mrs. Banto saw them. Did that mean that she was in danger?* Alana shook her head, as if that would shake away any danger. Then she pressed her back against the wrought-iron railing on Mrs. Banto's steps and waited.

In less than fifteen minutes, Keith was running down the street inside the trailer park toward her. She helped close the space between them by dashing to meet him.

"You don't know how glad I am to see you," she said when they were still a couple of feet apart. "What are we going to do? Come on. See for yourself what I mean." She didn't want him to think she had made it all up so he'd come back. Now that he was there, she felt foolish. What had really happened? She took a deep breath. "Look. I'm sorry. I know you have to get up early. It's nothing, really." She backed up and shrugged. "I shouldn't have called you. Maybe it was some of the kids fooling around inside my place. After all, nothing was taken."

"Kids brought you roses? That's an awfully expensive prank, even for kids with a lot of money. We're not going back there." He placed his hand at her back. "Come on. We're leaving. I'll come back later and check things out."

Alana went with him without protesting. The thought that he was acting as if he was more than capable of handling a situation that could be dangerous was comforting. She felt safe for the first time since she had gotten home tonight. At least until she thought of what it might mean if it hadn't been kids in her place. *Does that make me a female chauvinist?* She shook her head. *No. That makes me a person smart enough to know when the water is too deep for me to swim in it alone.*

Both of them scanned their surroundings as they walked. They didn't stop even after they reached Keith's car.

Alana sat in the passenger seat, refusing to think about her mood when she had sat in this same spot less than an hour ago.

"Where are we going?"

"You can stay at my place tonight." Keith pulled away from the curb.

"I'm not staying there with you."

"You'll be safe with me."

"I know."

He had made that more than clear before. How could she explain that she wasn't worrying about him, that she was concerned about her own ability to keep to business? The idea of sleeping under the same roof as Keith. . . .

She shook her head. "It wouldn't work out." He winced as she used the same words he had a short while ago.

"Do you want to go to your sister's, then?" He merged into the traffic on 192.

"No. I don't want to have to explain why I changed my mind about staying with her."

"You can't go back to your place."

"I know."

"My place is best. We need to talk about this."

"There's a motel not too far. I'll call and see if they have any vacancies." She took out her cell phone.

"You know the number?"

"It's posted outside the place. I pass it every day when I'm on the bus." She shrugged. "I have a thing about numbers."

She took out her phone and activated it. The static that burst from it was loud enough for Keith to hear.

"Hang up. We'll go there instead. If they don't have a vacancy, one of the others along the road will."

"But—"

Keith touched a finger to her lips, and no other word came out. Her glance was met by his. His finger brushed along her lips before he eased it away. Alana closed her eyes and relived the feel of his touch.

The next sound from either of them was after Keith parked along the side of the office of a small non-chain motel not even on 192. "Why didn't you—" He motioned for her to keep quiet, and the rest of her sentence never came out. They both went back to silent mode.

Alana spent the time trying to figure out what was going on, but she never once thought that he didn't have a reason for his actions.

He didn't touch her again before he left the car to go to the office, and she wondered why she was disappointed in that.

When he got back in the car a few minutes later, he parked around the far side, even though there were plenty of spaces in front of the units. Then he opened her car door and led her back to a unit near the end of the row.

"Now what?" Alana turned to him as soon as they were inside the room and the door was locked.

"Take off your shirt."

"What?"

"Take off your shirt."

"My shirt? I thought we were going to talk. What happened to 'We can't do this'? You could have taken me to your apartment if this is what you had in mind, although, with your approach, you would have been wasting your time and mine." She folded her arms across her chest and glared at him. "This doesn't seem like 'no involvement' to me. Besides, a little finesse would help." Her glare hardened. "And besides, I'm no longer interested in you."

"Ah, come on, sweetheart." His voice was a caress as he slowly pulled her to him. Alana was prepared for his lips to touch hers, but what she got was his hands unbuttoning her shirt.

"What do you think you're—"

Now came his kiss: his *shh* kiss, his stop-complaining kiss. His trust-me-on-this kiss. His kiss that changed from business to pleasure in two seconds or less and was now a let's-get-lost-together kiss.

Alana bought into it when it reached the trust-me stage. She was still with him when it deepened into pleasure: pure, sweet, torturing pleasure. And, if he was lost, she was definitely lost with him. She slipped her hands from his shoulders and wrapped them around his neck. As if on its own, her body molded against his.

She didn't know when he had changed his mind about them getting involved, nor why, and she didn't care. All she cared about was that he *had* changed his mind.

The kiss deepened and she became even more lost in it, going wherever he was leading her. Keith urged her closer still and she tried to obey without question even though she was as close as she could get unless and until they entered that final stage between a man and a woman. Together they would sort out reasons for the change later. For now, she'd enjoy being with him. She had been waiting for this ever since she knew about love, and she hadn't realized it. All those years she had been waiting for him.

She brushed her hands back and forth across his back. Her breasts were crushed against his chest, but still she tried to urge him even closer to her. She shifted slightly and sweet longing spread from her sensitive breasts throughout the rest of her body to collect in her rapidly warming female center.

Keith eased away from her and she felt a loss such as she had never felt before. She also felt the air on her body where her shirt had been. She shook away the fog clouding her mind. Her shirt was in Keith's hands. She frowned. *How did he do that?* She looked down at her own body and let her gaze follow the trail being made by his gaze.

It settled on her breasts, her tightened, sensitive breasts. Her lace bra revealed as much as it covered. Or more. She glanced up at him. His gaze was stuck on her breasts. She felt her fullness tighten even more, as if his hands were touching her, rather than his gaze. Her tips swelled and pushed against the lace as if waiting for him.

She stepped back and crossed her arms across her chest, trying to regain a little self-respect, trying to make her body ease back to normal, trying not to feel cheated and deceived. That kiss didn't mean a thing to him. It was just a way to get her shirt from her. *How many times will you let him make a fool of you?*

She turned her back to him, went into the bathroom, and got a towel. Her glance in the mirror caught on her kiss-swollen lips and her heightened color. She refused to examine herself further. She just wrapped the towel around her shoulders, clutched it to her front, and went back into the room.

Keith had taken her phone from her purse. She opened her mouth to question him, but the shake of his head made her change her mind. She kept quiet. She didn't want him to kiss her again. She shook her head. *That's not true. The problem is that I do want him to kiss me again. Heaven help me. In spite of his lack of caring, I would welcome him into my arms right now.* She sat on the edge of the bed and watched him.

Keith glanced at her. His hand holding the phone hung in the air, as if an invisible line pinned it there. His gaze touched her face, moved down to the towel, then went back to her face. Alana saw what looked like regret flicker across his face, but it might have been her ego making her imagine that. She continued to stare at him as if, if she stared long enough, she could see his thoughts.

Keith shook his head and tried to concentrate on the shirt again. He had never had so much trouble keeping his mind on a case before. A towel covered her, but he still had the image of white lace allowing a glimpse of tan skin to peek through, showing a preview of what was inside it. His mind kept trying to pull out his memory of how that fullness felt when he touched it, brushed against it, anticipated feeling it bare, weighing it in his hand. He shook his head again. He knew that memory wasn't going away; he just hoped it would ease back enough so he could work.

He passed the phone slowly over the front of the shirt. Halfway down the front a buzz jumped from the phone and startled Alana.

She watched with her mouth open as Keith pulled a tiny circle attached to a wire from behind the third button. He never looked at her. Instead, he held the wire and went into the bathroom. Alana watched from the doorway as he filled a glass, then lowered the thing into it by the nearly invisible line. The phone was now as quiet as it should have been all along.

She moved aside as he went back into the room, but she stayed in the doorway. She glanced at the glass, then back at him. Her frown deepened.

"What—"

Again he gestured for her to be quiet. This time she was too busy trying to sort things out to question why she should obey. She had no idea what was going on, but Keith seemed to.

He went back to the desk and picked up her purse. The phone buzzed to life when he slowly passed it over the bag. It got so loud that Alana expected it to jump from Keith's hands when he reached the place where the strap met the rest of the purse. He set the phone down, and again it went quiet.

Her frown changed to surprise as the explanation came to her. This time she wasn't surprised as she watched him pull out a twin to the other wire device. He glanced at her as he carried it past her and into the bathroom. Again, she watched him lower it into the glass on the counter, where it nestled beside the other one. He turned the water on, left the bathroom, and closed the door behind him.

She stood still as he again picked up the phone and activated it. He passed it slowly over her, ending at her shoes. Then he moved it back up. He went back to her purse, dumped it onto the bed, and passed the phone over the pile, as well as the inside of her bag. The phone kept quiet. He nodded. Then he turned on the radio to a talk show with callers discussing what Shaq was going to do to the Sixers before he finally turned to her.

"Why don't you sit down and get comfortable?" He sat in the chair at the desk. "This might take a while."

Alana glanced at the bed as if she was just now aware that she was still standing. "Comfortable? You think I can get comfortable?" She pointed to the bathroom. "Bugs? Those are bugs? Somebody bugged me?" She frowned. "How did they get to my shirt? And my purse? How long have they been there?"

"You're the only one who can answer those questions."

"I have no idea." She shook her head and frowned. "Did Miguel put one in the shirt when he gave me the uniform?" She shook her head again. Then she answered her own question. "No, he didn't have a reason to. Besides, I used my phone since then, and it was all right."

"Is that your only shirt?"

"No, I have another. I keep the extra in the closet at work. We're supposed to do dirty work, but our uniforms have to stay spotless. I once spilled coffee while I was emptying a trash can. I had a big stain down the front that Nelson was happy to point out. Since then I leave my extra shirt in the closet." She looked at him. "Do you think Nelson did it? He hasn't been at work."

"I don't know. How about your purse?"

"I keep it in the closet, too." She frowned. "It wouldn't be too hard for somebody to get into the closet if they had a key." She leaned back. "Why? Is it just me? Or was Corina bugged, too? Were they checking up on us for honesty?" Her face lightened. "Maybe Dave did it. With the problems DCS has had in the past, and since their work is so sensitive, it would make sense."

"It would, but it isn't Dave. I'm the one checking his security, remember?" He leaned forward. "As to why you—"

She nodded. "Yeah. I'm the one who was caught digging into computer files." She shook her head. "Something *is* going on."

"Somebody is afraid you might stumble onto something."

Alana gasped. "Maybe I already did. You know those

files I mentioned? The ones that didn't make sense?" A thin crease marred her forehead. "Do you solve the cryptograms in the newspaper? You know, the puzzles where you have to break the code, where one letter stands for another? That's what those files remind me of."

"When we were at my place you said that you forwarded some files to your laptop."

"I did." She gasped. "That's what they were looking for in my trailer. My laptop."

He stood. "Where is your laptop? Did they get it?"

"No. I leave it at Yvette's. I wasn't sure it would be safe in the trailer." She shook her head. "I was worried about kids breaking in and stealing it. I never thought . . ." She jumped up. "Do you think Yvette's in danger?"

"There's no way to link her to you. You never mentioned her full name; your last names are different. Still, we'll suggest she take some days off. I'll clear it with Dave."

He took out his own phone. In a few seconds he was telling Dave about the situation.

Alana tried to digest what had happened. It seemed as if they had gone from "probably no problem" to somebody aware of what she had done.

"Tell Yvette that Alana is all right and will call her later," Keith said into the phone. "Also, tell her to stay there until we get back to her." Keith's end of the conversation changed to questions. "When? Where?" He nodded. "Sure, I'll keep you informed."

"Where's Yvette? What happened?" Alana barely gave him time to disconnect.

"Yvette is fine. She's at a conference in Jacksonville. She was supposed to return tomorrow. I told Dave to find an excuse for her to stay."

"Oh, yeah. I forgot she went there." She frowned. "You have a funny look. What else?"

"They found Nelson."
"Did he talk? Is he involved?"
"He's dead."
"Dead?"

# Chapter 17

"He's dead." Keith's voice was too calm for his words.

"Dead? Nelson is dead? When? How?" Alana leaned back as if she needed extra space to absorb this information.

"This morning the mail carrier told the landlady that Nelson's mailbox was full. She went to his place. When he didn't answer, she went in." He stared at Alana. "It looks as if he's been dead since the first day that he didn't show up for work, but they won't know for sure until they perform an autopsy. The security company notified Dave as a courtesy."

"What—What did he die of? Do you think those same two men. . . ?"

Nelson was short of his share of congeniality and he had given her a hard time every time he saw her. *I had wished he would leave me alone, but I had never wished him dead.*

"It looks like a heart attack, but they won't know that for sure until after they run some tests." His stare got more intense. He hesitated before he continued. "I will be more than a little surprised if he died of natural causes."

"Those men—"

"Might have had nothing to do with this." His finish to her sentence was the opposite of what she was going to say.

"But you think they did, don't you?"

"I've been wrong before." His stare swung to the window,

as though he could see through the thick drapes. "Sometimes about important things." His last words were almost a whisper. Then he shook his head and that mood was gone.

Alana had forgotten that only a towel was covering her until he handed her back her shirt. "It's okay to put this on now."

The look he gave her was heavy with regret. It said "I don't want you to. What I want is to take the rest of your clothes off. What I want is to see you without any barrier between us. What I want is you."

Alana's returning look was a matching one. She read what was on his face and in his eyes. She knew what he wanted because she wanted the same thing. So much had happened between them; but so much more hadn't. Too much had been left unfinished. She sighed. *When something isn't meant to be, it isn't meant to be, no matter how much you want it or how right it feels.*

He turned his back to her at the same time she turned hers to him.

Before long she was fastening the last button on her shirt. She felt as if she was closing the door to something that should have been. *How long would it take this feeling to go away?* She frowned. *Will it ever?*

She turned back to face him, but she looked beyond him. She was not going to make an even bigger fool of herself by letting him see what was in her eyes.

"I'm finished." As she stared at him, she knew her regret was still visible, but she couldn't help it, no matter how irrational it was. *How can I be so hurt by something that didn't happen?*

"I think we should stay here for the night. We're safe. If they know that we're here, we'd know it by now. We can get the computer tomorrow." He glanced at the bed. "You take the bed. I have the chair."

"They call that a king-size bed, so it's supposed to be big enough for two."

"I don't think that's a good idea."

"You need your rest as much as I do. To say we'll have a busy day tomorrow would be an understatement." Her jaw tightened. "You'll be safe with me. I've never forced my attention on anybody yet, and I don't intend to start now."

"Alana—"

"I'm tired. Which side do you want?" Keith stared at her for a few long seconds. She stared back without blinking.

"I'll take the door side," he finally said.

Without saying another word, Alana walked to the wall side of the bed and pulled back the covers. She slipped off her shoes, got into bed fully clothed, and turned her face to the wall.

Keith turned the light off, but Alana never shifted positions. When the mattress dipped from his weight, she tensed, but she did not move.

Traffic hummed past out on the road. Alana was glad for the noise. *What was I trying to prove with my suggestion that we do this? I've had some ideas, but this one moves to the top of my Stupid Ideas list.*

She shifted to her back, but made sure she stayed well on her side of the bed. *How long before morning?*

Keith tried to get comfortable on one-third of the bed. He had designated the middle as no-man's land, or at least as not his space and, he hoped, not her space either. *What am I doing? Since when do I accept a challenge for no good purpose?*

He shifted over to cover the last two inches on his side. *What is that perfume she's wearing?* He didn't want to, but he inhaled deeper to catch more of it. He tried not to remember beautiful tan skin visible where the pattern of the lace left spaces. *Does she always wear lace for nobody but herself?*

He ignored the possibility that maybe she wore it for somebody else. He was busy trying not to imagine his hands covering those spaces; his fingers dipping inside the fancy edging; brushing across the tip, making it harden, making it know his touch. He didn't want to think about how it would feel to draw that tip into his mouth, lace covering and all; and how he would peel the wet lace from her so he could taste her, only her.

He turned onto his back, still making sure to stay in his own space when what he wanted more than anything was to close the gap and pull her into his arms and love the concern away from her, slowly, thoroughly.

*Did her panties match her bra? How much of her female lusciousness was hidden by lace and how much was revealed to eyes lucky enough to be gifted with the sight of her? Was the lace edge at the top narrow or a finger wide? Was the skin beneath it as soft as the skin he had touched?*

He shifted to face the door. If he stayed on his back, the covers would surely rise as evidence of his arousal. *Why didn't I pull a pillow and the spread onto the floor? Why didn't I just get down on the floor and use my arms as a pillow?* He'd slept under worse conditions many times, too many times. Surely that would be more comfortable than this. *How could my common sense desert me when I need it so badly?*

A different need coursed through him, aching to be met, a need that only Alana could meet, a need that he had to ignore. The regret was strong enough to gnaw at his insides; it was begging him to reconsider. Pleading with him to, just this once, do what he wanted.

Instead of obeying, he wadded his pillow beneath his head and closed his eyes. *Why didn't the motel have a room left with two doubles, like most of them do? How many people traveling together wanted to sleep apart?* He shook his head slightly. Maybe wants didn't come under consideration for them, either. He shifted closer to the edge. *Why couldn't king-size*

*beds be bigger? And how many hours until morning?* He sighed.
*One would be too many.*

Alana tried to shift positions, but something was holding her. She opened her eyes. Her gaze met a solid chest.
It was covered by a T-shirt, but her hands had found their
way under it and were resting against warm, hard flesh.
She snapped the rest of the way awake and tried to ease
away, but an equally solid, bronze arm tightened around
her. Strong fingers rested against her back. At some point
during the night her shirt had ridden up and warm hands
had found their way to her bare skin. She held herself still
for a couple of seconds; then she closed her eyes and
leaned back into Keith, into the space that had been
empty when she fell asleep last night, but which they both
now filled.

His eyes were still closed, but his fingers stroked up and
down her back. Alana eased closer, still refusing to question the situation, refusing to think beyond now. *I'll take
this gift.* She inhaled deeply. His aftershave reached to her.
*Is this better than nothing?* She let her actions answer for her.

She resisted the temptation to brush her lips across his
chin or to use her fingers to test the texture of his skin. Instead she settled for allowing her hands to explore. She
savored the feel of the hard muscles of his back. Then her
fingers inched up and opened and closed gently against
his shoulders, learning the contours, savoring the stolen
moments, knowing this would all end too soon.

Keith's hand brushed up and down her back. A hunger
that had nothing to do with food seeped through her and
settled in places that she wanted ignore. *He's asleep. He
doesn't even know it's you that he's holding.* She shook her
head slightly. *Not like this. I don't want him like this. I want him
to know that it's* me *in his arms.*

She poked him and tried to push away. At first it was like pushing against a smooth, brown rock. His hands tightened around her, but then they stilled.

His eyes flew open and his burning gaze settled on her. She knew the second he was wide awake because the heat retreated from his gaze and his eyes looked as if a glass shield had been lowered between her and him. The change in his gaze came too late; his fire had already reached her and caused the flames in her to flare up many degrees. In spite of the change, she didn't struggle to get free. It took a few more long seconds before he loosened his hold on her.

"I . . ." His hands left her back; his arms released her, and his eyes filled with the same regret they had shown her the day before.

"Don't." Alana pulled her hands away from him. She scrambled from the bed and went into the bathroom without saying a word. None were needed. She did not want to start the day with his apology in her ears. Especially when she had been tempted to stay there and let what might have happened, happen.

After a quick shower she went back into the room. "It's all yours. I mean the bathroom, of course." *The sooner we're out of here, the better.*

Keith must have been of the same mind. He took less time with his shower than she had.

"It's best we leave in heavy traffic. I doubt if our friends have a clue as to where we are, but we'll play it safe."

Alana followed him to the door. *I don't care why we're leaving, just that we are leaving.*

Neither one glanced back at the bed before they left, but they each remembered what had almost happened in it.

\* \* \*

When Keith left the narrow street and merged into traffic on 192, he was glad for the volume: happy that he had to give most of his concentration to his driving, wishing he could center all of it on something as safe as traffic. He drove past the street leading to the trailer park and kept going.

"Do you want to stop for breakfast?" he asked when they neared a fast food restaurant. As much as he tried, he couldn't ignore her.

"No. Let's get this over with." *The sooner we sort this out, the sooner I will not have to see Keith ever again.* Her heart lurched at that, but her mind went forward. *I'll move in with Yvette and get a job as far from DCS as I can.* She tried to be happy about that, but it was next to impossible.

"Good. We'll get your laptop, check those files, and take things from there."

"Okay." Her thoughts crowded in on her so much that she had to shake them away a short while later, when Keith spoke again, so she could understand him.

"It looks like we might have a problem."

"Problem? Is something wrong with the car?"

"I think we have company."

"Where?" Alana turned and looked out the rear view window.

"A car seems to move up whenever I pass another vehicle. It's still a few cars behind us, but it never allows the distance to widen."

"How did they find us?"

"I shouldn't have taken the direct route past the trailer park."

"What will we do?" She tried not to panic. She tried not to remember that in every movie with this kind of chase scene in it, the bad guys always caught up with the good guys.

"Lose them."

"Can you do that?"

"I hope so."

He zipped around a slow-moving truck, with its bed full of metal bars and cylinders. As soon as he slipped into a spot in front of it, he went around another truck. This one had its yellow cement mixer rotating slowly.

Keith held the new spot for a minute before he passed what could only be a tourist who was driving as if he hadn't a clue where he was, where he was going, or how to get there if he had. Keith would have put distance between him and them even if he hadn't been trying to elude somebody.

He widened the space, which other cars quickly filled. Now he stayed with the faster-moving traffic.

The faint sound of horns blaring and brakes squealing, followed by a loud crash a good distance behind them, pulled his attention to his rearview mirror.

Alana turned and looked back. Except for three cars immediately behind them, the rest of the traffic had stopped. She hoped the men following them weren't in one of the three cars.

"I hope the accident isn't serious, but—" Keith never got to finish his sentence.

More brakes squealed, this time in front of them. Keith uttered a word not meant for delicate ears as he slowed the car, then stopped it behind the car in front of him, which had stopped suddenly. He glanced to both sides.

Construction barriers had them boxed into one lane with no option of driving away from the snag.

"Come on." He left the car, opened her door, and grabbed her hand.

"We're going to just leave the car here?"

"We'll take care of it later."

Alana got out. She noticed the sky and frowned. Angry,

nearly black clouds were quickly rolling in. *Where had they come from so suddenly?*

Wind gusts worried the palm fronds of the trees lining the highway. Even as she looked, the clouds looked as if somebody above them was filling them with black ink. The wind increased. Shrubs along the buildings bent almost to the ground. *We're in for more than just a little liquid sunshine today.*

As if to prove her words true, large drops spattered her and Keith. The rain started slowly, but quickly increased, as if anxious to leave the sky.

"Let's cross here and stay low." Keith led her through the narrow gap between the huge concrete barriers. He hoped they would screen him and Alana from their tail. If not . . .

He scanned the area across the street, searching for the place that offered the best protection. The brush was almost nonexistent close to the road. Not too far behind the businesses where they were heading, on the side of the road, a narrow canal, which seemed standard for every strip of buildings in Florida, stretched as if waiting.

Keith glanced at the rain pelting them. Today the planners would know if the canals were large enough to do their jobs.

He swung his glance to a huge field behind the buildings but well away from them. It teemed with activity. Several vans parked at the edge, and a group of people bunched beside one of them, working with equipment and seemingly unaware of the rain soaking them. Keith's grip on Alana's hand tightened. She responded by increasing her speed.

Alana followed him as the large drops of water tried to cover their clothes. In the distance, lightning forked down, striking whatever was in its path, releasing claps of thunder to announce its presence. Other strikes followed as if playing a game of tag, but some things on the ground were It. Way off, the long, loud wail of a siren joined the thunder in trying to fill the air.

Keith looked back and increased his speed, pulling her with him. "Over here."

He dashed from the safety of the concrete blocks and didn't slow until he reached the van with the name of a company that sold hot air balloon rides.

Shouts came from somebody in the basket of a returning balloon, but the people inside scrambled over the sides before the basket touched the ground.

"Wait. We'll secure it and help you down," somebody on the ground yelled. Several people moved toward the basket.

The passengers clambering to the ground acted as if they couldn't hear.

"Come on," Keith yelled over the noise of the thunder. Rain hurled down as if it was fulfilling an assignment to get everything and everybody soaked as soon as possible. Alana was already beside Keith.

The basket teetered on its edge, trying to turn onto its side.

As the last of six people left the basket, Keith reached it and helped Alana scramble into it. She moved to the far side, and more of the basket touched the ground. Keith leaped in beside her, and that helped right it even more.

"Hey. What do you think you're doing?" The words came in a British accent from the tall man grabbing at Keith and the basket. "You can't do this. It's not safe. It's—"

"Sorry." Keith glanced up at the small opening in the very top of the balloon. He took a deep breath and grabbed a thick rope. The opening closed, but the balloon sat still.

Alana looked back to the road and saw two men trying to cross against the traffic zooming past from the opposite direction like ants from a disturbed hill. For once she hoped traffic would get even heavier.

Keith glanced far down the road. Although day was looking as if it had confused itself with night, he saw enough to know that a gap in the traffic was coming close. The men were poised to use it.

Alana pulled up a rope dragging from their basket. She and Keith both ignored the stream of profanity coming from the man with the ground crew, who seemed as if he believed that if he could find the right words, she and Keith would change their minds.

Alana frowned, took a deep breath, then pulled down on a lever joining two controls.

Fire roared from the burners and Alana jumped back and released the levers. The fire shut off, but enough air had been heated to cause the basket to first sway and then lift slowly. Suddenly a gust of wind grabbed it, and it soared as if it were late for something.

Alana pulled on the lever again, and the balloon rose higher, moving toward the storm but away from the treetops.

Not far enough away, more lightning speared the sky, followed by more deafening thunder. Alana didn't think it possible, but the rain increased until it seemed as if she were looking through one solid sheet of liquid.

The balloon soared higher still when she pulled the lever, and she wondered if it was possible for a balloon to go above the clouds, the way planes do. She glanced to the quickly shrinking ground below and then looked around at the fragile basket they were in. *I'm not sure if I want that to be possible.*

The wind grabbed them and shoved as if somebody was waiting to catch them on the other side, wherever that was. The rain turned the treetops below them black to match the dark sky now surrounding them. It was growing blacker as she watched.

Still the water fell as if the clouds were trying to empty themselves at once and be done with it. *I know that Orlando needs rain, but why does it have to come all at once and why now?*

She thought of the men chasing them. *Are we as hard for them to see from down there as the ground is for us to see from up here?* She closed her eyes. *Please let us be hidden from them.*

The force of a strong gust pushed against the balloon and the basket, sending them north and away from the road. Alana hung on to the sides as the basket rocked as if it wanted no part of this trip.

# Chapter 18

"Over here." Keith pulled Alana directly under the balloon with him. That did lessen the rain that reached them, but it didn't matter. They and their clothes had already reached the saturation point before they got into the basket. The water soaking them dripped onto the floor.

Alana pulled the rope and opened the balloon fully. Then she tugged the levers. The valves of the propane tanks attached to the burner opened. A finger of fire flared, heated the air, and sent it up into the balloon. The balloon lifted.

"What are you doing?" Keith crawled over to her.

"Trying to keep us up."

"You know how to fly this thing?"

"Ballooning is not called flying."

"Do you know how to make it work? Can you control it?" He tugged on the lever. A sharp whoosh of hot air blew into the balloon and soared them higher. The wind at that level rocked the basket as if to protest them disturbing it.

"Don't do that." Alana jerked his hand away. The balloon settled at one level.

"You do know how. Great. How do you know? Where did you learn?" He leaned against her and looked over her shoulder.

"I don't exactly know how." She glanced at him quickly and then back to up to the balloon. "Don't throw confetti just yet."

She tried to ignore the feel of him against her back. *Concentrate on what you're doing.* She barely tugged on a rope dangling into the center and stared up into the opening as it found a new wind current and shifted to the side.

She forced herself to focus on what the weather was doing to them instead of what he was doing to her. She shook her head. *He doesn't even realize the effect he's having on me.* She frowned. *Question. He asked a question. Concentrate on his question and on finding an answer.* "We wouldn't . . ." She shook her head again as he shifted and his shoulder brushed against her back. Then she started over. "Even in good weather we wouldn't have much control. We could change the altitude. Wind currents vary at different levels, and they control the direction. In this . . ." She nodded to the storm surrounding them and shrugged. "We go where the wind takes us and hope it takes us where we want to go."

"How do you know all of that? How did you know about the lever and what it does? How did you know about the ropes and all those gizmos?" He pointed to the instruments. "How many times have you been up in one of these?"

"I watch The Discovery Channel a lot." She refused to look at his reaction to that. She knew it was the same as hers would be if the situation were reversed. *How long before his reaction to that bit of news?*

She tugged slightly on the lever and the balloon floated up and shifted to the left, which was where they needed to go. It rocked slightly before it steadied, but the wind still pushed it left. *Not too bad.* In spite of her success, she still refused to look at Keith. *It will come any second now.*

"What? The Discovery Channel?" His tone of voice made her look at him. His stare, mixed with what could only be shock, held her. "You're controlling this from what you remember from a television program? That's all we have to rely on? How many times did you watch it?"

"I don't watch reruns."

"One viewing of one television program?" His words marched out one at a time, as if not wanting to get close to the others. "That's your entire experience with flying these things?" He shook his head and raindrops scattered from him. "No. We can't even call it an experience."

She let his use of the word "flying" slide.

"Hey, if you've got more, feel free to take over." She wiped at the rain that dripped into her eyes as heavily as if she were standing under a shower. She glanced at him and then away. "I figured we should try to head over there." She pointed way off to the horizon where the ground was slightly visible. "It looks as if the storm left there to move over here to us. This current seems to be taking us in that general direction."

Alana sent another short burst of air into the balloon. The now stronger wind pushed them toward where the sky was clearing. She hoped the wind didn't decide to change directions. "I'm not sure how far we have to go or what's over there or even if we can make it." A rumble of thunder acted as if they needed a reminder that the storm was still very much with them. "I think there are some developments being built near Clermont and I think that's where the clearing is, but I've only been up that way a couple of times."

She released a hard breath as another clap of thunder sounded even louder. It sounded as if the storm had decided to double back over their balloon and spend more time with them.

"It doesn't matter what's over there." Keith nodded

toward the clear section of sky. "It's out of the storm. It doesn't seem as if we have much say in that anyway." He shrugged and glanced down at where he knew the ground was. "It's also away from the road although, in spite of our bright yellow and red stripes, I doubt if anybody can track us in this darkness. Go ahead, Bessie Coleman." He shifted back from her. "Do your thing."

She was too busy to remind him that Miss Bessie flew airplanes. The balloon drifted down a little and shifted away from where they wanted to go. In spite of the situation, she smiled as she gave the lever a quick tug and they moved back up to the strong wind current that they needed. "Remember, the only thing we can control is the air going into the balloon." She shook her head. "Again, the wind is deciding our direction. Lucky for us, different currents exist at different levels."

A double shaft of lightning and near-deafening thunder reminded them that the storm hadn't gone anywhere. Keith stared down and to the left. The brightness of a fire lightened a small section of sky, but he couldn't tell what had been hit. "I hope the lightning doesn't take a liking to us."

"You don't want to know what they said on that program about storms while being up in one of these. I'll bet somebody from the company catches the devil for not anticipating the storm and canceling the flight."

She shivered as the cooler wind, caused by the combination of night and storm, pasted her clothes against her body.

"I can imagine what they said. I don't know about these balloons, but I do know something about thunderstorms. I also saw how those people were scrambling to leave this thing when we hopped in." He frowned. "Maybe grabbing this wasn't the smartest idea I ever had."

"Those men were after us. This is what was available.

I'd rather take my chances with it than on the ground with them. I doubt if they wanted to just talk to me." Alana touched his arm. "This was our only choice." She shook her head. "They must have been near the trailer when we drove past."

"I should have anticipated that. I should have taken a different route. It's my fault." Keith stared off as if to look at something outside their haven. He looked as if he were somewhere else.

"It's not your fault. I'm the one in trouble. I don't want to think what would have happened to me by now if you weren't with me."

Keith shook his head slightly and was back with her. "We'll manage." He sat on the floor. "Come down here with me. You're shivering."

He opened his arms on an impulse. His only intention was to ease her discomfort by warming her, to protect her from the wind, to stop her shivering. To innocently share body heat. That was all he had in mind, wasn't it?

His body tightened at the idea of sharing heat with her in a different way, a way that shouldn't happen. Still, he held out his arms and stared at her. *I wouldn't change my mind about holding her even if it weren't already too late.*

As she started toward him, he questioned his motives again. Still he waited for her, literally with open arms.

Alana took a step toward him, hesitated, and then joined him on the floor. They were still in the same situation: stuck in a storm, the highest target for the lightning, but she found his arms reassuring as she moved into the circle he offered. He folded her in his embrace and she felt as if she had found what she had been seeking forever.

"I—I'm soaked." *Why is my voice so breathless?* She wished she could blame the situation for that. She shifted in his arms. *It is the situation, but I can't claim that it's just the storm.*

"I feel like a drowning rat." *How much of what I'm feeling is because of the storm, and how much is because of him?*

"Trust me. You look nothing like a rat, drowning or not." Keith brushed her hair back from where it had curled around her face. A large curl had found a place beside her eye. *Beautiful, warm, brown eyes. Eyes showing the same want and need that I'm feeling, that I have been feeling since I first saw her.* "Nothing at all." His tone made Alana stare at him. His stare met hers and their stares held each other.

"We should . . ." She tried to find at least a little bit of sanity to use. Tried to point out in her mind a sensible approach to their situation, tried to reason herself out of getting lost in Keith's arms, in him.

"We should what? Land?" He brushed his lips across her cheek. "Leave?"

His fingers brushed across her back, warming her with heat that spread inside her, dissolving the last bit of reasoning that had started to form, making her speak honestly.

She shook her head slightly. "I don't want to leave you." Her words whispered from her.

"And I don't want you to." His stare shifted to her mouth.

"But back there you said—" Keith's finger barely touched her lips, but it was enough to make her words stop coming out. His mouth touched the side of hers before he eased back enough to look down into her face. "What are you doing to me?"

He brought his mouth against hers before she could try to find an answer in words. Instead her body answered for her.

Alana wrapped both hands around his shoulders—his strong, warm, sheltering, hard shoulders. His kiss was even more potent than she remembered. And she was getting even more lost than she had gotten before—

each time before. Still, the kiss deepened. She pressed closer, enjoying the way her breasts felt in contact with his hard chest, which was warming her through both sets of cold, soaking wet clothes. She shifted an inch and fire flared where her breasts rubbed against him. Her hard tips ached, wanted, needed more, so much more of him.

The basket wobbled on a wind surge, but Keith and Alana moved closer together instead of apart.

Keith shifted and Alana settled against him, her body settled within the space formed when his legs opened to her. His need pressed against hers.

The storm outside was nothing compared to that which was raging inside them, between them.

Keith shifted yet again, easing his shoulders to the floor of the basket and taking Alana with him. Then he shifted them both to their sides, still locked within each other's arms.

"This is madness." He placed a row of slow kisses from her mouth to the side of her neck. "Sweet madness."

His hand found her breast waiting for him, just for him. He covered it slowly, as if there was no need to hurry. His thumb found the tip, brushed it from the bottom of her fullness before finding the swollen end pushing against him. Then he brushed gently across it before filling his hands with it.

"Yes." Her answer was more a moan than a word. She thrust her breast against his hand. She wasn't sure if she was agreeing with his statement or with what he was doing to her; probably both. He closed his fingers over her fullness and gently squeezed. Both. Definitely both.

She shifted to give him better access to her breast, even though what he was doing to her, as his hand now barely brushed across the tip, was sweet torture.

Her own hand was busy: touching the side of his face, her finger finding and exploring the cleft in his chin, then finally brushing across his strong jaw to his mouth. She let a finger brush across his lips, slowly tracing around them, before finding the sensitive inside of his bottom lip and stroking there.

Keith's response was to allow his hand to leave her breast and to let a finger dip beneath her shirt, which was trying in vain to remain pasted against her body. He skimmed across the top of her bra, tracing its form as it followed the swell of her breasts, envying the lace which covered her, needing to replace it with his hands, his mouth. His finger found the hollow between her breasts and dipped into it as his teeth captured her finger and gently drew it inside his mouth.

Alana's quick intake of air as his tongue tasted her finger brought her breast tighter against her bra, closer to his hand. But not close enough, not nearly close enough.

As if on cue, his other hand found the buttons on her shirt at the same time hers found his.

The soaked shirts were plastered against their bodies, but Keith and Alana's needs were great enough to make their fingers work until, one by one, much too slowly the buttons were freed.

*I should slow down,* Keith thought even as he eased his shirt from his arms and as Alana eased her own off. Instead of following his "should," though, he followed his "must."

He gathered her to him again as soon as they shed their shirts so that not even air separated them. Then he took her back down to the floor of the basket, using the shirts as a cushion beneath their shoulders.

He reached around her back and freed the hooks of her bra. Gently, finally, he eased the white lace covering from her and leaned away. "Beautiful." He allowed his gaze to drink in what he had been resisting for too long. "Just as beautiful as I imagined." Alana looked away from his stare and started to bring her arms across her front.

"Don't. Please don't," he pleaded when she made to cover herself from him. "Let me see you."

She stared back into his face and slowly eased her arms back down. Heat flared in his eyes, strong enough to rival the lightning striking at targets on the ground. She held her breath as he met her stare and closed the space between them.

Then he drew her body against his again and she was back where she belonged.

His hand traced a hot path from h;r waist down to her thighs over the fabric which was covering her legs and still in his way. Then he inched a path down the front on her leg, leaving a trail of fire in his wake until he reached her soft mound. His hand stilled, rested there as if it had finally found where it belonged, then brushed back and forth as if to make sure she was really there and he wasn't dreaming.

Alana's hand traced down his thigh and slowly across his strong, hard legs, trying to ignore the way, in spite of his clothes, his muscles bunched beneath her hand wherever she touched. Then she hesitated before she moved on until her hand rested on his hardness.

Keith brushed his hand to her inner thigh and then back to the outside, avoiding exploring her hidden secret, teasing, taunting through the two layers of barriers. Then he traced the path again. Alana cupped her hand against his hardness, pressed, released, and then pressed again. It was as if they were playing a very adult game of "Anything You Can Do I Can Do Better."

Keith eased from her to his knees. "I'm not going anywhere," he said when she mewed a protest at his leaving. The heat in his stare eliminated any chill caused by the storm. "I couldn't even if it were possible." He eased his pants off his body, took out his wallet, and removed a foil packet. Then he tossed the wallet aside.

Alana's gaze widened as it found his desire pressing against his shorts. Then Keith moved back beside her. He placed a finger beneath her chin and eased her face up until he could look into her eyes.

"Are you sure about this?"

"Yes." Her words were husky with desire. "More sure than I've ever been about anything in my life."

Keith's smile would have made her change her mind if her answer hadn't already been "yes."

She answered his smile with a smile of her own as she undid the snap on her pants and slid the zipper down. She pushed at them, but the wet fabric clung to her legs, as if reluctant to let go. His hands helped her discard the one obstacle. Soon, but not soon enough, only the silk and lace barrier of her panties was left.

Keith's hand glided across them. He trailed enough heat so that the fabric should have dried on her body. His hand went up to her waist. Then he stroked up and down her silk-slick side, each time hesitating at the top, but then moving lower.

His finger eased beneath the lace edging at the top of her thigh and followed the contours across until he reached the middle.

Alana gasped as his finger skimmed then tugged the hair curled over her center. Keith swallowed her gasp. Then his fingers moved achingly slowly back to her waist, where they moved as if not sure of which direction to follow next.

"Please." Alana wasn't aware that she had spoken, but Keith was.

"Yes," he answered. He peeled the filmy obstacle from her and finally touched her smooth tan skin.

His hand found her soft mound again and his finger traced small circles of fire through the thick covering. Alana moaned and pushed her fullness against his hand.

Her own hand squeezed Keith's hardness and it hardened even more.

"Easy." He eased her hand away from him and brought it to the safety of his chest. Her fingers curled and uncurled in his coarse chest hairs as if searching for something. "We don't want this to end too soon."

He left her long enough to roll protection into place. Then he returned to gather her to him. His mouth found hers yet again. His tongue tasted hers as he eased her leg over his. He rolled to his back, pulling her on top of him.

Slowly, as if giving her time to change her mind, as if he thought that were possible, as if it wouldn't kill him if she did, he entered her. Alana shifted slightly as her body accommodated, then closed around him, welcoming him home.

Keith just held her for a few seconds, reveling in the way she held him tightly within her as if he belonged there. Then he eased back a little before he slowly thrust into her again.

Her hands tightened around his back, urging him closer still, as if that were possible. She arched into him, wanting more of what she was feeling coursing through her—wanting more of him, as if she wasn't already holding everything.

He increased the speed of his movements, and she clung tighter to him each time he buried himself in her. They matched rhythms as if this wasn't the first time they had shared this ritual, as if remembering something handed down since man and woman discovered each other.

The basket rocked as another gust caught it. The couple was too lost to notice as their own world rocked from the intensity of what was happening between them.

The force of the wind continued to shove them in the direction of the clearing, but they were too busy to notice.

Lost together, they soared higher than anything could take them, searching, striving to reach release, yet wanting their pleasure to never stop. The storm raging outside the basket was puny compared with the one building inside their woven world.

Finally they reached the pinnacle, spun off together, and drifted back to reality, still in each other's arms.

# Chapter 19

Alana shifted in Keith's arms, reveling in the feel of the coarse hairs on his chest against her still sensitive breasts. Her eyes didn't open, but she smiled. *Wow.* Making love with Keith had been better than she had imagined it would be. She thought of his conviction that nothing should happen between them; his assertion that she would be hurt if they became involved and her smile widened. *Wow.* The way she felt at what they had shared could never be described as hurt.

She nestled back against him and listened to the now gentle rain pattering against the balloon. The wind had tired itself out and the balloon was sheltering them from what was left of the storm.

That storm had been nothing compared to the storm she and Keith had created. She did not question how they could fall asleep during the fury that had controlled the balloon. She was just grateful that they were still all right. She shifted slightly. *We are more than all right.* Again her smile showed itself. *I should at least open my eyes and pretend to be concerned.* She paid no attention to those thoughts. Instead she drifted back to the serenity she had found at the end of their lovemaking. *Keith and I shared lovemaking.* She released a gentle sigh. Lovemaking. *The word doesn't do justice to the act we shared.*

She shifted her hand against Keith's chest. His answer

was to shift his body against hers until their fronts were nestled together again as they had been during the night. His hand found her bottom, brushed across it, then cupped it, easing her closer still. He was still asleep, yet his response hardened against her, reminding her of what they had shared; her body was ready again to join with his.

The bottom of the basket scraped against something and Alana's eyes flew open as the movement made her shift yet again.

For a few seconds Keith's arms tightened around her at her movement; then he sat up. He took her with him, but it was as if he wasn't aware that she was there. He scrambled to the side and Alana followed.

"Here." He tossed her shirt to her and she pulled it on. She ignored the rest of her clothes and rushed to stand beside him.

They looked over the side into the not-quite dawn of what would probably be a rain-swollen day. They watched soft but steady raindrops spatter into the tops of trees that were level with them.

Alana grabbed the lever controlling the propane flow and pulled. Her only reward was a weak "whoosh" that sent them a few yards back up above the trees. She tugged on the same rope again, but she may as well have saved her time and effort.

"We're going down."

As if to prove her right, the basket skimmed to the left, over some trees, closer to a clearing. Hoping that there was a little gas left, Alana pulled the lever again. The only reward she got was a slight burp. The balloon drifted forward as it drifted down.

"We'd better get dressed," Keith said as he handed her still-damp clothes to her. Alana's fingers grazed his as she took them. She stared into his eyes, not knowing what she expected to find, not sure what she saw there after she looked.

She frowned as she pulled on her cold, wet panties and pants, stuffed her bra into her pocket, then turned her back to him. She had to give her full attention to trying to coax a bit more help from the burners. Nothing. It was as if it were weary of the whole effort and wanted her to leave it alone.

The balloon continued with its determination to land. She pulled on the rope controlling the opening in the top of the balloon to try to ease the landing on a golf course.

"The first golfers teeing off today, if the rain clears, will not be pleased," Keith said as the basket settled on the ground at the edge of the thicket rimming the roadside of a golf course. "Ready?" He tied his shoes, and Alana did the same with hers.

The balloon gently collapsed in a long streak along the ground, with some of it draping over the shrubbery. In slow motion the basket turned onto its side. Keith held Alana's hand as they waited for the basket to settle. As soon as it did, they crawled from it and scrambled onto the soggy ground.

"Let's see if we can make this thing less visible." As soon as they were out, Keith started pulling the balloon toward them. Alana worked with him, gathering the many yards of fabric toward them and the basket. Together they pushed on the balloon, shoving as much of the limp fabric into the basket as possible before setting the basket upright. Then Keith climbed back inside to cram it even tighter.

When he was satisfied that no more of the balloon would fit, he jumped back down to the ground. He began to shove the basket further under the trees. Alana rushed to his side to help.

They gave the basket one last shove, sending it between

two live oaks spreading their shelter over the surrounding shrubs.

"Too bad we don't have a green cover," he said as he scanned the area around them. "Over here."

Keith began gathering downed limbs. Alana gathered fronds discarded by the palm trees. Carefully they covered the fabric and as much of the basket as they could. They finished, and Alana stepped back.

"Do you think they. . . ?" She shook her head, inhaled deeply, and looked around. The road was far enough away for her to think, to hope, that the basket wouldn't be visible to anybody driving past.

"The way the storm raged, I doubt if anybody could have tracked us," he responded to her unfinished question. He grabbed her hand and held it. "If that wasn't a hurricane, it was a good imitation of one."

Alana could tell that the word "storm" had triggered memories in him of their own storm of last night. Longing stirred in her at her memory, but she didn't dare hope that Keith was feeling the same. He was too businesslike this morning, too unemotional.

Regret nudged her longings aside. She wanted to nestle against him and feel his warmth again. She wanted things back the way they were during the night. Instead she contented herself with holding his hand. She made herself concentrate on his words.

"I do think they'll be looking, trying to guess the balloon's path." His gaze offered her reassurance. It wasn't what she had hoped for, but she needed this, too. "Besides," Keith continued, "those golfers, unless they are perfect on the nearby holes and are so wrapped up in their game that they won't notice the basket, are sure to report it. Then some reporter is bound to pick up the story, not to mention the owner of the balloon. We did

steal it." He stared at her. "About last night." He frowned.
"We have to talk."

"Yes." She barely nodded in agreement. "But not now."
Alana was surprised at how calm her voice sounded, considering the turmoil tumbling through her. "There's a
development that goes with this golf course, but I don't
know if anybody has moved in yet. Do you think we should
make our way to it?"

"It beats scrambling through those wet bushes and
climbing the fence." Keith pointed to the side blocking
the course from the road. He reached for her hand
again. "We don't want anybody questioning what we're
doing here at first light."

He led her around the perimeter of the smooth but
soggy green expanse. Neither spoke as they made their
way to the clubhouse. Keith nodded slightly as he noticed that the building was still dark, but he didn't say
anything. Neither did Alana. She kept her thoughts in
the present. Their talk in the future would come soon
enough and she knew she wouldn't like it.

They walked past the carts waiting for Tiger Woods
wannabes, and down the wide driveway. The only company they had was each other and the steady drizzle.

"I don't think we should bother with the development," Keith said when they reached the place where a
road broke off to go to the houses visible in the distance.
"We don't need questions from the sales representative
who is sure to be in the model home later."

"There are a couple of motels along the road, as well
as a few stores." Alana pulled at her damp shirt. "We can
at least buy T-shirts." She glanced at the sky still turning
on its light and shook her head. "They probably won't be
open yet." She pulled at her shirt again.

Keith watched her. When she let the shirt go, the fabric molded back against her as if it were reluctant to leave

her. He stared. *I know the feeling.* His pants were getting uncomfortably tighter, still he couldn't look away. The tips of her breasts, hardened by the cool damp shirt, poked at the cloth, as if trying to escape. In spite of his longing, his imagination wasn't good enough to let him think they were seeking him.

His thoughts flew to one of the reasons why her breasts had reached that same state last night and his hands itched to cover them again, to stroke his fingers across the silky hardness. He swallowed hard as his mouth remembered how they tasted. Dark chocolate, they were sweeter than any candy he had ever sampled.

His body tensed even more in spite of his efforts to prevent that from happening. *I should have been stronger. She's going to be hurt when she learns that what we had is all there will ever be. It will be my doing, but already it's ripping at my insides.* He shook his head. *Better now than later, after we get in deeper.*

"Okay." He led the way to the road but didn't touch her hand again. Alana tried not to notice. "Wait a minute." Keith stopped walking after they were away from the complex. He pulled out his cell phone, wiped the moisture from it, and punched in some numbers.

Alana watched him. *Reality is back.*

"Dave, it's me. We ran into a problem, but both of us are okay. I had to leave the car last night. I need for you to see that it's moved." He gave the plate number and location. "I'll call you as soon as we get situated." He broke the connection and looked at her. His smile made Alana determined to make sure that things weren't as hopeless between them as he thought. "The beauty of answering machines. You can communicate without having to deal with questions." His smile left. "Let's go." He watched as Alana yawned. "I figured we'd check into a motel, get a little sleep, since . . ." His sentence stopped as if the rest of his words had gotten tangled on something that kept them from coming out.

Alana knew what it was. She was caught in the same place. Neither the storm last night, nor the fact that they had been stuck in a balloon, was the main reason for their lack of sleep. Although he might try to ignore it, what they experienced with each other—that was the real reason. Everything else was a distant second.

Without giving him so much as a glance, she left him standing as she headed down the road. *He can try to pretend that nothing happened between us if he wants to, but that won't erase the fact that it did.*

Staying close to the brush, they walked along the side of the road together, but they may as well have been alone. The drizzle, which had seemed to be tapering off, now acted as if it had changed its mind. Alana didn't care. She couldn't get any wetter. She tried to ignore Keith by concentrating on where she was walking, as if gravel rather than tarmac covered the road.

They passed a store offering to let them pick their own citrus, but even if they had been interested they couldn't, since the store hadn't opened for the day yet.

Orange trees along the side of the road sent their citrus perfume to tease them. Alana's stomach reminded her of how long it had been waiting for a meal. The trees seemed to go on forever.

The clouds were almost empty by the time Alana and Keith reached a small motel tucked under twin live oaks and fronted by three palm trees. Hibiscus, as tall as trees, followed the line of the building, their red blossoms trying to sway in spite of the heaviness of the rain collected on them. It looked as if somebody had decided that the plants would make people decide to stay here instead of somewhere else. The plants could have been bare sticks stuck in the bare ground for all Alana cared. She was most interested in the vacancy sign posted under the name of the motel.

She walked to the door. The only way she knew that Keith was with her was the faint sound of his footsteps just behind her. She took a deep breath and pushed the bell. A man appeared at the night window as if he had been waiting for them. In spite of the early hour, his smile wasn't forced.

"Our car broke down." Keith didn't give Alana time to speak.

"How unfortunate." The man's accent gave away his East Indian heritage. "The telephone is over there." He pointed to the side of the parking lot.

"We need a room." Keith smiled at him. "After being in this storm for so long, we need time to get some rest." His smile widened. "We need your room farthest away from the road, please, nice and quiet."

Alana tried to keep from reacting. *His smile isn't for me.* She stared at the road as if she intended to go back to it. His smile would never be for her again.

"Very good." The man's grin got even wider. "I have a very nice room for you." He pushed the registration paper under the slot. Keith filled it out, gave the man his credit card, and got the key.

Alana followed Keith past the three cars parked outside of the units until he stopped at the last room in the row, opened the door, and stepped aside. Alana stopped just inside the room. Two double beds dominated the room. *That takes care of that.* She frowned. *I should be relieved.*

"You take the far bed. I'll take the one by the door." Keith didn't look at her. Instead, he turned the knob of the window unit to vent. "Maybe we can at least dry your shirt a little."

Alana could tell from his expression that he was back to last night, back when she took her shirt off, back to remembering that he had helped her with that. *He's thinking about what happened next.* She shook her head. *I'm struggling with memories of my own: helping Keith shed his own shirt, the feel of my hands on his bare chest, our shirts forming our mattress as we escaped the storm and created one of our own.* She looked away first. Then she walked away.

The bathroom was small, but large enough for her to put space between them. She took off her shirt and pants, refusing to think again about the last time she did this, wrapped a towel around her body, picked up her wet clothes, took a deep breath, and went into the room. She hadn't stayed in the bathroom long, not because she was ready to face Keith, but because enough time didn't exist for her to be ready.

She glanced at him without meaning to and saw him wrestling with his reaction to her. She pulled her glance away and, even though her legs threatened to quit working, walked over to the unit installed low in the window. She took longer than she wanted to, but she managed to drape all four pieces of her clothes over a chair in front of the stream of air pouring into the room. She shifted her chair to make room for a chair for Keith's clothes. Still not looking at him, she walked over to her bed and crawled beneath the covers.

She turned her back to the room and to him, and closed her eyes. Either Keith was good at walking softly, or he never moved from the spot that he was in when she had come out of the bathroom. Right now, and hopefully from now on, she didn't care.

Keith watched as Alana shifted the second pillow so she hugged it to her. She was covered, but it was too late to help him. The vision of her fine, brown, surprisingly long legs below the towel was so vivid in his mind that she could be standing in front of him now. The fact that she wasn't was his fault. He leaned against the wall and closed his eyes.

Last night had been more than he had ever experienced. It was the first time in so long that he had given in to his desires. He inhaled, hoping the air would be cold enough to help him get his temperature and his body back to normal. His groin hardened in spite of his efforts. The memory of her close to him, her body pressed against him, her firm breasts with their tips that grew harder under his caresses, was almost as strong as if it were real. It was killing him to remember and to realize that a memory was all he would ever have. He exhaled sharply. *A memory was better than nothing.*

Peace. While he had held Alana, he had found the peace that had been missing for so long. Peace that he didn't deserve. He glanced over at her. She was huddled against the far side of her bed, as far away from him as she could get. He sighed. She was a half day too late.

He went into the bathroom, hoping he could find his equilibrium, but not expecting to. He'd settle for finding a way to coexist with knowing that he'd never have her again. Finally he gave up and left the bathroom.

Too soon he was draping his clothes over a chair beside the one Alana had used. For a second he allowed himself to run a finger over the lace that had covered her breasts from him. If things were different, his hand would be on her right now and he wouldn't have to rely on a memory. He glanced at her. Not a sound came from her bed, but he knew she wasn't asleep. She was too quiet. *People who don't know assume that those sleeping are still and don't make a sound.* He knew differently. He pulled back the covers of his lonely bed and crawled in. He knew a lot of things that ordinary people didn't know. *Good for them.*

As he had been trained to do, in spite of the turmoil within him, he was asleep within a few seconds.

\* \* \*

*What is that?* Alana's eyes flew open and she turned over. She was trying to remember where she was when the sound reached her again. A low moan born in pain came from the other bed. Keith writhed as if in agony. The covers were tousled around him as if he had been fighting them for a while. His face told Alana that he was battling some demons and losing the fight.

She hesitated until another unearthly sound came from him; then she left her bed and went to his. He turned over to his back and his leg fought its way out into the open, but he continued to mutter and move restlessly, as if seeking something. Alana moved closer.

"Just a few more seconds. I'm almost finished." The urgency in Keith's voice grew with each word. "No." His head brushed back and forth on the pillow. "Don't you die on me, Sawyer. You hang on a little longer. That's an order. Do you hear me? You can't die. I lost Zee on the last mission. I refuse to lose you on this one." His voice became a plea. "We're almost there. Hold on."

The pain filling Keith's face was so strong that Alana felt it as if it were her own. Tears for him trickled down her face. She didn't know if she could help, but she had to try. *Nobody deserves the torture he's going through.*

Without thinking, she slipped beneath the covers and against him.

As if the rift had never occurred between them, as if it was the most natural thing to do, she eased him into her arms.

For a few seconds he resisted, as if his nightmare wasn't through with him. Then gradually his restlessness eased, the tension left his body, and he found peace in her arms. Still asleep, he turned to face her. His hand found her hip and molded to it, as if were his anchor. His breathing steadied until it was that of a normal person finding the restorative powers of sleep.

Alana continued to hold him as if she alone could help him get the rest he needed. *What demons haunted him? Is this why he's determined that we have no future together? What caused his nightmare and how can we make it go away?*

She fought the temptation to smooth out the last trace of a crease still showing between his eyes. Instead she held him as if standing guard lest his nightmare return. Holding him this way, she drifted off to join him in sleep.

# Chapter 20

Keith shifted slightly and Alana stirred. She opened her eyes, but she didn't move again. Instead she stole the few seconds that she knew were all she had left to stare at him.

His face, relaxed in sleep, made him look years younger. As she traced his features with her gaze, his eyes opened. His frown looked as if it had gained strength while he slept. He removed his hand from her bare hip as if it was burning him, but his stare still held her in place.

"You had a nightmare." She answered the question on his face before he had a chance to use words to ask why she was in his bed.

He seemed to suddenly be aware of her bare body pressed against the length of his, and he acted as if this was the first time they had been this close, as if, not long ago, they hadn't been even closer. Much as she wanted to, she didn't resist when he quickly untangled his legs from hers and put some space between them. She tried not to feel the loss. She had known the closeness wouldn't last. He had told her that it would never happen. He had been wrong about that. She doubted if he would let what he considered a mistake happen again.

She steeled herself and tried to protect her heart, as all she could do was watch Keith withdraw from her even further. He sat on the side of the bed with his back to her. *Is he trying to pretend that I'm not here? If he manages that, maybe he'll tell me his secret so I can do that, too.* She could see his back muscles rise and ease back into place as he practiced deep breathing.

"I have them from time to time." He didn't turn toward her, but she saw him shrug; at least he tried to.

"It was bad." Her heart caught in her throat at how tortured he had been and at how helpless she had felt for not being able to help him. It was her turn to shrug. *Maybe I did help him. Maybe my holding him chased them away. Does he believe that I helped?* She stared at his stiff back. *Probably not. He believes he doesn't need anybody.* She swallowed the tears that welled up in her throat. *Too bad for me.* She sighed. *Too bad for us.*

"So I've been told."

*By whom?* Alana bit back the question. *Do I really want to know? Would it make any difference if I did? Would it make him more accepting of a relationship between us now that I know about the nightmares?* She shook her head. *This isn't about me.* "Do you want to talk about it?" She watched as he calmly gathered his shoes and socks. *How can he be so casual about something that was tearing him up so badly just a little while ago? Something that evidently happens often?*

"I've talked with the best in the field." His shoulders lifted in what should have been a casual shrug, but he still didn't quite achieve it. "My dreams like me too much to leave me alone." His words had no room for bitterness; resignation filled all the space.

"But maybe if you try—"

"We'd better get dressed." His interruption was like a period at the end of a sentence, only more final. "We have a lot to do. Do you want the bathroom first?"

"You go ahead."

Alana watched him grab his clothes from the chair and leave her. The door closed behind him and she stood and wrapped the towel back around her. She wanted to search for a way to turn time and place back to the balloon. What she also wanted, even if it meant she wouldn't have held him last night, was to erase his nightmare. She didn't bother waiting for her mind to come up with a solution. Instead of looking for a way to perform the impossible, she did something that she *could* do: she gathered her clothes from the chair. They were dry. She nodded. She needed something to take pleasure in about now.

Keith in the throes of his terror came back in her thoughts to take away the little satisfaction that she had. *He must know how he is when he has a nightmare. Whoever witnessed one must have told him. He has to realize how it affects his sleep. How can he brush it off so easily? How can he accept it?* She frowned. *Maybe he didn't. Maybe the demons are with him constantly. Maybe they are always hovering in the background waiting for him to go to sleep so they can attack him.*

She had read a little about post-traumatic stress disorder. Was that what it was? She shook her head. *If it is, it's a lot worse when you witness it than when you read about it.*


Keith closed the bathroom door and leaned against the inside. *Why now?* The nightmares didn't come every night. In fact, it had been a while since he had had one. He couldn't have survived this long if they visited him every time he went to sleep. He closed his eyes. They didn't always start the same, but the endings were identical: Sawyer questioning him near the end of a mission gone wrong while he tried to salvage it, accusing him with his last breath instead of saving it until they could get him to safety. Then the nightmare moved on: he was carrying Sawyer onto the rescue chopper even though he knew he was dead, refusing to leave him in the jungle. *Would I do it again the same way?* He pushed off from the door and turned on the shower. It hadn't really happened that way;

his mind had created its own version. He knew that, but he couldn't make the nightmares stop.

He turned the water lever to hot and watched as steam rose from behind the plastic curtain.

Each doctor had told Keith that his conscience was responsible for the haunted dreams, that he had to accept that losing Sawyer wasn't his fault. He stared at the curtain as if he could find peace rising from behind it, as if he could see a way to undo the damage inside him.

*It was my fault. It was all my fault. I was in charge of the team. It was my decision to continue instead of aborting the mission when the scouting reports proved wrong.* He closed his eyes. *Why can't I focus on the lives that were saved because of the information that we obtained? Why does my mind stay stuck on what happened to Sawyer?* He didn't try to stop his mind from answering the question that always came at the end. *Because you would have insisted on finishing the mission even if you had known the outcome.*

He adjusted the shower to hotter. *Why had the nightmares decided to show up last night when I was with Alana? Why then? To show her what my nights are like? To give her a hint as to how terrible I am? To show her why nothing can ever be between us? To prove how people near me get hurt?*

He stepped into the shower. Maybe it was a good thing that it happened. Again he remembered how she had felt this morning; her soft skin pressed against his down the entire length of their bodies, as if they had made love and making love again this morning was a probability. Then his memory skipped back a little further, back to that other time, that glorious, perfect lovemaking time, the time when it seemed as if their bodies had been formed with each other in mind.

His body reacted to the memory now as if they would fit their bodies together when he left the shower; as if

Alana was waiting for him to do just that. As if that was the fair thing to do to her.

He stepped into the shower hoping for two things: for the water to wash away his guilt and for his body to accept that what had happened with Alana would never happen between them again.

Finally he gave up and left the bathroom. "All yours." He fastened the last button on his shirt.

"Are you all right?"

"Yeah." *As all right as I can ever be.*

He tried not to notice her full tan legs below the towel. He tried to ignore the way the knot she had tied nestled in the space between her breasts. Struggled to *not* remember how he had caressed, how he had tasted, those full, sweet breasts with dark chocolate tips. Wished he could forget how it felt to explore the secrets of her body, how right it felt to be sheathed inside her, held in place by her tightness as if he belonged.

He pulled in a deep breath and shoved it out. He had as much success with that as he had keeping the nightmares away.

He heard her turn on the water. He had just finished his shower and gotten dressed, but he had to fight the urge to go share her shower with her in spite of everything. Now he had to fight that need as well as his memories.

Alana had been in the bathroom long enough to be halfway through her shower and he was still trying to control his memories, still trying to keep from doing something stupid.

Finally he gathered himself together and took out his cell phone. He used all of his learned discipline to concentrate on the call he had to make.

By the time Alana came out of the bathroom, Keith had successfully stored his memories and had accomplished what he had planned. He allowed himself to stare at her and hoped it didn't trigger his desire, which was waiting barely beneath the surface. *She's dressed. Good. Maybe that will keep me from going off on a sensual tangent. And taking her with me.*

"I called Dave. He got the car and turned it in. I also made arrangements for us to get a rental car from this area. They'll pick us up in about twenty minutes. Dave is going to see that the guy gets his balloon back and will take care of the expenses for that. When this is over, I'll go talk to the owner, too." He gave her an all-business look as if that was all that was going on between them. "I asked Dave to hold off on the balloon part until later this evening to give us a chance to get away from here." He shrugged. "I don't want to take a chance on somebody being able to track us. Given the strength of the storm, I don't think we have to be concerned about that, but it doesn't hurt to be cautious. As soon as we can, we'll get your laptop from Yvette's."

"Okay." Alana smoothed her hand down the front of her slacks.

*If I hadn't witnessed it, I never would have known about his nightmares of such a short time ago,* Alana thought as she gazed at him. *He's fully in charge now. And just as appealing as when I first saw him.*

The impact he had had on her from the first hadn't faded at all. If anything, after last night in the balloon, after making love with him, after sharing her body so completely with him, the pull he had on her had grown stronger. *Why couldn't we have. . . ?* She shook her head slightly. *I refuse to try to change our past together. What would be the point? The sooner I can get out of this mess, the better for me.* She ignored the fact that her heart didn't agree. It knew that when that happened, she'd never see Keith again.

Her plans to uncover a big story, to gain door-opening

journalism credits, and move her career ahead seemed unimportant now. *All I want to do is get on with my life without getting hurt any more; I need to put time and space between Keith and me. Hopefully, soon I can do just that.* She frowned. *Focus on the situation, Alana.*

"Yvette is still away from work, right?"

Keith nodded. "She's okay. Dave assured her that you're okay, too. He sent her to Tallahassee to do some running around for the company that will keep her there for at least a week, maybe longer."

His smile, meant to only reassure her, did much more. It made her forget her vow of a few seconds ago, made her determination to see the last of Keith as soon as possible fade to nothingness. It made her want to try again to gain the closeness they had found in the dark and to hold on to it in the daylight. It made her want him.

She glanced away from him to try to break the hold that he wasn't even aware he had over her. Then she picked up the conversation without looking at him again.

"What did Dave tell her about what we're doing?"

"He told her that you and I are working on the story and that you're safe with me." The last of his words forced her to look at him. She steeled herself before she allowed her glance to find him, settle on his face. "You are, you know. I won't let anything happen to you. I promise."

All she could do was nod. *Doesn't he know something already happened to me? Isn't he aware that my only hurt is coming from his refusal to let a relationship develop between us? How can he not know that I'm in love with him? That I have a first-hand knowledge that love is illogical, beyond your control and more persistent than a child learning to walk?* She sighed. *I thought that when I fell in love it would be with somebody who would at least give it a chance.* She shook her head.

He had warned her. He had told her from the start, from the time they had felt that first attraction, that there could never be anything between them, that he couldn't have a relationship with anybody. Her heart hadn't listened. It had allowed her feelings for him to grow as if both she and Keith had cultivated them. She was usually an intelligent person, but in this case her head had followed her heart as if it had forgotten that it was supposed to be the voice of reason. She had gone ahead and gotten involved. She had offered and he had taken. She blinked and turned to stare out the window to keep him from seeing her feelings, which she knew were showing on her face.

She had to be truthful about this. They had both taken, and, Heaven help her, in spite of the pain, she wasn't sorry. If nothing further happened between them, she had tasted love.

She closed her eyes at the memory of exactly how he tasted when their mouths explored each other's. How the tight hairs on his chest had roused her breasts and made them impatient for more from him.

Her mind decided to bring along the smell of his aftershave mixed with his own Keith scent, and Alana rocked with the double assault. She had never known that memories could be so accurate, so strong, but then, she had never had such experiences to test.

She shook her head. *I don't regret one second of making love with Keith. It's hurting me now, but for a short while he was mine.* She blinked rapidly. *I will not cry. I will not.* She took a deep breath and let it out silently.

The sad thing was that he didn't have a clue to how deep her feelings for him had already grown. *Doesn't he realize that the body isn't the only thing that can get hurt?*

The muffled scrape of the desk chair made her glance at him. He was writing furiously on the note pad, probably planning their next five moves. The vulnerable man that he had been in sleep was nonexistent now. She looked at him a few seconds before she stared back out the window.

The rental car came and she traded sharing a small space with Keith to sharing an even smaller one, but she was grateful that they were on their way.

They stopped for a breakfast sandwich before going back to Orlando, but there was no conversation beyond the casual level during the meal. It was as if they weren't even close enough to be friends, as if they were only sharing a table because all of the others were taken.

She glanced at Keith several times while they were eating, but he was lost somewhere. Probably finetuning his strategy for dealing with the information that the e-mail message contained. *In spite of the way things are right now, even with his no-commitment insistence, I wouldn't mind being close with him.* She frowned. *Stay away from there.* She moved her mind to another track. *Maybe he's anticipating his move after this is over and he can get on with his life. Will he stay in Orlando? Will I? Will I ever see him again after this is over?*

They got back in the car, and Alana's thoughts kept going, too. *I don't know what he really does. He's definitely more than a business consultant, but what?* She remembered his nightmare. *Where did that come from and from how long ago?* She swallowed hard. *And what business is it of mine?* She let the answer come in spite of the hurt. *None.*

She wouldn't think about what Keith would do once they were finished. Nor would she make plans of her own. She did allow herself to think about the e-mail message and what it did or did not contain. It wasn't as important to her now as it once was, but she was determined to unlock it. It had cost her too much to ignore it.

*Is more than the security of DCS involved? Would somebody bent on stealing software programs go so far as to send an encrypted message? Why not just steal the program itself? Had*

*Nelson been involved? Was he the inside man? Keith and I caught him at the computer. Did that have anything to do with this, or was something else going on?* She frowned.

Who had gone to her place, obviously looking for her laptop? In all the things she had read about corporate espionage, she had never come across anything as complicated as this. Had she and Keith uncovered something that had to do with the government? If they had, and if it was as big as it seemed, the story wouldn't be allowed to be told to anyone outside some government inner circle, regardless of her and Keith's part in the discovery. The information would be on a need-to-know basis, and those in power would never decide that the public was part of those who needed to know. Her jaw tightened. *I have a need to know. I want to know exactly what somebody is hiding and why we're in danger. Because of this, my life will never be the same again. I* earned *the right to know.*

As they got close to Yvette's street, Alana's attention was pulled to the present. Keith tried to be casual as he checked the rearview mirror, but Alana noticed it. She wasn't worried, though. She believed him when he said that he wouldn't let any harm come to her.

If somebody had plotted Keith's trail as he drove the few miles left to Yvette's house, they would have thought he was way past lost. Still, he glanced into the rearview mirror almost as much as he did the road.

When they finally reached the house forty-five minutes after they should have, he circled the block twice before he parked three houses down the street, then rushed her to the house.

Alana used her key, glad that she didn't have to explain anything to Yvette yet.

She stepped inside and Keith shut the door and stepped in front of her before she could move further into the room. He motioned her to wait and she did. She tried not to worry at the thought that maybe somebody had linked her to Yvette. She was relieved when he came back and his face looked a little more relaxed.

"Where's your laptop?"

"In the bedroom closet. I'll get it."

"The bedroom closet? Did you have a reason to hide it?"

"Nothing to do with this." She shook her head. "Yvette has the same kind of laptop and we didn't want them to get mixed up." She shrugged. "Besides, there wasn't any reason for it to stay out since I only came by on weekends."

As she turned to leave the room, Keith's cell phone rang. The conversation was short. As soon as he clicked off, he turned to her. She couldn't read the look on his face, which, in itself, was a reason for her to be concerned.

"That was Dave. It seems that Nelson's heart had help in stopping."

# Chapter 21

"What?" Alana's gaze widened. She had heard him. And there was nothing complicated about his words. It was just a lot to digest. She frowned. *I shouldn't be so surprised. I never did believe in coincidences. That must have been Nelson fooling with that computer. Why would a security guard risk his job to mess around on a computer while he was supposed to be on the job, when computers were so cheap that he could have one at home and visit all of the porn sites that he could stand? Warnings were posted all around the office about not using the Internet for personal business, and anybody who knew anything about computers knew that it was easy to tell which sites were visited and when. Why would he take a chance like that?*

"They don't think Nelson died of natural causes."

Keith's words were filtered through the "When a site was visited" part of her last thought. She paced around Yvette's living room as if it were a miniature track. She couldn't go far before she had to turn around, but she had to move to keep up with the speed with which her mind was connecting ideas like dots in a child's game.

"He was on the computer that night when we were checking computers," Alana said. "He had to know that the time logged on was recorded. He knew somebody could find out that the computer was used when he was the only one there. Still he took a chance. Why?" She frowned and stopped pacing. "He discovered us together." Her words stumbled at the image of how she and Keith were together when Nelson walked in. Then her thoughts marched around that memory and went on. "Nelson is probably tied to the reason why somebody is after us." *Had he suspected that they were into something besides what it looked like? Had he really believed that he had stumbled on just a sexual encounter between them?*

The memory of the kiss she had shared with Keith kicked in. *"Sexual encounter" sounds so cold a description for the heat that had been building between us and had exploded in that kiss.* As her mind reran the scene, she didn't know how Nelson could *not* believe that what he saw had nothing to do with computers. At the time her body had reacted to Keith's kiss as if it believed that to be true. Anybody looking at them should have gotten the same impression.

She was tempted to turn up the air-conditioner and hope it could cool off the way her body was reacting right now. Then she forced that memory back to the past, where it belonged, and hoped her body would go back to normal on its own. "What did they say about Nelson?"

"Not much." Keith rubbed his jaw and continued. "The preliminary autopsy showed something in his blood that shouldn't have been there. The authorities are still trying to find out what it is and how it got there." He stared at her. "I told Dave what we found out. Maybe I should have told him to call the Feds." He shrugged. "Or maybe I should call them myself, but we have no idea what's going on. I'd rather know more before we decide whom to go to. If this is big, it could involve somebody in any department at any level. We'll check first ourselves and take it from there."

"The government? You think the federal government is involved?"

"I don't know. We have to act as if that's a possibility."

Alana nodded. Then she got her computer, hooked it up to her printer, and pulled up the file she had forwarded to herself. She didn't even try to read it before she printed hard copies.

Keith took the first copy as soon as the printer paused. A few seconds later, Alana grabbed the next. They decided at the same time to move to the dining room table.

"See what I mean?" Alana held up the paper before she sat. She tried not to notice that Keith hesitated before he sat beside her. "A cryptogram."

She got pencils and put them on the table between them. Keith got up and went to the computer. Alana followed. "I want to check something." He touched a key and the computer woke up. Then he scrolled to the top of the message. Alana looked over his shoulder, so engrossed that, for once, she didn't notice how close she was to Keith. That wasn't the case with Keith.

He was aware of every inch where her body came in touch with his. When she shifted for a closer look at the screen, her breasts brushed against his back and he had to struggle to remember his name, not to mention what he was doing.

"What's the matter?" She leaned her head closer still to the computer screen and her shoulder pressed against his. That innocent part of her body kicked off a heat spike in him that would be off any temperature scale known to man.

Now the smell of her soap teased him. *Who knew motel soap could be so tantalizing?* He struggled for control. *I do, now.*

He shifted, but not away from her. That's what he should have done. If his common sense had been in control, that's what he would have done. But, when he was near Alana like this, he had no sense at all, common or otherwise. His body shared control with his feelings. *I*

*want her. Right here, right now, when the only thing on my*
*mind should be decoding this message and solving this case; I*
*want her. I want to make love with her until all this goes away*
*and then I want to love her some more.*

"Do you see something?" She shifted yet again and
only brushed against him slightly this time, but it was
enough to send him closer to the edge.

The warmth from her body decided to transfer to him.
He felt his body begin to prepare to take things further.
*How can I begin to try to see anything on a computer screen when*
*my other senses and my feelings have taken over?* He did not
turn to look at her, but he knew that Alana didn't have a
clue as to what he was going through.

"Not yet." He answered her and warned his body at the
same time. It was one of the hardest things he had ever
done, but he made himself concentrate on the message.
Mercifully, Alana shifted away from behind him and sat
beside him. Her leg brushed against his as she got settled
in her chair, but better her leg than her breasts. *Her firm,*
*beautiful, tan breasts. Breasts that fit into my hand as if meant*
*for me. Breasts with sweet chocolate tips meant to be tasted.* He
shook his head slightly. *The message, Keith. Focus on the*
*message.*

"Do you want me to try?"

"No." He stared at the top of the message and was
grateful that he could force his mind to focus on that. His
fingers moved over the keys as he tried to coax the computer to give him first, the source, and then the intended
receiver of the message. He kept bumping into a wall as
solid as any in the real world. He couldn't backtrack, nor
could he go forward. The message was guarding its secrets
at both ends.

"Try this." Alana's fingers replaced his on the keyboard.
*Her talent is wasted on journalism,* he thought as he
watched with admiration as she tried first one way and

then another to make the message give up its secrets to them. Finally she quit and leaned back and shook her head.

"I'm impressed."

Alana frowned at him. "Why? I couldn't get in."

"But you got pretty far."

"Not far enough." She frowned at the computer as if it were at fault. "We already knew the message came from DCS and we knew at which computer it originated." She folded her arms across her chest. "I didn't find out anything we didn't already know. We still don't know who sent it, or even what it says."

"We're not finished yet. I'll be surprised if we're successful, but let's try to decipher the message itself," Keith suggested.

They went back to the table. This time Keith sat across from her. Soon they were so lost in the letters on the paper in front of them that they may as well have been alone.

The erasers on the pencils were used up, and a pile of papers covered with their attempts sat in front of them before Keith spoke again. He set his pencil down but he stared at the printout a second longer.

"I know you're good." He glanced from the paper to her. The regret showing on his face at his choice of words had nothing to do with Alana's ability to decipher anything. She watched as he took a deep breath, as if that would pull back the words and give him a second chance. Of course it didn't. "But I don't expect either of us to be able to break this." His voice was all business now. "Can you copy this to a disk? We don't know how long it will stay on your drive."

Her answer was to get a blank disk and do just that, after which she handed it to him, being careful not to touch his fingers when she did so.

"I know somebody who's much better at this than I am. If anybody can break it, he can."

"Who? How?"

"Tommy has a knack for this sort of thing." He paused as if he didn't want to continue. Then he went on. "I used to work with him." Keith's stare snagged on something far away from them, something not even in the present. "It was a long time ago. Back in a different life. I'll see if I can contact him."

"Okay."

Alana didn't ask for details. She kept herself from voicing the many questions pushing from inside her to be heard. She wasn't sure she was ready to hear how he knew somebody like that. She chewed on her lip. She doubted if he would answer her even if she did question him for details. "Now what? Do you want me to wait for you here?" She was still trying to decide which answer she wanted from him when he answered.

"No. You'd better come with me." He fixed her with a hard stare. "I don't need to tell you how easy it is to trace who received a message." He hesitated before he continued. "Especially one like this." He hesitated again. "You know you made it to that list when you forwarded it to yourself."

"I know." Alana's voice was a lot steadier than she expected it to be. She felt as if she had gone fishing and caught a shark instead of the sea bass she had expected. In this case, though, cutting the line wasn't an option.

"I'm sorry." Keith shook his head.

*Was he sorry because she got involved in something dangerous or sorry that he was stuck with her?* She knew not to ask the question. The answer was probably both. "This isn't your fault. I pushed myself into this."

"No sense going into that. We have to move, but not to my place." He shook his head and slipped the disk into his pocket. "They might have linked me to this, too. We'll find a place and stay put for a while." He looked back at her. "Do you have any clothes here?"

"Yes."

"While you pack a bag, I'll call Dave again."

*This is the story you wanted,* she reminded herself as she sorted through the clothes she had left and put some into a suitcase. She started to go back and ask Keith how much she should pack, but changed her mind. *A writer once said "Be careful what you wish for." Now I know exactly what he meant.* She looked at the pile and then added a few more things. Then she took off her uniform, put it toward the back of a drawer, and put on a pair of jeans and a T-shirt. She took a deep breath, lifted her packed suitcase from the bed, and went back to Keith. *However this turns out, I want it over.*

"I spoke to Dave," Keith said when she went back to the living room. "The police aren't through, but it seems that Nelson took something. Or, most likely, somebody gave him something. It was either mixed with his food or in something he drank. They're still working on that. They're also digging into his life."

"That should be interesting. We know he was more than a security guard. Maybe they can find out what else is in his past." She stared at him. "Do we tell anybody what we know?"

"Not yet. Let me contact Tommy first. Get the papers and the computer and let's go." He pointed to the printer. "Is that yours?"

"Yes."

"The printer also copies, scans, and faxes. Right?"

"Yes."

"Let's take it, too." He didn't wait for her okay. He unhooked it, tucked it under his arm, and picked up her suitcase with his other hand.

After they stepped outside, he automatically scanned their surroundings while she locked the deadbolt. Then they wasted no time getting into the car.

They left Orlando and headed north.

"Where are we going?"

"Jacksonville."

"Jacksonville? Why?"

"It's far enough away so they shouldn't think to look for us there. It's also big enough for us to get lost."

Keith left I-4 at Jacksonville. It was obvious to Alana that he knew the area. He never hesitated at an intersection, nor did he stop until he reached an executive hotel right at the outskirts of the city limits.

Alana knew to wait in the car. *I'm getting good at covering my tracks. After this is over, I could give lessons.* She swallowed hard. After this was over, it would be completely over. No dangling ends. Everything in her life that had to do with Keith would be tied up tight. She blinked hard. She knew that. She just didn't know how to keep the knowing of that from hurting.

She was still working on that thought when Keith came back with a key. Soon they were in their suite. Alana glanced around enough to determine the size of their quarters.

*Too many doors for a one-bedroom unit.* She convinced herself that this was a good idea. She didn't try to convince herself that Keith had gotten two bedrooms so he wouldn't disturb her at night. She wouldn't have minded being disturbed by him. She shook her head. *Fool.*

She closed the drapes, not because she wanted to shut out the world, but because she needed something to do. *Maybe his nightmares wouldn't reach into my bedroom, but he's already disturbing me, just as he does whenever I'm close to him, or farther away, or just thinking about him.* She frowned. *How did I get to this point?* She didn't wait for her mind to provide an answer. It didn't matter, anyway. The fact was that she had reached this situation and no explanation would change that fact. She slipped the laptop strap from her shoulder and placed the unit on the desk.

"Let's set up the computer. I'll send a message to Tommy, and then we can go get something to eat. Okay?" He pulled a chair besides hers.

"Sure." She set up the laptop on the counter, hooked up the printer, and was on the Internet almost immediately. Keith sat beside her. "Here." She shifted the computer until it was in front of him. Then she watched.

He gained access to his own mail site, then typed a sentence describing the weather, which was nothing like the way he described it. Then he asked about a dog named Skipper and how well he had adjusted to the change. Next he asked if there was any problem. He clicked the automatic "save draft" default to nullify it, clicked "high priority," and then hit "send."

"You have a dog?"

"No." He stood. "Ready to go eat? We should have an answer when we get back."

Alana got her purse. *Whoever sent that message we were trying to decode isn't the only one who knows about codes.* She glanced at Keith. *At least his reads as if it's real.*

The restaurant where Keith took her was large, busy, and impersonal, just as Keith hoped it would be. Without discussing it, they both ate quickly. He paid cash and they left. After stopping at a store so Keith could buy some clothes and a small suitcase, they returned to the suite.

Keith went straight to the computer. His server was telling him that he had a message waiting. His fingers flew over the keyboard as he answered.

Alana was curious, but she didn't go to him. She knew he would fill her in as soon as he finished.

He slipped the disk into place and must have forwarded the contents. Then he stood. He left the computer on.

"Tommy is good. It might take a while, but, if anybody can do it, he'll break the code." He stared at her as if to see her reaction to his next words. "He's got somebody working on the other aspects of our situation."

"You were in the service together."

"He's the best there is."

"Is he still in?"

"No."

"What branch?" *Would knowing that help me understand what's hurting him?*

"That's not important." He glanced at her, but his face told her nothing. Then his gaze slipped from her. "You can take the far bedroom. It has a private bathroom."

*He acts as if I don't already know that he made sure that I wouldn't be anywhere near him tonight.*

"What do we do after we hear from Tommy?"

"Depends on what he uncovers."

"Of course."

"You know, there is still the possibility that what we uncovered was a scheme to steal software engines. It could be that somebody plans to claim them as their own. There are millions to be made in bootleg copies. Maybe this has nothing to do with the government at all."

"Somebody killed Nelson over a game?"

"Millions of dollars," he repeated. "Maybe he got greedy and wanted to freelance."

"You don't believe that's all there is to this."

"It's possible."

"Sure it is. Just as much as it's possible that there's a tooth fairy who makes house calls and loves to collect kids' teeth." She stared at him. "What do you think is really going on?"

For a few seconds he looked as if he wasn't going to answer. Then he must have decided that she could handle what he had to say.

"I've seen cases of computer espionage before. It was never as elaborate nor as heavy as this. Usually the object is to get in, take what you want if you can, and get out undetected." He fixed her with his stare as if gauging how far he should go. "In spite of the potential for big money, it rarely gets violent." He hesitated. Then he continued. "If this were simply a case of stealing plans, they would have moved on as soon as they were detected. I've never known anybody doing stuff like this to go after the one who might have uncovered their operation." He frowned. "You're sure that it wasn't one of your relatives who stopped by your trailer?"

"The bottom line is that nobody would know where to find me." She took a deep breath. "At least not a relative. Remember, not even Yvette knows exactly where I live. Even if she did, she wouldn't tell anybody. She knew I didn't want anybody to blow my cover." She stared at him. "You don't think those men gave up, do you? You think they'll continue to look for me."

"We'll find them. Tommy has some friends who are as good at what they do as he is. Then those two guys and whatever friends they might have play by our rules." His face softened. "I won't let them get to you." He glanced at his watch. "It's late. We'd better get some rest." His gaze was full of regret. At least Alana thought so. She knew hers was.

She got her bag and went to her room like a child being punished. She shook her head. *There's not a thing childish about my feelings.*

She picked up the remote and flicked on the television in her bedroom. As she surfed the channels, she paused at a movie she had wanted to see. It was just starting, but she surfed on without thinking further about it. She was not in the mood for a spy movie tonight.

She propped both pillows behind her back and settled for an old comedy. *I could use a lighthearted laugh about now. If it's good enough, it will make me forget that Keith is right down the hall.* She sighed and shifted. *They haven't made a movie that good yet.*

In the meantime, Keith wrestled with Alana's closeness. *Two bedrooms was the smart thing to do.* He stared into the empty hall. *Even if it doesn't feel like it.* He walked to the living room window even though it took all of his determination not to go in the opposite direction. Not to follow her into her bedroom, not to make a second bedroom useless.

He checked the parking lot four floors down. Nothing out of the ordinary. He frowned. *I wish I could say the same about the way I feel.* He glanced at the hallway again and ignored the inclination to follow where his glance went. *Why her? I've dated a few women since I came back and feelings like this never kicked in before.* He shook the rest of the sentence away. Surface relationships: he'd never been involved in anything deep. He'd never been what anybody would call involved. He frowned. *Why her? I've dated more glamorous women, and my heart was still intact when things ended. What is it about her that lets her burrow inside me?*

The answer came in the form of an image. Alana: nestled against him. Alana: soft, and warm, and responsive. He resisted the urge to turn up the air conditioner, but he let her stay. Her full lips had opened under his. She had let him taste her. Her hands on his body had explored it as if staking a claim. He checked the door one last time to make sure the deadbolt was in place.

*I told her that nothing could develop between us, and then I let something get started, as if I hadn't meant what I said. I never should have touched her.*

Even as he thought that, his hands ached to do it again. He wanted to walk down the hall, take her into his arms, and tell her that he had been wrong—that they had a chance together after all. He wanted to feel if her skin was as soft as he remembered. He wanted to cover her with kisses, to erase the hurt he knew he had caused her. He wanted to fill his hands with her smooth as satin tan breasts, to brush his thumb over the tips until they were pebble hard and then flick his tongue over them to taste if they were still as sweet as the dark chocolate that they resembled, as sweet as he remembered from that brief time he spent making love to her. He wanted to close his fingers in her thick curls covering the place that was secret to everyone except him.

Then he would explore inside her place to make sure she was as ready for him as he would be for her. Right now he needed to bury himself inside her, to feel her muscles lock him into place as if he belonged, as if they could be like that forever, as if his past were just a story somebody had made up and had nothing to do with him.

Keith's body hardened as if it would be all right for him to go to her and satisfy his need. His heart urged him do just that. He wanted to. More than he had wanted anything in a long time, he wanted to forget the past and let his life go on from this point. He wanted a future with Alana. He wanted Alana.

He ignored his wants and his needs and did what he knew was right for her.

He went to his own room and hoped his nightmares would take tonight off. If they did decide to come, he hoped Alana wouldn't hear them, that she wouldn't come to comfort him. It wasn't that he didn't want her in his bed; it was that if she came to him there was no way he could let her leave him without making new intense memories with her.

His mind drifted to what path his life would have taken if he had made different choices. *What if I had gone to work at the post office as I had thought about? What if I had used my computer major to work in the corporate world? What if I hadn't decided it would be interesting to see the world at Uncle Sam's expense?* He turned over and punched his pillow. *What if those last two missions had never happened and Zee and Sawyer were growing old somewhere instead of where I put them?*

He turned over onto his back. *How can I deserve a happily-ever-after when the only thing left of Zee and Sawyer are what somebody remembers about them?* He sighed. *Will I ever stop paying for my mistake?*

He glanced at the clock. Too many hours of darkness left for his questions, without answers, to pick at him.

# Chapter 22

Keith opened his eyes. Daylight. The clock said 6 o'clock and the light slipping through the slits around the drapes was weak, but it was good enough for him. Sawyer had taken pity on him and let him sleep through the night. That didn't have any effect on the questions that appeared every morning as if, if they came enough times, he would also receive answers.

*Could I have made things turn out differently? Could I have used the bad info from the scouting recon and still made it work so that Sawyer would have stood for his medals to be pinned on him, instead of having them and a folded flag given to his father?*

No answer came to him, but he hadn't expected one. He had gone over the plans so many times that it was as if he expected to have to put them into operation again. He sat on the side of the bed, but he didn't stand.

He had lost men before. Everybody understood that not coming back was a definite possibility. Everybody knew that casualties aren't always on the enemy's side. Even Sawyer had accepted that. He had comforted Keith after a particularly rough op. "You did everything you could, sir," he had said. "You got to let it go and move on." *Why can't I take that advice this time?*

Keith got up and walked over to the window. He hoped his thoughts would decide to stay in bed so different ones could show up. *I only needed a few more seconds. Why was that too much to ask for?*

He made the unanswered questions pull back to wherever they went during the day so that he could function. He glanced at his bed. The bed looked as if a battle had been fought in it. That was nothing new. If the dreams let him sleep, he wouldn't worry what they did that he couldn't remember. He got dressed and left the room.

He paused in the hall. Did she sleep well? Silence came from her room and filled the gap between him and her.

*What does she sleep in? If things were different, maybe she would have let me help her take it off. She cares about me. If she didn't, she never would have let me make love to her.* He shook his head. *Correction. She let me make love* with *her.* He closed his eyes. *She was definitely a willing participant.* He could almost hear her soft moans and feel her hands pulling him closer as their desire built, demanded release, made them climb the elusive peak before they flew off together in each other's arms. *His arms ached for that again. For her right now.* He made his feet take him in the opposite direction.

He reached the kitchen and kept his hands busy making the coffee. Maybe that way they wouldn't miss her so much.

He got out cups and set the table. The bagels, cream cheese, and jelly in the welcome basket would hold them until they could go out. He didn't think about Alana much during the whole ten minutes that all of that took him.

He turned on the computer. He was always able to elude his memories when he was on it, but this wasn't busywork. They needed some answers and fast. They had to know what they had uncovered so they could plot their next move.

He got to his site. Tommy had gotten back to him. Keith

glanced at his watch. Not good news. Then he started typing.

"Are you there?" Keith didn't have to wait for the answer.

"Right with you, good buddy. I see you haven't learned to stay in the safe zone."

"What have you got?"

"Nothing."

"I guess it is too soon."

"Time doesn't matter. You sent me nothing. The files were empty."

"Both of them?"

"This isn't the first time. What are you into? If it's something big, you know how it often goes."

Keith explained about DCS, about how somebody stole a software engine before, and how he was checking computer security to make sure it wouldn't happen again.

"Tell me you have a hard copy of the elusive message."

"The fax is on its way."

Keith took the paper he had been working from, slipped it into the machine, pushed the proper button, and watched as the paper slowly eased from the bottom of the machine. Then he went back to the computer and waited.

"Got it. I'll get back to you later."

Keith stared at the screen. Then he logged off. *I hope that Tommy is as good as I remember.*

Alana came into the kitchen. One look at her and he knew he'd have to start over sorting things out. His mind had scattered his thoughts like a deck of cards in a gale-force wind. *How can Alana in a too-big T-shirt and loose jeans look like a custom-wrapped gift?* Reality kicked in. *A gift that I don't deserve to open.* His desire ignored reality. He looked at her longingly. *We have to get this over with so I can get away from her. I can control my temptation only so long.* His gaze found her face.

*No makeup covered it; this was pure Alana. Alana, with her luscious mouth waiting for me to sample a morning kiss, just to compare it with a kiss shared later today. Alana's smooth cheek, waiting for me to feel if it is as soft as my fingers remember.* He swallowed hard. *Alana within reach, and I don't have the right to touch her.* He curled his hands into his pockets.

"Good morning." Alana's smile tried to be strong. It didn't make it, any more than his would. He knew that she was fighting her own battles. "What's on the agenda for today?" she asked.

He knew what he wanted to be on their schedule. He knew what he wanted to be their schedule for at least the rest of the day. He also knew it wouldn't happen. Not today, not ever again.

"I heard from Tommy." He poured her a cup of coffee and himself another. Then explained what had happened with Tommy.

"Blank? Both messages were blank? But they're on my computer."

"Probably not anymore."

Alana rushed to her computer and pulled up her messages. Keith stood behind her, looking over her shoulder.

"They're gone." She checked the "Sent Mail" file. "Not a trace." Then she checked every other folder, and finally the drive itself. It was as if the message never existed. She removed her fingers from the keys and stared at the screen as if expecting the message to emerge from some hiding place that she hadn't thought to check. Finally she leaned back. "So. That's how self-destruct works. I thought that ancient television program was only fiction."

"It probably was at the time."

"So now what?"

"We wait. May as well have some breakfast." Keith went into the kitchen and poured fresh coffee. "Come on. A watched screen doesn't reveal any more action that a watched pot." He tried to keep his features relaxed. *I hope Tommy doesn't take too long. I feel as if we're on borrowed time.*

"How long do you think it will take him?"

"He's good." *I hope he's better than whoever designed that message.*

They sat across from each other, each one acting as if the food in front of them came at the end of a long feast instead of first thing in the morning.


Twenty minutes later the computer signaled that e-mail had come in. Both of them left the cold coffee and crumpled bagels and rushed to receive it, but it was only junk.


An hour later, Keith suggested they go food shopping.

"Great. My ears hurt from listening for the incoming message signal." Alana got her bag.

When they returned an hour later, no message waited from Tommy. They waited for the rest of the evening, staring at one television program after another, but watching nothing. Finally, after the eleven o'clock news went off, Alana stood.

"Good night," she said to the space above Keith's head. Then she went down the hall to her bedroom.

Keith wasn't surprised at the regret that swept over him as he watched her go. *I'll never get used to her leaving me as long as I'm with her.*


The next morning Alana and Keith reached the desk at the same time. Alana reached the mail site and smiled.

Then she opened the message they had been waiting for. She slid the keyboard to Keith, who sat next to her. He knew what words to use with Tommy.

"Somebody has been very bad and very busy," Tommy wrote. "You said your partner downloaded the package at DCS?"

"You got it. Or at least I hope you do."

"Right. Your messenger isn't a thief. I didn't find any plans to steal software engines or anything else. In fact, the developer plans to give away something to as many places as he can reach. The program is a very nasty virus."

"Virus? It didn't look like one."

"New things are developed every day. You know that, good buddy."

"What would it do to the games if it were attached to them?"

"Let them share the virus the same way folks pass colds from one to another. Only this would work a whole lot easier than sharing a cold."

"I see. The kids put the game in the computer and the virus attaches to everything it finds. A lot of computers would crash. DCS would probably fold. It's on the financial edge now. That would be terrible." Keith hesitated. "But from the reactions we've gotten, I think there's more to what we're mixed up in than viruses and games."

"You always were a smart guy. I've been working on this all night. I made some progress, but it's like wading through that thick mud we encountered more times than I want to remember on more missions than I care to count."

"I didn't expect you to drop everything to work on this."

"This chair doesn't take me out dancing much. Besides, you know I always did like puzzles. I don't know how long it will take, but I think I can make it give up all of its secrets. That's the good news."

"What's the bad?"

"I can't tell if it's been used yet. I hope not."

"I have faith in you."

"Hold off on that for a while. This baby makes everything that came before it look like something a kid dreamed up. Your program can embed itself so deep that it would be impossible to detect it until somebody or something woke it. It's gonna take a long time to break it."

"Games and motherboards? This is about programs for games?"

"You've been off the field too long. You forgot rule number one: Don't underestimate the opposition. This is not about games. It's designed to attach to *any* program. It will bury itself so deep that, unless you know it's there, you won't find it. Even if you do know, you'd still have a hard time digging it out and neutralizing it. As I said, this is one mean baby. Let's hope that I can be meaner."

Keith knew the answer to his next question, but he asked it anyway. "What would happen if government programs were put into the equation?"

"We don't want to go there." The cursor blinked impatiently waiting for Tommy's next input. "Our guys aren't on board at DCS, are they?"

"Not yet, but Dave was planning on it as soon as I got through checking things out. I know the Feds have their own screening devices. I just wanted to make sure they wouldn't find something to get DCS's bid denied."

"You know I know all about their devices. I know their capabilities, as well as their limitations. I helped develop one or two." There was a long gap of time before Tommy continued. "They'd have trouble with this one. It falls under limitations. If this thing gets loose in some sensitive program, what it does will make somebody who doesn't like us very pleased. You name it, and this thing can shut it down." Keith waited for another silence gap to close. "It frightens me, and you know I can give lessons on how not to be afraid. I hope we are at the beginning and not even a little later. From what I can tell, that's the case."

"You know somebody to alert?"

"I already did." Letters stopped appearing and the cursor blinked like a waiting person tapping a foot. Then Tommy started again. "You know, good buddy, there's something to be said for the old-fashioned mechanical devices. No outside influences; what you see is what you get. Every computerized development isn't a plus."

"What do we do now?"

"Fax me details of what else you got going on there. Descriptions, MO, that sort of thing. Anything that happened that shouldn't have. I'll get back to you ASAP. I'm gonna go give my mind another workout with the message again. Things would be easier if I had a clue to the program. You set up to receive faxes? I think I'd feel better with that option. Besides, if my contacts come through, I'll have some photos to send and I don't want to use a scanner."

"We can do that." He gave Tommy the phone number.

"Good. Be talking to you."

The screen went blank and Keith left the site. He was still digesting all that Tommy told him when Alana spoke.

"What do we do now?"

Keith took in a heavy breath. *I hate this part.* "After Tommy faxes us some info, we go back to Orlando. We have to check with your landlady. She's the only person who can describe the men. Hopefully, even if the pictures that Tommy sends don't match, she might still be able to use one of them as a starting point." He frowned at her. "Do you think she would talk to me without you being there?"

"No. She doesn't know you."

"I'm trying to keep you safe."

"That's not your job." Her chin went up in a way he

had come to recognize as her digging-in-my-heels mode. "I'm working on this with you. You are not my keeper."

"I never said I was."

"Yes you did, when you said that you won't let anything happen to me." She stared at him. "I appreciate your concern. I really do. But I'm in this and *I'm* responsible for me." Her stare intensified. "Okay?"

"Look, I just—"

"I know you mean well and I know you have had more experience with this kind of situation." Her stare intensified. "Even if you didn't tell me how. But I need for you to back off. Okay?"

"I'll try."

She continued to stare at him. "I guess that will have to do for now."

They cooked the food they had bought. Alana acted as if the subject was closed. Keith hoped he didn't have to open it again.

The kitchen was cleaned and both of them had packed. Now came the hard part: waiting for Tommy's next move. Alana leafed through a magazine in which she had no interest, while Keith alternated between pacing and staring at the printer. Finally, the fax machine shifted to life.

Both of them stood over the machine as if trying to see the papers before the machine printed them. As they came off, Alana examined the pictures as if there were a chance that she would recognize somebody.

By the time the machine quit, it had spit out enough pages to make an oversized deck of cards. Keith piled them neatly before he unplugged the machine.

"There's no reason for us to stay here any longer." He handed Alana the papers and tucked the machine under his arm.

Alana packed the laptop and picked up her suitcase.

Keith got his and they left for the next part of the case. Neither one talked about going back to what could be danger. They both knew it was illogical to think so, but maybe if they didn't discuss it, danger wouldn't show up.

# Chapter 23

Alana shuffled through the papers during the ride back as if she expected one of the pictures to change to somebody she had seen before. She knew there was little chance of that. Mrs. Banto was the only person who saw the two men who came to the trailer park. If a picture of anybody who worked at DCS were in the pile, Keith would have recognized them even if she didn't. She stole a glance at Keith. Determination had hardened his features, but it hadn't made him any less attractive.

He wasn't pretty-boy handsome, but that type had never appealed to her. She shook her head. She had been so focused on her career that her personal life had suffered. She smiled slightly. *Yvette would ask, "What personal life?" and she would be right.*

Alana inhaled deeply, which was a mistake. *Keith must have bought aftershave when he shopped. Why do makers use scents to entice, when the ones wearing them are not interested in that reaction?* She shook her head. *Change that to singular.*

She wanted to brush her fingers across his forehead to smooth out the creases. She wanted to touch his hand, the one that wasn't needed to drive since he didn't have to shift gears. She wanted him to hold her hand as if they had a future together. She wanted him to touch her; she didn't care what the reason was. Instead, she settled for his nearness and didn't let herself dream that, just maybe, later today, he'd change his mind and want her touch, too.

She shifted a different picture to the top of the pile as if it could derail her train of thought. *Maybe if I were different he wouldn't have brushed me off. Maybe if I were prettier, thinner. Maybe then he would want me.* She frowned. *I know it's not like that. I don't know him as well as I'd like to, but I do know he's deeper than that.* Her frown dug in. *Why is it, when I've finally found somebody I can get lost in, he makes it clear that we are not meant to be? Why won't he let me in? Why won't he trust me?* No answer came for even one of her questions, but she wasn't surprised. She hadn't expected any.

Keith had to force his mind to concentrate: on his driving, on the road, on the information they had received from Tommy, on anything except the beautiful, sexy woman sitting beside him in the too-narrow, supposedly full-size car. He didn't dare think ahead to tonight. Didn't dare zero in on the fact that again, they would be sharing spaces the way people involved did, people involved in each other, not just in a common problem. He frowned. It was hard, but he didn't even glance at her. He didn't dare take the chance. If he did, she might see the longing in his eyes and think that he had been wrong and that they did have a chance for a future together. His frown deepened. *I'd give anything, everything, if that were possible.*

During the rest of the drive his mind was working on strategies, something that he knew he could do about their other situation, something that was far removed from anything personal.

"Where are we going?" Alana asked when they were back in Orlando and Keith drove past the turnoff to go to the trailer park.

"I figured we'd find a place on Orange Blossom Trail."
He glanced at her. "I think it will be safer if we don't stay
too close to your place. Okay?" He smiled at the end.

It was barely there, but it was enough. Alana blinked.
It was more than enough.

"Okay." Anything was okay when he looked at her like
that.

Keith skipped several hotels until he came to one that
advertised suites.

*It doesn't take long to develop a routine, does it?* Alana
thought as Keith parked well away from the door. Without his reminding her, she stayed in the car and watched
him go in to register.

Soon they were inside their suite, bags by the door and
computer in place and hooked up.

"I figured we should check for messages from Tommy
before we decide about meals. Is that all right with you,
or do you want to go eat now?"

"That's all right. I can wait." She made the last connection to the printer, just in case.

Tommy had nothing further, but expected more information later from his sources. Alana tried not to be
disappointed. *Now that things are moving, I just want to
reach the end of this whole mess and get back to the real world.*
She shook her head. *Or the world as I know it.*

"We can get something to eat, then pick up a few things
from the supermarket to supplement the nonperishables
we bought before. That way we won't have to go away
from the computer whenever we get hungry." He glanced
at her and smiled. "This time we buy enough for today
only. I have never gone food shopping so much in my
life." His smile faded. "I think, when we get something
from Tommy, we'll have to act right away."

"Sounds okay to me."

Within forty-five minutes they had eaten and were in the supermarket.

"What do you usually eat for breakfast?"

"Cereal."

"Me, too."

"Is this brand okay?" She nodded and Keith put a box into the cart, then moved down the aisle. Each time they came to a section, it was time to make a decision.

*This is how it is for people whose lives are connected,* Alana thought, *people who spend a lot of their lives together, who live together, who care about each other in a special way. People living a normal life.* She sighed. That wasn't the case with them.

"Is that a yes or a no?"

"What?"

"I asked if you have a favorite brand or flavor of jelly."

"No. It doesn't matter." She watched as he put a jar into the cart. It didn't matter how much they knew about each other. In a short time that information would just be mind junk.

They continued through the store, buying a variety of things, but not a lot of any one thing. Then they went back to their pretend life together.

*How right this seems,* Alana thought as she put the jelly into the cupboard. *This could be our life together. There has to be a way to get past the barriers that Keith thinks are in the way.*

She was still trying to figure out a way when they were finished and back in the living room.

They connected to the Internet and read Tommy's latest message.

"Nothing so far. Don't expect anything until at least tomorrow. If we're lucky, that is. Get some sleep. I have a feeling things are going to break loose soon."

They clicked off the connection. After facing the blank screen for a few seconds longer, Keith turned to her.

"Tomorrow we can show the pictures to Mrs. Banto."

He stared at Alana as if seeing her for the first time in a long time. Then his gaze slid away from her as it usually did ever since that night they. . . . She stared at the side of his face, wishing she had the right to demand that he look back at her. Then she gave his words the attention that he wouldn't allow her to give to him.

"Tommy is right," Keith continued to speak even though he never pulled his stare from the wall. "We should get some rest. We need to be fresh for whatever happens next." This time he made himself look at her again.

Alana stared back at him for a few seconds, neither agreeing nor disagreeing. Then she made it all the way to the bedroom door, but stopped outside. She took a deep breath and went back to him. *It's not fair. He cares about me as much as I care about him. I can't leave things like this. This might be my last chance to try to get through.* She took another deep breath, but it didn't really steady her voice.

"I want to know about them."

"What?"

"Your nightmares."

"No, you don't."

"How do you know that? What makes you think you know what I want?"

At her last words desire flared in his eyes but died quicker that a lone spark. Alana knew her emotions still burned in her own eyes. She had always been terrible at hiding her feelings for very long. She sighed, as if that would help. *We both know that's a lie: Keith knows exactly what I like, at least about some things.*

Her words hung between them like a physical obstruction, but she shoved past them. Now that she had started, nothing was going to prevent her from finishing what she had to say. *Please let me find the right words to use.*

*Even if it doesn't mean that we'll be together, let me find the right thing to say to help him.*

She shook her head. If the first words she chose were wrong, she would keep talking until she found the right ones. Keith needed this out in the open as much, or maybe more, than she did.

"You've let something shackle you, keep you from living. I assume it's something in your past, although you won't even say that much. You stay so weighed down that you can't live." She paused, but she had no intention of stopping. She had started and she would finish before she quit. "As for us, you haven't given me a chance, haven't given *us* a chance. Why won't you tell me about what haunts your sleep? How much worse could it make things between us?" She shook her head. "You're—you're preventing something special from developing, something that comes only once, and then only if a person is lucky." She stared at him, waiting for him to answer. When he didn't, she swallowed hard. *At least he hasn't turned away.* "Maybe I'm the only one who thinks that. Maybe this is your excuse to get rid of me."

She bundled her hurt and shoved it out of the way, even though she knew it would find its way back soon. She bit her lip to keep it from trembling. She tried for strength in her words, but it didn't work. "Maybe to you I was just an easy lay." She stared at him for a second longer. Then she abandoned her resolve to get through to him. "Well, I quit. I'm through trying." This time when she stopped talking, she turned from him and walked away.

"Never that. You can't believe that's how I thought of you." Keith's words stopped, but the desperation in them made Alana stop, too. She didn't come back, but she stopped moving away from him. She would wait as long as it took for him to finish. For the first time, she understood what the phrase "waiting forever" meant.

"I was responsible for getting a man killed. It's the same as if I pulled the trigger myself."

His words lay in the air as if to make sure Alana had heard them, as if waiting for her to gather them up and examine them closely so she could condemn the man who had released them, as if waiting for her to feel about him the way he felt about himself.

Instead of putting more space between them, she slowly walked back to him, not stopping until she stood just in front of him. Once there, she allowed her gaze to scan his face as if looking for evidence of truth in what he had said. He stared back at her and she could see him struggling to control the pain his words were causing to himself.

"Actually, I was responsible for more deaths than I want to remember, but this one . . ." He took a deep breath. "This last one . . ." Another deep breath found its way in. "I think I could have prevented it if I hadn't been so stubborn. It was my fault. I should have . . ." He shook his head. "If I had just . . ." His stare slid to the floor and then back up to her face. "You deserve better than me. I'm sorry I let things between us go as far as they did."

"I'm not. You can regret it if you want to, but I am not sorry that we made love." Her eyes were open, but her mind was playing the scene of her and Keith over as if she were watching a movie. Her eyes filled at the thought that it would never happen again.

"I don't mean . . ." Alana waited as Keith searched for words. She would wait as long as it took him to find them. "The reason I'm sorry is not because we made love." A small amount of the pain retreated from his face. "Your sharing yourself with me was the best thing that ever happened to me." He held open his hands as if his explanation was a physical thing and he was presenting it to her. "I'm sorry because I feel as if I used you. I knew that we had no future together; still I acted as if we did." Again he struggled. His words were softer, but they were still loud enough for her to hear. "After you hear what I have to say, you won't want to have anything more to do with me. You'll be sorry, too." He released a heavy breath. "Sorry you let me get close. And you won't want it to happen again." He frowned. "I don't use people." He shook his head slightly. "Not usually. But with you, I . . ." He shook his head.

"You didn't use me." Her hand ached to smooth out his forehead, to caress his cheek, to help him through his pain. To make it go away forever. "You tried to warn me. I didn't listen. I'm not sorry for that. I will never regret what happened between us." A gentle smile filled her face. "Making love with you gave me the greatest pleasure I have ever known." She felt her face heat up, but she continued. "If you're honest, you will admit that it brought you pleasure, too."

"I-I never said it didn't." He wiped a hand across his forehead. "You are the one good thing that has happened to me in a long time, and I don't deserve you."

"Tell me. Make me understand." Alana took a deep breath and walked over to sit on the arm of the couch. She had come this far, and she would wait until he was ready to share his entire story with her.

Keith paced a few steps back and forth, but his stare found the floor and stayed there. It was as if he had forgotten that Alana was waiting, as if the last thing he wanted to do was wake up the terrible incident that still ruled his life and let it loose again. Then he stopped at the window and stared out as if his next words were written there.

"Our mission was to get information from enemy headquarters located deep in the jungle. It was supposed to be a simple in-and-out without detection. That's what the recon report promised." His words stopped and he struggled to make them start up again. "We were to find information showing enemy positions and immediate plans, and relay it back to headquarters."

Again his words stopped as if reluctant to come out. Again he forced them into the open. "Things went wrong almost from the beginning. Enemy headquarters wasn't where our reports said it was. Twice while going in we were almost detected, but we found what we needed." He stopped and his hands bunched at his side.

Alana waited. She was anxious to hear the rest, but she knew that Keith had to tell it in his own time.

"We heard the noise outside, but I took pictures of the papers anyway. I had to complete our mission. The men . . ." Pain etched even deeper into his face. "All while I was taking pictures, Sawyer kept saying we should leave, but no, I was determined to finish. In spite of the movement we heard coming toward us, I kept us there." He stared at her. "We were already in. The information was needed immediately so our troop movement could be planned. I only needed a few more minutes. That's all. I told them that. I figured we could still get out undetected." Alana knew that he was trying to convince himself, not her. "This wasn't our first mission of this kind. We had done this before and been successful. Why not this time, too?"

His stare slid to the closed drapes as if something interesting were there, maybe a different ending. "I had known Sawyer for a long time. We went way back together, completed a lot of missions together." His gaze swung back to Alana. "That was the last one." He wiped a hand across his eyes as if to erase what he had just seen again. "I carried his body out myself. I insisted on bringing him back. I put him into the chopper. I owed him at least that." Keith paused again and nothing filled the space he left. "We got the info and Sawyer's father got a flag folded into a triangle. We got medals pinned on our uniforms and Sawyer's dad got one in a small box. A flag and a medal with a piece of ribbon are poor exchanges for a son." His stare fixed her in place. "That was my last mission, period."

"Keith . . ."

"Now you see why we can't have a life together. Anybody who did what I did doesn't deserve happiness. I could cause something bad to happen to you, too. Sawyer was a friend and look what I did to him."

Alana's heart ached at the pain etched on his face as if it was there permanently. She struggled to find words to remove it or at least shrink it to a tolerable level.

"What did they do with the information that you got?"

"Used it to revise our troop movement."

"What would have happened if they didn't have the info?"

"I got Sawyer killed."

"What would have happened if you had aborted the mission?" She repeated the question that he needed to answer. *Please don't let him close the door. Not now that I finally got him to open it.*

"Our troops would have been deployed elsewhere."

"And what difference would that have made?"

"Sawyer would still be alive."

"How many others would be dead? How many more flags would have been folded and given to families?"

Keith still didn't look at her, but she could see him wrestling with what she said, trying to accept her words, trying to focus, for once, on what he kept from happening. His words struggled out as if they had to fight him for release.

"There's no way to know."

"Maybe you should try to think about that instead of staying stuck on what *did* happen." She walked to him. "I don't know about these things, but from what you said, Sawyer knew the risks. I doubt if he blamed you. Let it go, Keith. Just let it go."

"He blames me every time I have that nightmare."

"No, he doesn't. That's your mind's doing." Finally, she found the courage to touch his face. She allowed her fingers to gently try to rid his forehead of the proof of his pain. "Keith, you have to let it go." She wrapped her arms around him and lay her head against his chest. After what seemed to her like forever, he allowed his arms to close behind her, holding her against him.

They stood like that, with Alana trying to give Keith comfort, and with Keith struggling to give himself permission to take it. As they remained enfolded in each other's arms, Alana felt some of the tension leave Keith. It was a baby step, but it was forward and she'd take it. Keith broke the contact first.

"I'll see you in the morning. You've . . ." He stared at her. "I have a lot of thinking to do."

It might have been Alana's wishful thinking, but he seemed less intense. *Patience*, she told herself. *He's been carrying this load for a long time.*

"Okay."

Keith's hand on her arm was barely a touch, but it stopped her.

"Good night." He stared for a second, and then he leaned down and quickly pressed his lips against her cheek. Then his finger traced down the side of her face. "See you in the morning."

If Alana hadn't known that it was impossible, she would have sworn that she floated to her room. The impossible seemed possible now.

# Chapter 24

Time had long since passed over the midnight hump, and Alana was still searching for sleep. Hope and despair took turns nudging her each time she thought she had found rest. Questions pounded at her, keeping away her peace of mind. *What if Keith's sharing his story makes no difference at all? What if guilt and blame stay with him? What if, in spite of what I want, we were never meant to be together?*

Finally her exhaustion was stronger than the concerns keeping her awake, and she slept. It wasn't restful, but it was better than nothing.

Daylight came and had been in charge for a while before Alana awoke. Hope seeped into her. It was weak, but it was there. She tried not to let it grow. She had no idea what state of mind Keith was in this morning. She could only pray that he hadn't retreated behind his wall. She was out of ideas about what to say to break it down again.

From her scant possibilities, she took out a red blouse to go with a pair of jeans. Nothing like red to boost the spirit. She refused to ask herself how she expected a color to do something that words couldn't.

She got dressed, anxious to see Keith but fearful that she would learn that nothing had changed for him.

Then she gathered what strength she could find and left her bedroom.

"Morning." Keith spoke to her without looking at her. Although the set was turned off, he stared at the television as though he expected something to appear on the screen any second.

Alana stopped just inside the living room. She frowned as she noticed that he still wore yesterday's clothes. Her hope plummeted. "You didn't sleep well."

"Not at all."

"Oh." Alana's hope vanished. *Who did I think I was? Some kind of miracle worker? He's talked with people who know about things like this, people who have helped others with his kind of problem, experts. How could I think that talking with me would make a difference?*

She walked closer to him, but stopped before she was close enough to touch him. The only way she would do that was if she thought it might help him.

"I'm sorry. Nightmares again?"

He shook his head. "Uh-uh. Not this time. Thinking." He stared up at her. "I can't blame Sawyer for last night's lack of sleep. He didn't visit me."

"Well, you said that he doesn't visit every night." *I will not risk letting myself hope again.*

"That's true, but last night was different. It's not that I didn't wake up. I never went to sleep. My mind kept me awake." He shrugged. "Of course, the doctors have been telling me for years that it's all my mind's doing, anyway." He stood and faced her. "I just wasn't ready to accept that." His voice had a calmness to it that she had never heard before. Was it her imagination working, or was his face more relaxed? He shrugged slightly again. "It's been said that there's a time for everything."

A bubble of hope formed inside her in spite of her resolve. Her gaze examined each part of his face, looking for signs to allow her hope to grow, not knowing how to recognize them if they were there. *Maybe, just maybe.* A slight smile struggled at Keith's mouth. Her spirits soared a little more as he continued to talk.

"Last night, you didn't tell me anything that the psych doctors hadn't said more times than I can remember." His stare intensified. "But it was different coming from you." His voice was definitely calmer, easier. "For the first time I thought that maybe they had been right." He glanced away from her and shrugged. "Maybe it really is time to let go. Or maybe for the first time, I wanted something badly enough to believe it was true." His stare found her and a slight smile came with it.

"Oh."

Alana was afraid to say more, afraid to break the spell that had Keith believing, hoping for the future. It was a struggle, but she kept her own hope from soaring, kept herself from running to erase the few feet between them. *There has to be more that needs to be done. That couldn't be all that was needed.* She frowned. *Could it?* Her heart lifted. *Could it? Is it finally time for this? Can Keith move on at last?*

"I'm going to get cleaned up. Then we can check with Tommy before we go see Mrs. Banto."

Keith's gaze felt like a caress, but Alana was afraid her imagination had taken control. Her fear retreated a bit when Keith brushed his hand down the side of her face. Her fear shriveled up and disappeared when he replaced his hand with his lips. Hope came back full grown when he gave her a real smile, not just an attempt at one.

Slowly he backed up two steps, smiled, then turned away.

She watched him go down the hall because she couldn't move from the spot, afraid that if she did, his mental progress would recede. *Is this our second chance?*

She ditched caution and embraced that possibility as she went into the kitchen and put on a pot of coffee.

"I'm sorry." Keith, looking as if he had had a good night's sleep instead of none, came into the kitchen a while later.

"Are we back to that?" She tensed. *How could I think that it was that simple? That if I wished something hard enough, it would happen?*

"I'm sorry for what I put you through."

"Are you looking to take a new guilt trip?" She allowed her body to relax a little.

"Uh-uh." He shook his head. "Trying to clear an old record." He leaned against the counter casually, as if he had put away his old baggage and was free to be himself.

"Consider it cleared."

Alana had trouble locating the cereal bowls because she refused to take her gaze from Keith. Her hand groped the shelf where she saw them last. At least she thought she had the right shelf.

"Let me help you with that."

He closed the space between them. His hand brushed against hers. This morning, his aftershave held a promise instead of a taunt. This morning, dreams and wishes seemed possible.

Even though he wasn't looking where he was reaching, his fingers closed over the bowls. But he only held them long enough to set them on the counter. Then his hand went back to hers. Gently, as if it were fragile crystal, he removed her hand from the cabinet and held it against his chest. His thumb stroked across the back.

His gaze never left her face. It told her that he wasn't interested in cereal. Her gaze said the same.

"Alana, later, when this is over . . ." The rest of his sentence got lost somewhere. "Alana." Her name came from him as a groan, a plea, and he reached for her even as she closed the space between them.

"Yes." She brushed her hand across his chest.

"The hell with later." His hands found her back and stroked up and down. "I need you now."

"And I, you."

His lips met hers. Too many days without this urged them on. Problems, the situation, everything else was forgotten as they tried to make up for time lost.

Keith's hands urged her against him, as if she needed urging. Her hands brushed a path to his neck and clung there, finally home.

She felt his hardness pushing against her and she tried to move closer still, tried to let him ease her ache, needing to let him in. The kiss deepened as their tongues mated, trying to erase the long span of time since they had touched, giving a preview of what would soon happen between their bodies.

Keith's hands brushed from her back to her sides. Then they found their way to her aching breasts, which were pushing against his chest. He filled his hands with them, marveling again at how perfectly they fit, wondering how he could have gone so long without them.

His fingers brushed across a hard tip. Alana moaned and he swallowed her moan. His fingers left the tips and her moan was a protest.

"Please."

"Too much between us," he growled, but he wasn't talking about words or past events. "Way too much," he mumbled as his fingers worked the buttons of her blouse loose.

Her fingers agreed and fumbled to find a way under

his T-shirt. His hard buttons were hiding within the coarse hair, but she found them. She rubbed the palm of one hand over the first one, and then the other. It was Keith who moaned this time.

Then he eased away, but only far enough to lift his shirt over his head. "Still too much." He pushed her blouse down her arms. It bunched on the floor, but he didn't see it. He was looking at the plain cotton bra covering her fullness. Fancy lace had never looked as sexy. He watched as the tips that he had just brushed hardened even more under his gaze, as if they didn't already have his complete attention. He leaned forward and captured one through the fabric. Alana gasped as he pulled gently. She urged his head closer as he tugged again.

"Still too much. We'll have to fix it."

Keith's words were full of promise as he reached the back clasp and Alana was anxious for him to keep his promise. Soon, but not soon enough, the bra joined the blouse on the floor.

Alana felt her nipples pucker more, but cold had nothing to do with it. Anticipation was at work and impatience was with it.

Keith unsnapped her jeans and slid the zipper down as she returned the favor with his pants. Their gazes held each other as their pants met the other clothes around their feet.

Keith kicked his pants off and held her hand for balance as she did the same with her jeans. Then his mouth found hers again. Still locked in the kiss, he lifted her into his arms. Her arms found his neck again and stayed there. Her fingers stroked him as if wanting to make sure he was real.

Once in the bedroom, he eased her gently to the floor, but he didn't let her go once she stood. His hands found her hips and rested there. He rubbed his lower body slightly against hers and she tried to move her hips closer to him.

His finger slipped inside the elastic at her waist and traced a short path. His other hand helped shimmy her panties a few inches lower.

Alana flicked her tongue across his chin, then moved her mouth to the side of his neck. She bit gently as her own hands moved to the inside of his shorts.

Groan met groan as two pairs of hands worked themselves lower. Keith found the thatch of thick hair hiding her pleasure spot. Alana found his fullness. They both found a promise of fulfillment too long denied.

Keith lifted her to the bed and stared down at her, marveling that someone as beautiful, as desirable as she was, wanted him. Reluctant to look away but managing it because of the promise in her eyes, he gave his attention to the nightstand. He smiled at her as he took a small packet from his wallet, a packet that he had had no idea he would need, but that he carried anyway. Still looking at her, he opened it.

Quickly he rolled the protection into place, then returned to her waiting arms. He was anxious, but he found her center again, and stroked gently, slowly across it.

"Please." Alana's plea confirmed what her body had already told him. She was as ready for him as he was for her. He eased himself between her thighs. His hardness probed, searching, needing to find release. Alana pulled him closer. She gasped as he entered her, but lifted her hips to meet him.

He entered her, freeing them both from want long held in check, from need that had made their lives unbearable.

Together they moved as lovers have since man and woman existed; together they climbed the mountain of desire before soaring together to fulfillment. Together. Together. Finally together again.

\* \* \*

Alana opened her eyes and met Keith's gaze. His arm tightened slightly around her, easing her closer, claiming her as his own. She brushed a finger across his mouth, marking him as hers.

He said, "I don't ever want to leave this place, this bed. Now that I've found you again, I don't want to ever let you go."

"I was never lost. I was here all the time, waiting for you. I'm yours for as long as you want me."

"How does forever sound?"

"Perfect." She shifted a little. "Much as I hate to say it, I think we'd better get up and go see Mrs. Banto before it gets too late."

Keith glanced at the clock on the dresser. "It's true."

"What?"

"Time really does race when you're having fun." He sighed. "You're right. We have to go. The sooner we sort this mess out, the sooner we can concentrate on each other."

"I thought we did a good job of that earlier."

"Better than good." He rested a hand on her hip and massaged it gently. "However, I think in the interest of science, we should see if we can improve on it."

"I think if we're going to leave this bed, we'd better do so now, because if you keep that up—"

"Did you say up?" He brushed his body against hers.

"Behave." She touched his face and then forced herself to sit on the side of the bed. "At least until later."

He chuckled, but the sound died within him when she stood. The silky smoothness of her backside begged to be caressed. It was a struggle, but he controlled the urge, at least for now. He was only able to let her go away from him by promising himself "later."

Less than an hour later they were ready to leave.

"I thought we'd grab something to eat on the way instead of eating here."

"I don't trust us together, either." Alana smiled as she picked up her purse. Keith grabbed the papers from Tommy that were the reason for going.

The lunch crowd filled the restaurant when they stopped at a fast-food place. Then they drove the forty-five minutes to the trailer park. *Please let Mrs. Banto recognize somebody,* Alana thought as she rode beside Keith with her hand in his. This time she had a different reason for wanting this to be over. She glanced at Keith and smiled, looking forward to when this would be history and what was now the future would be the present.

They arrived at the trailer park to find a note on Mrs. Banto's door saying she'd be back later.

"I wonder how long ago she left." Alana stared at the paper as if waiting for more information to appear.

"No way to tell."

"She probably was here for lunch."

"Maybe." He stared at Alana. "Regrets?"

"Never."

"Good." Keith looked around. "Maybe she knows." He pointed to a young woman sitting on the step of a nearby trailer.

Alana walked over to her, but was soon back.

"Mrs. Banto left about ten minutes ago. Let's go to my place. I may as well check my messages while we wait."

She led him to her trailer. "It seems like months since I've been in here." She unlocked the door and stepped inside.

"A lot has happened since that time." Keith ducked his head and followed her. "So. This is your home."

"For a little while."

"Don't you get claustrophobic?" His head was a few inches from brushing the ceiling.

"I'm not here much." She smiled at him. "And I have a little more headroom than you would. It's really not that bad. I even have a bathroom." She opened the door to show him.

"That's the smallest bathroom I ever saw."

"But it has the essentials. It's okay for one person."

"Then I guess you'll have to say good-bye to it, huh?" He covered the few feet between them. "We'll need a place big enough for two." He brushed his lips across hers. "Unless you'd rather stay by yourself."

"You know better." Alana's hands traced a path down his back.

Keith brushed across her lips once more before he captured them. Alana's hands tightened. Keith's tongue urged her mouth to open to him. Promises of later filled their thoughts before, reluctantly, Alana eased her mouth away.

"I know there's a bed in here." She moved her hands to his waist. "And I know we can prove that this place is big enough for the two of us, but I think we should focus on why we're here." She stepped back. "If we keep this up, neither of us will be able to remember the reason for a long time."

Keith dropped his hands from her waist. "Much as I wish I could, I can't disagree. You'd better check your messages so we can leave this temptation."

"Okay. I'm sure we'll find another easily enough." She grinned as she looked at the steady red light on the answering machine, then she read the count. "Twelve messages. I didn't realize that I'm so popular." She pressed the play button and Yvette's voice greeted them.

"This is your sister. You know: Yvette? Yvette Duke? Remember me? Girl, where are you? Are you in trouble? I have called so many times that I'll have to take out a loan to pay my cell-phone bill. Alana, you have me worried. You call me as soon as you get this or I'm coming home. Dave can send somebody else up here. It's not necessary, anyway. Everything I'm doing can be done from DCS. Did you put him up to sending me here? Call me." She gave her Tallahassee motel phone number. "That's in case you want to say you lost the number. I swear, if you don't call me soon, I'm going to quit talking to you as soon as I see you, but after I lay you out."

Alana checked the other messages. Except for a tele-marketer who had a deal for her that she couldn't refuse, all of the other messages were from Yvette.

She frowned and immediately she punched in the number.

"I'm here," she said when her sister answered the phone. "I'm okay and I'm very sorry that I didn't get back to you. I haven't been home for a while." She glanced at Keith, who smiled at her. Then she turned away from him and nodded. "Yes, I know there's a phone on almost every corner. Yes, I know cell phones can reach across the country, so the miles between here and Tallahassee are no distance at all." She nodded again. "Here's my number where I'm staying, but I don't know how long I'll be there." She gave her the number of the motel. "Yes, I'll call you if we move and yes, I promise to keep in touch. Gotta go." She hung up and sighed. "I should have called her before. I didn't have to tell her what's going on. I knew she would worry." She frowned at the phone as if it were at fault.

"Guilt is an easy thing to pick up, isn't it?"

Alana looked at Keith. His smile helped her let go of her frown. "It sure is. Too easy." She shrugged and stood. "Shall we see if Mrs. Banto is back?"

The note was still on the door. Alana knocked just in case, but she didn't get an answer.

"Now what?"

"Let's wait a little longer."

They both leaned against the porch railing. An easy quiet blanketed them. Except for the sound of occasional traffic on the narrow street outside the park, nothing except the songs of birds and the rustling of palm branches broke the silence. Finally Keith glanced at his watch and spoke.

"It's after one. Let's go back to the hotel and see if there's anything more from Tommy." He shook his head. "I should have thought to bring the laptop with us, but for some reason my mind was somewhere else."

"I know the feeling. I should have called first." A sparkle in her eyes accompanied her grin. "My mind was with yours."

Alana wrapped her arm through his, and they walked to the car that way. Holding hands seemed natural as they drove to the hotel. They paused for a lingering kiss after they entered the suite, then they turned on the computer and got to work. It didn't take long. The message box was empty.

"I'll give Mrs. Banto a call." Alana didn't take long. "She's still not home. Should we wait a while before we go back?"

"Uh-huh. I guess we'll have to find some way to fill the time." Desire filled Keith's eyes.

"I guess so. Tell me what you have in mind." Desire made Alana's voice husky.

"I'd rather show you than tell you."

"Sounds like a plan." She helped Keith close the space between them. "A good plan."

Arm in arm they walked to his bedroom, and both had time to show their feelings.

* * *

Time was winding down the afternoon when Alana opened her eyes and stared into Keith's. "What are you doing?"

"Looking at you." He sighed. "I'd like to do more than look, but we'd better get back to Mrs. Banto's. If she's still not there, we can wait." He glanced at the clock. "It will be around six by the time we get back over there. Maybe she'll go home to fix her dinner."

After quick separate showers, they were on their way back to the trailer park.

Mrs. Banto opened the door on the first knock. After introducing Keith, Alana gave her the pictures.

"Sí. This one was here that day." Mrs. Banto handed Alana one of the pictures. Then she turned her attention to the rest.

"And this one. This is the one who says he is your cousin." She frowned. "He is not?" She handed the pictures back.

"Somebody is playing a joke." Keith smiled at the woman and held out his hand. "Thank you very much."

They left before she could question them more.

"Now we give Tommy our information," Keith said when they were back in the car.

As they drove away from the trailer park, Alana and Keith discussed their next step, but their minds were on each other.

They had to send Tommy the identity of the men, check for his latest information, and act on that. They had to find out which government agency to contact. They had to notify Dave about what was going on. But most of all, they had to figure out how to concentrate on all of that when what they wanted most was to get lost in each other again.

# Chapter 25

Alana and Keith stopped for a quick lunch before they went back to their place. The blinking light on the telephone told them they had a message. Alana checked while Keith checked the computer for word from Tommy.

"Oh, no." Alana gasped and shook her head. "No." She sat down hard.

"Who was that?"

"Housekeeping."

"What did they say to upset you?"

"How could I miss it?" She shook her head again. "How could it not register?"

"Baby, what's wrong?"

"Yvette."

"Yvette? You said the message was from housekeeping."

"The light was blinking."

"It was supposed to."

"The light on *my* answering machine was steady."

Keith took in a swift breath. "Somebody had already listened to your messages." Alana nodded.

"So-called investigative reporter and I didn't even pick up on something as obvious as that. It should have come to me right away, but it didn't. How could I miss it?" She jumped up and rushed back to the phone. "I put Yvette in danger." Her hand shook as she reached for the phone. "I have to call her."

"I have to make a call, too. You use your cell phone and I'll use mine. Leave the room phone free in case she tries to reach us on it."

The sight of two people punching in numbers at the same time while staring at a third phone would have made some people either laugh or admire at how technology had taken over. The situation, however, was terrible. Keith got an answer first, but this wasn't a contest. If they were lucky, everybody would win.

"Dave," Keith said, when he got an answer. "Call Yvette and tell her to go to the closest police station and wait there. We're on our way to Tallahassee. Tell her that we'll explain when we get there." He nodded. "Maybe. We're not sure. We'll explain when we can."

He looked at Alana, who was again punching in the same set of numbers. Concern and frustration were on her face, but concern, mixed with fear, was the stronger emotion.

"I can't get through. What did Dave say?"

"She's probably running around doing the latest task Dave gave her."

"What if she isn't? What if they already have her?"

"We'll assume they don't." He booted the laptop and barely gave it time to come to life before he was giving it orders. He checked for e-mail again, and then sent a message to Tommy. It was a short one, but Keith hoped it did some good.

"Looks like things are going down in Tallahassee. Can you get somebody there?" He got Tommy up to date, checked "high priority," and then sent the message. Alana, cell phone to her ear, watched.

"There should be a choice above 'high priority.'"

Keith unplugged the computer and grabbed it.

"She'll be alright."

He hoped Yvette was safe for many reasons. One was he

didn't want Alana to go through what he was still going through. He didn't want guilt to burden her for the rest of her life. He knew too well what that felt like. He squeezed her shoulders, then opened the door. "Let's go." They rushed to the car with his hand on her shoulder, trying to reassure her, trying to put her mind at ease.

As Keith took I-4 to the Florida Turnpike, and still as he took Route 75 toward Tallahassee, Alana had wishes for the past and present, and hope for now and the future. She wished whoever had decided on Tallahassee for the state capital had liked Orlando more. She glanced at the palm trees and Florida brush speeding past her window and wished for a way to teleport instead of having to use ground travel. She didn't wish for a higher speed limit. They didn't need it. Keith was pushing the car to the limits. What she did wish for was that all state troopers were taking care of business somewhere else.

Her hope was bigger than all her wishes put together. She hoped, she prayed, that Yvette was all right.

She alternated phone calls between Yvette's cell phone and her hotel room, but this time she was the sister who had to leave messages. She knew how Yvette had felt when she had to do the same thing at the trailer park; only Alana's own concern was multiplied many times over. She knew Yvette was in trouble. *And it's all my fault.*

"I should have gotten that device that lets you check e-mail without being plugged into the phone line." She shook her head. "I didn't think I'd ever need something like that, but if we had it, we could check with Tommy again. We could find out if he was able to do anything. I should have told Yvette to be careful; I should have let her know what we're working on. I should have called her so she wouldn't have had to leave that sarcastic message that told everything." She took a deep breath. "I never should have started this. I should have gotten a regular job. I should have—"

Keith glanced at her but quickly returned his attention to the road. An accident would steal time, time they couldn't afford to waste. He did reach over and squeeze her hand.

"No second guesses. 'Should haves' do no good. They're self destructive. They will sink you and not let you back up. Believe me, I know first hand. Yvette will be all right. Nobody has any reason to harm her. Just because you can't reach her doesn't mean something's the matter. Maybe somebody broke into your place because they could. Kids do that sometimes, just to see if they can."

"Do you believe that's all it was?"

"Why would anybody want to harm her?"

"Somebody listened to her messages to me."

"The messages they listened to just happened to be from her. We don't know who listened, nor why. All we know is that somebody accessed your messages. They might have just done that because they could, too. They might have picked your trailer because it was empty. You know how kids are."

"It's the men who were following us."

Keith didn't disagree. "Even if it is, they don't want her."

"No, you're right." Her words shook. "They want me. And they can get me through Yvette."

She struggled to control the fear that fought to fill her at the idea. Her struggle was even harder because the fear was even stronger at the possibility that they would use Yvette to get to her. She had placed Yvette directly in harm's way. *Please let her be all right. Don't let anything that I did cause her to be hurt. Please keep her safe. It was my actions, not hers. Please don't let her pay for them.*

"If somebody does want you, they'll contact you." Keith glanced at her. "Either way, Yvette's safe."

"For how long?" She swallowed hard. "I'll do whatever they say if they'll let her go." She frowned. "Why would they want me, anyway? I can't undo what I already did. I can't take back the message that I sent to myself. And we sent it to Tommy, who sent it on."

"They don't know what you already did. If anything, all they know is that you're a reporter doing a story. They can find out that you forwarded that e-mail to one address, but that's about it. They don't know whether or not you could do anything with it. They don't know anything. If Yvette tells them anything—" Alana's gasp made Keith stop. He tightened his hold on her hand. "*If* they have her and if she tells them anything, it will be that you're a reporter working on computer theft. Remember? We never told her what we uncovered. She's safe. If they even have her."

He changed lanes to get around a truck loaded with gravel and moving as if the driver was getting paid by the week instead of the job. Then he continued to try to reassure Alana.

"We don't even know that she's with them. She was fine when you called her back. That wasn't very long ago. Your messages were in Orlando, not in Tallahassee. Tallahassee is a big city. They'd have to locate her. She's all right. Dave said he gave her a lot of running around to do to keep her busy. That's why we can't reach her. She has no reason to expect another call from you."

"If you believed all of that, we wouldn't be flying down the highway."

"Alana, I repeat: even if they have her, they have to talk to you. At the most, she's their bargaining chip." He placed his hand on her knee and patted. "Look, we'll take this as it comes."

The car consumed the distance like a hungry dog eating its first meal in weeks, but the miles that they still had to cover seemed to be in the thousands. As they moved along, Alana alternated between calling both the cell phone and Yvette's hotel room. By the time they were a little more than halfway to Tallahassee, Yvette's cell phone mailbox was full, and Alana still hadn't talked to her.

"I'd better check my own messages. Maybe she called me back at my place." She managed a shaky laugh. "She couldn't get anything but a busy signal from my cell phone."

Alana punched in the different set of numbers. Only one message was waiting on her machine. It wasn't the one she had hoped for. In fact, it was the one she was afraid of getting.

"Your sister is visiting with us for a while, Miss Reporter. Bring your laptop." His voice was muffled but Alana didn't have trouble understanding the message. "We have to talk. Face to face." He gave a Tallahassee intersection. "I'll call you at the phone booth on that corner at eight o'clock. You'll get further instructions there. I don't think I need to tell you to come alone and tell nobody, not even your nosy boyfriend." Her hand was shaking, but Alana gave the command so the message played again. Then she held the phone to Keith's ear. He nodded when it finished playing to let her know it was through.

*It seemed like a scene from too many mediocre movies.* He shook his head. *Maybe it was still used because it worked more often than the authorities wanted the public to know.*

"We have an advantage. Don't we?" Alana's voice wobbled almost as much as her hands. She took a deep breath to try to steady both. "They don't know that we left Orlando as early as we did." Her attempt at reassuring herself was not working. Panic tried to wrestle control from reason. Still she continued to try. "We've got lots of time." Again she paused, closed her eyes, and tried to let deep breathing overcome her panic. "How much longer before we get there?"

"About an hour to the city limits."

Alana looked at her watch. "We'll still be way early." She frowned. "Do you know Tallahassee? How far is that corner from the limits?"

"Not far."

"Good. I'd rather be early than have something make me late. When we get about a block or two away, you get out and I'll go the rest of the way alone. I'll wait by myself."

"No, you won't."

"He said I have to come alone."

"You can't—"

"I know it's dangerous. I've watched old movies. I know there's no guarantee that they'll let Yvette go once they have me. I know that we don't even know if she's still . . ." Her voice wobbled badly. "I know I'll be in danger once I give them the laptop." She swallowed hard. "I *know* all of that, so don't tell it to me because I also know the alternative: they definitely *won't* let her go if I don't meet them. I *am* going alone even if I have to walk from here."

Keith didn't argue. It wasn't open to discussion. *Alana is not going to walk into danger alone.* His mind went into battle mode in case Yvette wasn't with the police.

The setting was different, but the situation was similar to several others he had experience with: locate the objective to be liberated, move in, finish the mission, and get out. He frowned. *It doesn't always work that way. Sawyer is proof of that.* He shook that thought away. This scenario had a big difference from any of the others: if Yvette wasn't with the police, Alana might have to be placed in danger until they found out where Yvette was.

He needed to forget his feelings for her, needed to

take his personal feelings out of the equation. He sighed. *As if I could. She's more important to me than anyone or anything else has ever been. No way am I going to lose what it's taken me my whole life to find.* His frown deepened. *Too many variables: Do they have Yvette? If so, is she still alive? If she's alive, where are they keeping her?* The only thing he and Alana had was a Tallahassee corner in the 'hood. He shook his head. They might not have her. They might still be trying to find Yvette. Still, he had to go on the assumption that she was with them. He had to plan for that possibility. If they had her, he had to find a way to locate her without Alana's life being on the line.

He released a hard breath and shook his head. *The phone booth angle was brilliant. Never let the enemy know more than the next step. No wonder it was used so much.*

"Why did he muffle his voice?" Alana broke his train of thought.

"What?"

"His voice—would I have recognized it?"

"A distinct possibility."

*That had to be the reason. But who? Who would know to go to the trailer park? Who would know to even follow us in the first place?* He thought about Nelson. *He was the only one who had seen us together at DCS, but he hadn't caught us at the computer.*

Keith's mind eased back to what had happened that evening. His body tightened at the memory of when Nelson had confronted them. So much had happened since then, between him and Alana and otherwise, but the incident was still strong. It had been the first time he had held her like that.

"Held her" was not the right way to put it. Melted into her, molded to her, wanted to make love with her right then and there among the computers, deep passionate love powerful enough to make every motherboard in the room fry just from being close.

He took a deep breath, but it didn't help. It never did take much for him to call back the feel of her body against his, her sweet, sensual mouth against his, letting him in, letting him taste. Her body: breasts to sweet mound to thighs, warm against him, kindling heat as if building a fire in Alaska in January. Her body welcoming him as if he was home, accommodating him, closing around him, holding him inside, making him whole again.

He shifted to try to find a cool place, a place where his body would let his mind work. Finally his body eased to let his mind do its job.

He drove to the next block, still sifting, still analyzing. *Nobody at DCS had actually seen Alana doing anything except clean. Had they? Could somebody have seen her and she hadn't realized it? There was a reason why they zeroed in on her. Did Nelson have anything to do with this? Who helped his heart stop? If so, whom had he given information to?*

"What do you think?"

"What?"

"It would have to be somebody from DCS. I don't know anybody else in Orlando."

"You're right." Another variable. *I should have picked up on that right from the get-go.* He shook his head. *You're getting sloppy. Focus, man. Focus on the mission.* "I should have caught that instantly. The phone call should have made me think of DCS first. They told you to bring your laptop. Only somebody from there would know that you forwarded the message to yourself. He's guessing that it's a laptop, and not a desktop. I should have realized—"

"Stop the car. You missed the turn back there. You just passed one of the streets." She stared behind as if to pull the street along with them. "Go back. We can follow it to where it intersects with the other."

"We'll check police headquarters first."

"Stop the car. I don't want to be late meeting him. I can't be. He'll hurt Yvette if I am."

"Alana, we won't be late. We're still way ahead of his timetable."

"*I* won't be late."

"We have to check the police station. If she's there, it calls for a whole different set of plans."

"And if she's not?"

"We'll have a set of plans for that, too." He glanced at her and then back to the street. "For now, why not think of the glass as half full?" Again his glance found her. "She will be safe." *And so will you.*

Alana didn't answer. Keith knew she hadn't changed her mind about anything. He knew that she had already decided on her own plan if Yvette wasn't with the police.

He reached Seventh Avenue and turned. He didn't use the few blocks left to try to persuade her to his way of thinking. It didn't matter. Whether they found Yvette at the station or not, Alana was not going to go to the next step. Not alone, not with a whole battalion. *I'll have them throw her into a cell if I have to. She's not going. I'll deal with her anger after this is over. I'd rather take a chance on that than having nothing but memories to hold. Memories are a poor substitute for the real thing.*

He continued to the police station, hoping they would find Yvette waiting for them, but prepared for action in case they didn't.

# Chapter 26

Keith waited for two police cars, sirens blaring, to leave the parking lot. The sign posted at the entrance said "Police Vehicles Only." He made himself hold on to his patience as he drove past the building, looking for a spot on the not-wide-enough street. *We're way ahead of the meeting time,* he reminded himself. *Way ahead. This is necessary before we go to the next step, before we even decide on the best next step.*

Alana asked, "Why don't I get out here and you go park?"

"Why?"

"I could check inside."

"That wouldn't change the facts."

Her stare said she still liked her idea.

"We'll go in together." He wanted to be with her in case Yvette wasn't waiting for them. "We need to plan our next step regardless." He stopped his sentence before it included "of whether or not we find Yvette inside." It was true, but he didn't need to state it. The thread that Alana was holding on to was quickly unraveling.

"It's *my* sister's life on the line." A crease showed along her forehead. "I-I appreciate what you're doing, I really do, but I am not some helpless female who needs to be protected by the strong, handsome hero. It's *my* sister at risk, and I'm going to do what I have to do to change that."

"I know all of that." *I also know that you and I differ on exactly* what *you will do.* "I have a friend who works here. I can cut the time we spend here."

He glanced at her as he continued to drive slowly down the block, knowing that she couldn't hear his thoughts no matter how strong they were, but checking just to make sure.

"I understand your feelings, but please, Alana, just be patient a few minutes longer. I know I've taken charge. It's just that I've had experience in dealing with situations like this. So have some females, but not you. You have to admit that to yourself. The fact that you're a female has nothing to do with my concern." *The fact that you're the particular female involved in this has everything to do with why I'm having trouble keeping my emotions out of it.* When she didn't say anything, he continued. "We both want the same thing: Yvette safe."

He stopped in front of an empty space, glad that he had opted for a compact car. He was also glad that he had found a spot. He knew Alana's patience was gone and nothing he could say could get it back.

She left the car before he turned off the motor. He had to run to catch up with her. When he did, he wrapped a hand around her shoulder, hoping it would not be needed for support because of what they would learn once they were inside, but merely to show that he was with her. They each took a deep breath, sent up a prayer, and then went inside.

Various activities were taking place in the large waiting room. Very few people were just waiting. Even though it seemed as if nobody noticed when they entered, two men came over to them before they took two steps toward the desk. One separated himself from the other man.

"How's it going?"

"It's going."

The face of the man who held out his hand to Keith was from a time that he tried every day to forget. Now it was staring at him, trying to pull him back to the past, where names weren't important unless they went into the "for posthumous recognition" file. Keith shook the hand and stayed in the present. He was needed here, where he could make a difference.

"We got a call from Tommy. We can use the room down here." He led them to the narrow hall.

"Wait a minute." Alana stood at the edge of the room, staring down the hall. "Is Yvette here? Did you reach her before . . ." Alana swallowed hard. "Is she safe? Tell me. Is my sister all right?"

"Please come this way." The man glanced at her, then continued down the hall as if he hadn't heard her.

Alana stared after him. She wanted to grab his arm and not let him go until he answered her. She would have if she had thought it would have made him answer her. Instead, using the little patience she had left, she followed. *He has two seconds. Then I shift into Crazy Woman mode.*

They passed several empty rooms but didn't stop. The agent's time was up just as he stepped into the room at the end of the hall and moved aside so the others could enter.

"Okay. Enough. Tell me—"

"Alana?"

"Yvette?"

The two women stood facing each other, but still a room's width apart, as if afraid to move for fear of disturbing an illusion, afraid reality was the complete opposite. Finally, at the same time, they met in the center of the room.

The men, along with a woman who had been with Yvette, gave them time to make sure that they both were all right. Keith was glad they waited. This was far from over, but Alana and Yvette needed a few seconds of assurance before they could move on.

"Thank you, Mister . . ." Alana shook her head. "I don't know your name." He hesitated, then answered.

"Agent Grant."

"Agent Grant," Alana repeated. Tears started when she saw Yvette and continued to race down her face. "I don't know how I can thank you." She hugged Yvette to her and held her there, but she reached to the man in charge and grabbed his hand. She shook it as if it were a stubborn water pump in the cold of winter. "Sorry." She let him go, but no sorrow showed on her face, only gratitude, happiness, and relief.

"What now?" Keith asked the man who said his name was Grant. Keith knew him by a different name, but that wasn't important. *Maybe it is his real name. Maybe the other was fiction. Maybe policy has changed since I got out.* He stared at the man. *I doubt it.*

He moved his stare to Alana and Yvette, each still making sure the other was really all right. He hated to bring them down to earth, but reality would come to Alana any second.

"Who had her? Did you get the man who called me? Who is he? How did you rescue her?"

*Reality with a vengeance.* Keith thought he knew the answers, but he hoped he was wrong. He hoped it was really over, but he knew it wasn't. What Tommy had found out proved it. The fact that these men were here added to the proof. He walked over to her and stood beside her, ready to be there for her when they heard the truth.

Yvette said, "I was on my way to the courthouse when I got Dave's call. He told me to come here and wait. He didn't answer my questions. He said he couldn't, but I thought he meant that he wouldn't." She took a deep breath and shrugged. "I came here anyway." She struggled several seconds for control. "Dave swore you were all right, but I wasn't sure if he was telling me the truth." Again she stopped. "I didn't even know if he *knew* the truth. I . . ." She shook her head. "He gave me a code so I would know who I was supposed to trust after I got here." She frowned at Alana. "What have you gotten yourself into? What is this all about?"

"We're not sure." Keith answered. Then he turned to Grant, who stepped forward as if that were his cue.

"We need those guys."

Alana said, "I'm supposed to answer a phone in"—she glanced at her watch—"an hour. They'll tell me my next step from there." She told the location.

Grant punched numbers on his cell phone, recited the location, and drilled orders to whoever was on the other end. Then he turned back to Alana.

"She's not meeting them." Keith moved closer to Alana. "She's not even answering the phone in that booth. She's not going anywhere near it. She's out of this."

"We need her."

"Work around her." He took a step from Alana and toward the man.

"We can't."

"Find a way." Another step would take him seriously into Grant's personal space. "Use an agent."

"He's right." Alana touched Keith's arm.

"You're out of this." His glance at her was full of anger, but she knew it wasn't for her. She touched his arm as if he were the one in danger, the one needing reassuring. She smiled at him. In a way that was true.

"The caller knows my voice. He has to if he knew how to reach me. He muffled his voice so he must think I can recognize his. If I *can* recognize it, it's only logical to believe that he can recognize mine." She squeezed Keith's arm. "Even if the authorities get the voice right, I doubt if there's anybody here who can pull off a Philadelphia accent like mine, especially on such short notice." She squeezed Keith's arm again. The muscles remained rock hard. "I have to do this."

"It's too dangerous."

"You know what will happen if I don't do this. You know what Tommy said. They have the capability to do things I don't want to imagine, things I probably *can't* imagine." She hesitated. "If I don't do this, nobody, including me, will be safe in the long run."

"Baby, you can't go."

He didn't address her logic, but he knew what would happen better than she did. His imagination could pull from his experiences and show him exactly that. On a personal level, he knew what effect *not* going would have on her life. She'd never be safe. They would come after her no matter what. *She's the unknown factor, and in operations like this, you tie things up tight even after you put your plans into action. Especially if somebody can identify you.*

Grant broke into Keith's thoughts, trying to use reasoning to convince him.

"Look, it's just until she makes contact, and we'll be there all the way. We have this planned out. Nothing will go wrong."

"Quit talking about me as if I'm not here. I'm doing this. I want them to go down."

"This can't be about revenge," Grant said. "You have to remember that. Revenge can make you do dumb things."

"I'll remember."

Grant turned to Keith. "She'll be safe. I promise."

Keith almost said that he knew how promises like that went, but he didn't because of Yvette and Alana. Instead he just said, "I know how that goes."

*Only too well. I know how "nothing can go wrong" can fall apart until you can't recognize it enough to pick up the pieces.* He frowned. He also knew that they were right. Alana had to do this, at least the next step of it. But he'd be there. All the way. If the least thing went wrong, the second it went wrong, he'd be there to do whatever was necessary.

"Let's get things ready." He hated saying those words.

Grant pulled out a chair and motioned for them to sit. Keith, mind still racing, still searching for a way to keep Alana out of the operation, held out her chair, then sat beside her. He grasped her hand as if that would keep her with him, keep her safe, keep her from going where he knew she had to go.

"We have a lot to do and less than an hour to do it." Grant shifted a sheet of paper in front of him, but the marks he made must have been just to help him think. Alana looked at them. They made no sense and he didn't even look at the paper as he explained his plan.

"Why do you need people around the phone booth? I mean, I appreciate your efforts, but he can't hurt me over the phone. He's going to call me."

"That's what he told you. He might have been telling the truth." Grant stared at her. "Or maybe he wasn't."

Alana didn't want to think about that part, but she knew he had a point. She didn't ask another question as he continued to explain the plan.

Keith sat quietly, a scowl planted on his face, his whole being filled with anger at the situation, feeling impotent because he couldn't think of an alternate plan that would let Alana wait here.

"I don't think you should go." Yvette, who had been standing silently watching, touched her shoulder. "Keith is right. There has to be another way to do this without your going. You don't have any training in this kind of thing."

"I'll be okay. I just have to talk on the phone." She tried to reassure her with a smile. "We both know how good I am at that." Yvette's expression didn't change. Alana adjusted the awkward flak jacket under the sweater she had been given to hide it. She fought the temptation to check for the thin wire that Marge, a female agent, had taped to her. This would connect her to everybody while she was in the phone booth. She knew it was still taped between her breasts. When this was over she'd almost need dynamite to get it off. She touched the spot anyway, just to make sure.

"Sorry about the wire. We'll have the phone covered, but we need the wire just to be sure." Alana nodded. "As for the jacket, that's just a precaution," Grant added as she tugged on it again.

"Do I look that stupid, or do you think I'm super naïve?" She glared at him as she adjusted the jacket, trying to make it more comfortable, knowing in the short time that she had it on that that was impossible.

"Just trying to reassure you."

"Truth does that, not obvious lies." She exhaled. "Look, I know the danger involved. I also know I have to do this. Don't try to snow me." She glanced at Keith. His scowl was still in place. She smiled and walked over to him. "Are you all right?" She smoothed a finger across his forehead.

"Not as long as you're in the middle of this."

"It won't be much longer." She drew him closer and spoke into his ear. "After this is over, we'll see what we can do to make you all right again." A twinkle appeared in her eyes as his body tightened against hers. She brushed her lips across his and stepped back. "Be patient." Then she turned to look at Grant. "Let's go."

Marge, her hair pulled back the way Alana wore hers, a sweater that matched Alana's covering her upper body, followed behind Alana and Keith. *Maybe, if the area around the phone booth was dark enough, she would be mistaken for me,* Alana thought as she looked at her. *Maybe.*

They reached the car and Alana had to tug to free her hand from Keith's.

"I'll be okay."

"You'd better be." He directed his glare at Grant, but it was really for himself. *I should have come up with a better plan. One that would guarantee Alana's safety, one that would keep her here.*

Alana got behind the wheel, Marge slid in beside her and huddled out of sight. Keith opened the back door.

"You don't go." Grant stepped forward.

"Wanna bet?"

The staring contest lasted only a few seconds, but it was long enough for Keith's point to get across.

"I don't think this is a good idea."

"Point taken. I need a weapon."

"You're a civilian."

Part two of the staring contest ended as soon as it began. Grant handed him a gun; Keith checked it and then climbed into the back. He settled himself on the floor in a way that allowed him to see between the front seats. The gun never left his hand.

"The area is well covered. You won't see them, but our people are already in place." Grant nodded. "You'll be safe." The look on his face showed that he wasn't as sure of that as he wanted Alana to think he was. She understood what was involved; she knew the danger. She knew he was afraid that she'd change her mind. He didn't know her, didn't know about her stubborn streak, which her father had once told her was as big as she was. Her chin lifted. *Daddy, you were right. I hope you'll never know that.*

She glanced toward the back seat once. She couldn't see him, but, in spite of the danger she was in, it was comforting knowing that Keith was with her.

She took a deeper-than-usual breath. Then she drove away from safety and to a dangerous unknown.

For somebody who was supposed to be alone, she had a lot of company.

# Chapter 27

A third passenger riding with Alana, along with Keith and Marge and just as silent, was apprehension. It wasn't tangible, but it was as real as a person would be. The quiet inside the car gave Alana's thoughts a chance to be heard.

*I'm scared. Plain and simple.* She made her breathing behave. *Do I wish I were out of this?* She nodded slightly but quickly. *No question.* She stopped for a red light and used the opportunity to gain control of her thinking. *I had a choice. This is my choice. No arm-twisting, no coercion. My decision.*

She waited while one last car stole her green light; then she moved forward.

*I can't even comprehend what will happen if they don't catch these guys. I have to do this.* Clichés bounced around in her mind: "make the world safe for democracy"; "it's a dirty job but somebody has to do it"; "if not me, then who?" She shook her head slightly.

"What's wrong?" Keith's voice from the back seat interrupted.

"Nothing. Just thinking."

"Change your mind?"

"I can't."

No other words came, so her thoughts took over again. *All of those sayings are appropriate. Maybe that's how they got to be clichés.*

They all also sounded so noble, but she didn't feel noble. That didn't have anything to do with what she was doing. She felt a little like the little boy with his finger in the dike and afraid of what would happen if he let go. Fate had put her here, and she was the only one who could do this.

Alana reached the street where she had to turn. She stopped at the stop sign and stayed longer than necessary.

"You can change your mind, baby. Yvette is safe. Somebody else can do this. It doesn't have to be you."

Keith's voice sounded as if he was more worried than she was. She knew how that was: it was always harder on the one waiting. She thought back to a short while ago, when she thought Yvette was in danger. What could have happened was too fresh in her mind. But, thank Heaven, the fear was wasted. She glanced back even though Keith couldn't see it.

*I know why he's scared for me. Nobody, no matter how many people there are watching over me, trying to protect me, nobody can really keep me from being hurt. The most that they, even Keith, can do is catch the person afterward.* She swallowed hard. "I'll be all right." In spite of the situation, she smiled. "I'll be all right," she repeated. And, all of a sudden, she believed what she was saying. All she had to do was follow the plan.

She moved from the safety of the sign and turned the corner. She felt extremely relaxed for somebody driving to what could be her end. She smiled slightly again. Keith was with her. And she was going to get the chance to get the ones who had put her through hell. Her jaw tightened. *Payback time.*

She reached the intersection, and the phone booth stood out as if waiting for her. She took a deep breath and opened the door.

"No. Wait." Keith's voice from the back seat and Marge's "no" from beside her made Alana freeze in place. "Stop.

Wait for the phone to ring." The intensity of Keith's command made her obey. "You'll hear it from the car."

Alana closed the door. She glanced at her watch. *Five minutes early.* She shook her head. *Ten minutes, when she factored in the five minutes she kept her watch set ahead so she wouldn't be late for things.* She frowned. *Were they really that precise, or did something scare them off? Had they seen the people Grant had put in place and changed their minds?*

Alana had looked all around when she stopped the car. She had let her gaze touch everything within range, but she didn't have a clue that anybody was out there besides the four of them in the car.

Maybe Grant had changed his mind. Maybe he had decided that it was just going to be a phone call. She shook her head. *Uh-uh. I don't know him that well, but I know he's thorough. His people are out there.* She looked at her watch again. *What if the man who called me got scared? Then what do I do? Wait for them to contact me again?* She frowned. *They can't. They know I'm not home. They know I'm here in Tallahassee and they don't have any way to reach me.* She swallowed hard. *Do they? Do they know my cell phone number? Do they know the description of this car? Are they watching me right now?*

The phone rang, stopping the flow of questions tumbling through her mind. She took a deep breath, made her hand stop shaking enough to open the door, commanded her legs to support her, and then stepped out.

"Leave it open," Marge whispered loudly as Alana reached to shut the car door.

"The phone booth door, too," Keith reminded her.

Alana did as she was told: left both doors open just as they had decided when they had worked out this plan. She didn't want to allow herself to think of the reasons for the open doors. Didn't want to think about making a smaller target, about giving them as little light as possible. Refused to consider the reason for that, too.

She glanced at the streetlight high up on the pole beside the booth. The light in the phone booth wouldn't have made a bit of difference. She took a deep breath and forced her mind to focus on what she was supposed to say, touched a quick finger to the wire taped to her body, then went to play her part.

"Do you have the laptop?" The voice asked as soon as she said hello.

"Not with me."

"Why not?"

"I'm trying to stay safe. If I give it to you, how do I know you'll let me go?"

"Clever, aren't you?" His chuckle made her skin crawl. "What did you do with the e-mail message you stole?"

"Nothing. I-I couldn't read it. I still have it on my computer. I should have deleted it. It's-It's just taking up memory."

"You never should have forwarded it in the first place. Why did you?"

"I thought it was somebody trying to steal another game engine and I could get a story out of it."

"Stupid Nelson." A stream of choice words about the dead security guard came through the phone.

"It makes no sense." Alana steadied her voice. "I figured that it's in a format that my computer can't read."

He laughed, but that only made Alana shiver. "Who did you show it to?"

"Nobody. I'm a reporter working on an in-depth story of the theft of the game engines. I—I'm freelancing now. I was planning on selling it as an exclusive after I uncovered everything about the problem."

"Too bad your paper in Philadelphia folded. You had to give up your nice little home. Maybe you should have gone to New York like so many of your colleagues. Jack is doing well up there."

Alana gasped at the reference to the reporter whose desk had been next to hers. *What else does he know about me?* She shook her head. *I don't want to know.* She took a deep breath. "I want to speak to Yvette. How do I know you really have her?"

"You don't want me to dump proof on you, do you?"

"No." Alana's answer was swift. She swallowed hard. *I know Yvette is safe at the police station, but he sounds as if he has her.* She shook her head. *I can do this. I know things that he doesn't. He needs something from me.* She gulped another deep breath. *And I need to help get him.*

"Quit playing games. Where is the computer?"

"I—I put it in a safe place. I've seen enough movies to know that after I give it to you, you won't have any reason to let me go."

"Smart girl, but not smart enough."

Alana held her tongue to keep from telling him that she wasn't any kind of "girl." Instead she listened as he went on.

"I don't need to hurt you, not if you hand over the laptop. You can't identify me. You wouldn't know me if I held a door open for you and smiled." His voice got harder. "Remember that if you try to back out of this. You're in as much danger as your sister. I can get to you whenever I want, wherever you are. I know more about you than you know about yourself. Computers are very helpful that way. Enough of this." The cold in his voice made her shiver as his threat continued. "One last chance and then I come for you. Understood?"

"Yes."

"You better be able to get your hands on it in fifteen minutes. You and I are going to the park." He told her the street. "Once you get inside the entrance, count three benches, then sit on the fourth, the one in front of the fountain."

"I don't know where that street is. I—I'm not familiar with Tallahassee. You know that." *Take as much time as you can. Give Grant enough time to get set up over there.*

A stream of profanity reached her. She cringed, but she endured it.

*Go ahead. Use up time,* she silently urged him.

His words changed to giving directions in the same harsh voice.

"You want me to leave the laptop there?"

"Oh, no, pretty lady. I want *you* to wait there."

"But I'll see you. I'll be able to identify you. You said—"

"Fifteen minutes."

"But . . ." Alana stared at the phone when no more sounds came from it.

She got back into the car. "I almost recognized his voice."

"Wasn't it muffled?"

"Yes, but for a second it wasn't, and I heard something familiar in it. Also, there was something in what he said . . ." She shook her head. "Something that should have given me a clue." She started the car. "I know him. I just can't identify him. Not yet."

"Don't worry. We'll all know him very soon." Keith held his cell phone to his face. "You got that?"

"We're covering the park right now," Grant's clipped voice said. "You can move."

"We'll have to switch places," Marge, still crouched in the passenger seat, told her. "I'll tell you when to pull over. I'm afraid to do it too soon. We don't know where he is. Our guys are out there, but he might have somebody out there, too."

Alana forced herself to stay within the speed limit as she drove down unfamiliar streets, hesitating at each corner even though Keith was directing her. Finally a red light caught them.

"Now," Marge said. "Pretend to pick something up, scoot over here, and I'll move over there. But stay down."

"I'm not sure this will work. Maybe I should meet him—"

"No." The word came from Keith and Marge at the same time.

"But if it's light enough, he'll see that you're not me. As much as he knows about me, he must know what I look like." She shook her head. "You don't look anything like me."

"Maybe he'll think you lost your tan."

"The one I was born with?" She stared down at the face that would have to spend hours in the sun before it could come close to her color.

"We didn't have much time to work with. We had to go with body build and size rather than color. Come on. Let's switch."

"I've got a bad feeling about this," Alana said as she crawled past her and slipped to the floor.

"This is the best we can do." Marge settled into the driver's seat and eased into traffic.

"What if there's a street light by the fountain?" It was Alana's turn to crouch down in the seat. "There probably will be one by every bench. You know there'll be one by the fountain. What if he sees that you're not me? What if you have to say something? You know he'll at least ask if you have the laptop. You can't sound like me. What if he asks something that only I can answer?"

"Alana, you are not getting out of this car." Keith's voice rumbled from the back. "Marge knows her job. Let her do it."

"Yeah. That's why I get paid the big bucks." Marge smiled, but her attention was on the turn she was making. "Almost there. Hang on. I'll get close, but I have to leave us room to work."

She reached the park, hesitated, then drove up over the curb and across the grass. She moved slowly and stopped near the fourth bench. The light hanging over the bench made the moon unnecessary.

Alana looked out the side window. *The power used by this one lamp would take care of my whole house for a month.* She frowned as her mind raced. *This is not going to work. Not like we planned it. He'll see right away that she's not me. He won't even have to get close.*

Alana popped upright, reached back, snatched the laptop from beside Keith, and scrambled out. Marge automatically ducked down so they both wouldn't be visible at the same time. "Sorry," Alana muttered. "This is the only way it will work." She opened the door and dashed out.

She wasn't going to think about him seeing her come from the passenger side. She wasn't going to wonder if he saw Marge before she ducked out of sight. She wasn't going to think about what he would do. She refused to think about. . . . *"Preston,"* she spit out as she looked back to the car. "It's *Preston* from DCS. He chewed me out once because his wastebasket was overflowing by the time I got to it. A few times he also told me I was making too much noise outside his office." She nodded. "It's Preston."

As soon as Alana had grabbed the laptop, Keith grabbed, too, but the only thing he caught was air. He released a stream of words that Alana had never heard before, but he stayed in the car.

"Get back in here." Marge slid toward the open door.

"Don't. Let her go. It's too late to stop her." Keith hated to say that, but anything they tried to undo the situation would put Alana in more danger. *When this is over and she is safe, I am going to wring her neck.* He breathed deeply. *Please let her be safe.* He tried not to think of that last mission that went wrong. *Please.*

*Please let this turn out okay,* Alana thought as she stood beside the car.

For someone as nervous as she was, her legs shook very little as she walked the few yards to the bench. She looked around, then stood at the end of the bench that was closest to the car.

"Bring it over here," a voice called from the dark under a maple with branches spread out as if to provide shelter to dozens of people. Tonight it was hiding only one who was blending in with the trunk.

"Don't go. Make him come to you." Keith's voice was as loud as he dared.

Alana heard him, but she felt that she didn't have much choice. She did have a little control, though. She moved sideways instead of forward. By the time she stopped walking, she was beside the fifth bench and the car was off to the side.

"You come over here. It's too dark over there. I can't see you." She took a deep breath. "Preston." She watched a shape separate from the tree trunk.

"What gave me away?" The man, who had worked with Dave since DCS opened, eased a few feet closer. The gun in his hand was small, but large enough.

"Something in your voice." She saw the face she had seen many times as she cleaned the offices. He always wore a scowl. Her stomach tightened. *The last time I saw him was late one night when he was working on a computer in somebody else's office.* "When I saw you that night, were you . . ." Alana caught herself before she mentioned the virus. "Were you stealing the search engines?" Alana didn't know why she was still playing dumb about what was going on. She shifted slightly, making him face away from the car.

"It doesn't matter to you." The look on his face was deadly.

"Where's Yvette?" She knew what it meant that he no

longer minded her seeing him. She had expected this all along. She just wasn't sure what to do now. *Time. Play for time. Give somebody time to do something.* "Why did you do this? Dave is your friend. He has been for years."

"Enough money can make friendship unimportant." He shrugged. "I owe some people. Some other people made it possible for me to pay them." He took a step closer, and the gun looked larger.

Alana inched closer to the clump of bushes to the side until a branch brushed against her leg. The shrubbery was dense, but not thick enough to stop a bullet. *How good was a flak jacket at close range?*

"What's this about?" Maybe, with more time, Keith could do something.

"I told you. Money. Some people are willing to pay obscene amounts to have control."

"But . . ." She almost asked him how he could put everybody in danger, how he could sell out his own country. Then she remembered that she wasn't supposed to know anything about that. "Take the laptop. Just let me go."

"Sorry." His hand moved slightly toward her. "Nothing personal."

Alana stared at the gun, as if waiting to make sure Preston would use it before she moved.

# Chapter 28

Everything happened at once, as if a time limit was about to expire.

Alana heaved the computer at Preston, who ignored Keith when he flung a "no" at them as he opened the back car door. Keith cursed the angle of the car and dashed around it, gun ready.

Preston grunted as the case hit him in the arm, but his aim went back to Alana. She dropped to the thick grass and winced as her shoulder made contact with the ground, but she rolled behind the bush. A bullet kicked up the dirt at the spot where she had been standing less than half a second earlier. She stopped rolling, tried to make herself smaller since she couldn't make the bush bigger, and looked for a branch, for a rock, for something else to throw at Preston. Another shot shattered a branch just as another, along with Keith's shout, came from a new direction.

Finally Preston turned toward the car and his gun's aim moved with him. His next shot went toward Keith at the same time that two more shots from Keith's direction joined the one that Preston sent from in front of the bush.

Alana found a rock and stood to throw it while Preston was turned away from her. Her hand closed around it and she gathered her strength to put everything into her one chance. Instead of throwing it, she held onto the rock as Preston fell like a slowly deflating human-size balloon.

"Stay down." Keith yelled. Alana crouched back down, but Keith didn't obey his own order. Instead he, followed by Marge, raced toward Alana as if he could undo what had just happened.

He kicked the gun out of Preston's reach without stopping. Then he ran to Alana and hauled her from the ground. Alana winced as his hands tightened on her shoulder, but he didn't let go. He didn't seem to notice her reaction. Still holding her, he positioned himself between her and Preston. Keith's grip tightened and he pulled Alana closer still as Marge spoke.

"Hold it right there." Alana glanced around Keith's shoulder and saw Marge standing with her gun aimed at Preston. "Roll onto your stomach and put your hands behind your back." In spite of the growing red stain on Preston's shoulder, he obeyed.

A groan escaped from him as he brought his hands together behind him, but Marge acted as if she hadn't heard it. She fastened his hands together with handcuffs, but made him stay face down.

Keith glanced at what was going on, but when he saw that Marge was in charge, he gave his full attention back to Alana.

"Are you okay? Did a bullet hit you?" Gently he probed her, not willing to take her word for it.

"Don't you think that should wait until we're alone?" Alana, surprised that she could speak at all, was proud that her voice sounded as if this were a daily happening in her life.

"Don't joke. How could you do something crazy like that?" Anger was in Keith's words, but fear was much larger. "Do you know what could have happened to you?" He pulled her close, then pushed her at arm's length. He stared at her hand. "A rock? You were going to throw a rock at him?" He snatched the rock and flung it away.

"It was all I could find."

"Do you realize how much danger you were in?"

"I know. I just—" The sharp intake of breath as he touched her shoulder made her stop speaking.

"What is it? Did he shoot you?" Keith's fingers barely touched her. He started at her neck and slowly skimmed his fingers over her shoulder. He stopped when she winced again.

"I'm not shot. I hit the ground hard." She rubbed her hand over the sore spot.

"You could have been shot. It's a miracle that you weren't. You could have been killed. Do you know that?"

"Yes." She moved her shoulder as if trying to get rid of a kink.

"It's going to take more than that to get rid of the soreness." He glared. "And it serves you right. Alana . . ." He pulled her close, then turned toward Marge. "You okay?"

"I got it covered. Company should be here any second."

As if a director had given a cue, four people came running toward them from all directions, identifying themselves as they ran, as if the bold white letters on their jackets weren't shouting "FBI."

A van pulled up alongside them. Grant was the first person to spill out. He glanced at Preston, who was now standing in front of Marge. Then he looked at Keith and Alana.

"We'll take it from here."

"What's going to happen to him?" Alana's voice shook a little.

"We'll take care of this."

"What if he comes after us?"

"He won't. That I can guarantee." Alana was glad that the look on Grant's face wasn't for her. "I think he'll have more important things to worry about than you. Somebody isn't going to be very happy at what he's going to tell us. And he will tell us. We're his best chance of survival. His friends won't like his failure." He nodded to Marge and she put Preston into the van.

"What about the message? What if they already sent it on?"

"They didn't." Grant nodded toward Preston. "In order to protect himself, he had to make sure he hadn't been discovered. He couldn't afford for his colleagues to find out how careless he was about a loose end, so he had the message held. We got it in time." He stared at Alana for a few seconds. "Sorry you can't write your story, but I'm sure you understand." He didn't sound sorry at all. Neither did he sound as if he cared whether she understood or not. "You folks have a safe trip back to Orlando."

The van left as soon as he got into it with the other agents. He never glanced back at the two standing with their arms around each other.

Alana knew that not writing the story wasn't important. She had known, as they got in deeper, that the story would never come out. What should have been disappointment was, instead, relief that the message had been discovered in time. She shuddered at the thought of what could have happened if it hadn't been. If it had been put into operation, a newspaper story would have been the last thing anybody would have worried about.

She and Keith watched the van drive away. The sound quickly faded and, except for the crushed grass showing its tracks, it was as if it had never been there.

"Are you really okay?"

"Yes." Alana touched Keith's face and traced a path down his cheek as if her touch could reassure him.

"I thought." Keith stopped. "I was afraid." Again he stopped. "I don't know what I would do if I lost you."

"That will never happen. You're stuck with me forever. You will be sick of me and I'll still be around."

"That could never happen." His lips captured hers. The possibility of what could have happened, that this moment might never have taken place was in their kiss. Dreams coming true, a future together, gratitude for the chance at such a future, all were in the intensity of their kiss. Reluctantly, a minute, or an hour later, they separated, but their arms stayed around each other as if the danger still hadn't passed. They walked slowly toward the car. There was no longer any reason to hurry, nothing to worry about.

They stopped when they reached the car, but Keith held her back when she started to get in.

"Why did you get out of the car? We had a perfectly good plan. Why didn't you follow it?"

"I suddenly realized whose voice it was and put a face to it. I saw him one of the nights when I had been on a computer. He didn't chew me out, so I thought I had covered up pretty well, but obviously not." She shook her head. "He must have checked up on me because of that." She paused. "A few days after that I saw him on the computer in somebody else's office." She took a deep breath. "He must have been working on the virus." She frowned. "That was just before somebody went to my trailer." She shook her head. "I never put the two things together." She exhaled sharply. "He was at a computer in somebody else's office. That alone should have raised a red flag for me."

"That still doesn't explain why you ignored the plan."

"It was so bright at the bench. I knew he'd see Marge's face in the light. That's probably why he picked that spot: so he could make sure I was the one meeting him. He would have killed her. I couldn't live with that."

"He could have killed *you*." His hands tightened at her waist.

"No. He wouldn't have." She shook her head. "He

needed me. He still wasn't sure that I had the computer with me."

"Marge would have been all right. She knows her job. She would have improvised. Besides, if something had happened to her, it would not have been your fault. It was a good plan. Sometimes we have to adjust as circumstances change. No matter how much you plan and how much you need for plans to go right, they don't always work that way."

He knew hearing those words didn't mean you believed it. Even saying them didn't guarantee belief. He didn't want to, but he thought about living with being responsible for something exactly like what Alana talked about.

"I know Marge knows her job." She stared at him. "And I also understand what you're saying." She brushed her hand along his arm. "Now you need to accept your own words, too." Her voice was soft. She placed her hands against his chest and stared up at him. "Can we go now?"

"Yeah. In a minute." Keith brushed his lips across hers. "Or a few." His mouth met hers again, and his arms tightened around her. Her hands moved from his chest to his neck. The kiss deepened, as if both needed proof that the danger was really gone. Finally they separated, but only long enough to get into the car.

As they drove to the police station, Keith thought over what he had said. This was a true case of several clichés coming into play. "Do what I say and not what I do" tried to assert itself, but it didn't have the power it would have had a few minutes before. A more appropriate saying insinuated itself to the front of Keith's mind: "No matter how much you want to, you can't change the past." He focused on that last saying, but he hung onto Alana's hand. With her help, he'd work on accepting that last adage.

They reached the station and, after a tearful reunion with Yvette, Alana left her to remove the flak jacket.

As she held it in her hand, she stared at it. She felt as if a weight had been lifted, one that was much heavier than the jacket weighed. It was really over. They were safe. All of them. She felt the tension, which she hadn't realized was so strong, ease from her. She took a deep breath, smiled and gave the jacket to Marge. After she thanked her and said a last good-bye, she left the small back room.

Once in the main room again, she took one last look around the station. Nobody even noticed that they were still there. Everybody had moved on to the next incident, the next piece of police work, the next crisis.

She inhaled and let it out slowly. *None of this has anything to do with us anymore.*

She walked out the door with Yvette and Keith and shook her head as they walked to the car. She tried to pay attention to what Yvette was saying, but her mind was still on what had just happened in the park. Keith had been worried about her, but all of her fear had been about "What if something happens to him?" *This love thing isn't easy.* She reached over and held Keith's hand.

He closed his around hers. They only let go long enough to get into the car.

Soon, hands back together as if something might try to separate them, they were on the road back to Orlando.

"Okay. Tell me. What happened? I want to know everything. Why did Dave tell me to go to the police station? They didn't even try to come up with a reason for my being there, just kept telling me that it was for my own good and assuring me that I wasn't under arrest. Why was I even in Tallahassee in the first place? The work Dave gave me could have been done more easily and more quickly from the office. What is going on?"

Alana looked at Keith. His gaze met hers.

"We discovered . . ." *How am I going to explain this? How much should I tell her?* She inhaled deeply. "We—"

"We uncovered another attempt to steal software engines. Preston was involved." Keith's voice was calm.

Alana shook her head. *If I didn't know the truth, I would believe him.*

"Preston? Are you sure? He's Dave's friend."

"He was," Alana said.

"Why did he do it?"

"Money."

"Money? That's enough to make him throw away a friendship that goes back years?"

"Evidently."

"What happens now?"

"Now Dave goes for the government contract. He's sure to get it now," Keith said.

Yvette let that sink in for a few seconds. "That doesn't explain everything. Why did Dave send me up here?"

"Because we didn't know exactly what was going on at DCS and he didn't want you to be at risk." *At least that part was true,* Alana thought. "And I was afraid you'd blow my cover."

"I'm not buying that cover bit. I did okay when I ran into you at DCS. Why all of a sudden did I have to come to Tallahassee? And why did I have to go to the police station?"

"I had been discovered at DCS." Alana chuckled, trying to be casual, hoping it would help make Yvette accept her explanation. "I wasn't very good at the undercover thing." She paused. When Yvette didn't respond, Alana went on. "Somebody listened to my messages, the ones from you. I was afraid that they would try to hurt you. Stealing software engines is big business."

"You were in danger?"

"Just a little." Keith cleared his throat, but Alana refused to look at him. She had to make Yvette accept this explanation. "Things are all right now." That came out a little better.

"You're sure?"

"Yeah." Alana knew that was the truth.

"Now you can write your story."

"Yeah." She nodded. "'An In-depth Look at Computer Espionage.' That will be the working title." She hesitated. "Nelson was involved, too."

"Nelson? The security guard?"

"That's the one. His heart didn't stop on its own. Maybe he decided that he wanted all the money for himself."

"All of this was going on and we never had a clue? How did he manage it?"

"After hours, during lunch, when all of you were at meetings," Keith said. "If somebody wants to do something like this, there are lots of opportunities. The more money they stand to make, the greater risks they'll take.

"Was anybody else involved besides the two of them?"

"Not that we know of." Alana hoped her hesitation wasn't long enough for Yvette to notice. *I know that's not true, but Yvette doesn't need to know the whole story. Nobody ever will, except for those working on it. Nobody beneath Grant's group will ever know how close they came.* She shook her head. *Quit thinking about what could have happened.* She glanced at Keith. His nod told her that he agreed with what she said. Yvette's questions stopped. Alana leaned back. It was over.

Each one's adrenaline rush had run its course. A sense of calm settled around them like a security blanket. At a normal speed, they covered the miles back to Orlando.

# Chapter 29

"Are you sure you're going to be safe?" Yvette looked at Alana as they stood outside Yvette's house.

"I won't let anything happen to her." Keith put his arm around Alana's shoulder.

"You can always stay here, you know." Yvette glanced at Keith, then looked back at Alana.

"I know, Sis." She smiled. "It's not necessary."

"But where are you going? You said it's over. You don't have to stay at the trailer park anymore. Besides, you and I have to talk."

"I have to get my things. I-I spent a few days at a motel before we went to Tallahassee." She shrugged. "We left in kind of a hurry."

"A motel? Why?"

"I wasn't sure what was going on." She hesitated. "I didn't know who was involved and I didn't want anybody to find out what I was doing at DCS. They could have messed up my research."

"Research, huh. And I guess Keith is with you for the same reason? Research, I mean." She stared from one to the other. Then her stare planted itself on Alana. "I know you well enough to know there's something more to this. I'd have trouble accepting that so-called explanation from somebody I barely knew. Knowing you makes that more than a little lame." Her stare held. "I wish I could let you slide on this one, but you know me: I like things tied up in a neat little package, maybe with a bow on top. I left it alone in the car because I didn't want to mess with your concentration. No distractions now." She unlocked the door and opened it. "You may as well come in. I'm not letting you leave until I hear it all." When Alana didn't move, she continued. "You'll be more comfortable inside instead of talking out here, don't you think?"

Alana sighed. Then she shrugged. "Okay." As soon as they were inside the living room, she turned to Yvette. "This is going to take some time."

"It may be late, but I'm not in any hurry. Take what time you need." She leaned back in the armchair. "Whenever you're ready."

For the next half an hour Alana gave the barest possible explanation about what had happened. Whenever she hesitated at a particularly sensitive part, Keith filled in. When Alana reached the end of the story of how somebody had tried to use DCS to spread a virus, she held her breath. They hadn't told of the potential for damage from the virus. She relaxed when, after staring for a long time, Yvette nodded.

"So. It's over now?"

"Yes."

"No more danger?"

"No."

"You're sure?" Yvette let her stare stay on Keith. He answered.

"Yes. It's over."

"How do you know it won't come back? That they won't try again?"

"The authorities will see to it."

Yvette frowned, as if having trouble reaching a decision. She stared at Alana and then back at Keith. "I'm trusting you to keep my sister safe."

"You can count on it."

Yvette used her stare a few seconds longer. "I guess I'll let you guys go." She moved her stare to Alana and stood. "You call me tomorrow." She glanced at her watch and shook her head. "No. I mean early this evening." She gave Alana a hug and kissed her cheek. "Night. Or, I should say, morning." She smiled. "I have to decide whether to fuss at Dave or thank him when I get to work."

Alana listened for the click of the deadbolt after she and Keith got outside. Then she turned and, followed by him, went to the car.

"Is it really over?" She fastened her seat belt. "I'm having trouble accepting that I can go around without wondering if somebody is after me." She looked at Keith as he buckled himself in and started the car. "It's as if I just watched a realistic ction movie and my imagination pulled me into it." She shook her head. "I'm really safe?"

"You're really safe." Keith drove down the street toward the highway.

"We won't hear any more about this, will we? I mean, from the Feds."

"It will be as if it never happened."

Neither found more words to say as they rode to the motel. They each had their own thoughts speaking to them. Alana tried to sort hers out.

*It's over. Now what? We go our separate ways and I try to go on without him?* Alana frowned. *He said a lot of things after Preston was captured. He talked about being afraid of losing me, of needing me, but that was the situation talking, wasn't it?* She frowned. *Was it really just fear of being responsible if anything happened to me?* She thought of how Sawyer's death still haunted him and nodded. *Probably so.* She swallowed hard. *He probably feels that what happened tonight, that this whole situation, is his doing. He probably feels that if it weren't for him, I would never have been involved in anything so dangerous.*

She twisted and untwisted her hands in her lap, staring at them as if they belonged to somebody else. *In a way, he's right. I didn't have any connections. I would have gone on digging, looking for one thing and stumbling into another and never realizing it until it was too late. I would have been in more danger without him; I just wouldn't have known it. How can I make him see that?*

During the ride to the motel she tried to find the right words to convince Keith that he hadn't been the cause of her being in danger, that he had kept her safe. By the time they were inside their unit, she still hadn't found the right words to make him believe that.

"Let's get our things and check out. We can go to my place." Keith avoided eye contact.

He went about gathering the few things he had taken from his bag as if in a hurry to put this all behind him. And he probably was. *Including me.* Alana stood in place.

"They won't pack themselves, you know." Finally he looked at her.

"True." Her voice felt shaky, but Keith acted as if it sounded all right. Still she didn't move. Loud talking from the parking lot should have gotten her attention, but it didn't. She swallowed hard. *He warned me.* She took in a deep breath, hoping it would help her phrase her words so that she would get through to Keith. *This is my last chance.* "It wasn't your fault. My being in trouble, I mean. None of it was your fault."

"Trouble is too mild a word for what almost happened to you." He glanced at her, then collected some of her things and put them into her bag. Next he checked the drawers.

"That's true also." *Why won't he look at me?* "But if you weren't there, if Dave had never called you in, if you hadn't accepted the idea of us working together, I still would have found a way to dig out information. It would have been more difficult, but I would have found a way." She waited for him to speak, but he stared at her with an "oh, yeah" look on his face. She went on. "I already had their message. That's what brought Preston out. The only change would have been my trip to Tallahassee. It would have been unnecessary. He would have caught me here in Orlando. And I would have been alone." Her voice softened on that last sentence.

Keith stopped. The things from the bathroom that he was holding stayed in his hands for a few seconds. Then he placed them into her bag. "You want to check to see if I missed anything?"

Alana stared at him. Then she gave up and went to check. When she came back empty-handed, she closed her suitcase. She had to let her ears tell her when Keith did the same with his. He reached for her bag, but she picked it up before he could. She left the room and walked to the car without looking at him again. *I should have gotten my car from Yvette's while we were there. Why prolong this?* She still could go back to her sister's place.

"If you take me back to Yvette's, I can get my car. I won't have to bother you anymore. There's no reason I can't stay in my trailer until I can sort things out. I'm not in any danger. I'm just out a laptop. My budget can swing for another one. I can move in with Yvette while I look for a job. I—"

"We need to have a serious talk. We can do that at my place."

Alana shrugged. Their last serious talk was about how he couldn't get involved with her. She stared at him. *I don't know about you, but, as far as getting involved is concerned, I'm already there.* She didn't tell him that, though. She didn't tell him anything. She just gave up and walked out.

When they got to his place, he grabbed both bags. She followed him in. *I have to try again. And again.*

"None of my involvement in what went on was your fault. I would have done what I did even if you weren't there. I—"

"Marry me."

"I just would have been in more danger without you." She stared at him. "What did you say?"

"Marry me."

"But you said you can't get involved. You said I'd get hurt by you." *Why am I trying to talk him out of it?*

"I was wrong. I said a lot of stupid things." He closed the space between them.

"You want to marry me? Are you sure?" *Shut up, Alana, before he changes his mind.*

"More sure than I have ever been about anything." He slowly pulled her against him.

"But—" Whatever she had been about to say was replaced by his lips touching hers, claiming hers, persuading her, as if she needed persuading, as if she didn't want this more than anything, as if she hadn't been afraid that he would walk out of her life leaving a hole that would never be filled. She put her soul into her kiss, telling him, showing him how she felt.

Keith broke the kiss slowly, as if he didn't want to. Alana smiled up at him. She knew the feeling.

"Is that a yes?" He smiled. A real, honest-to-goodness smile. The first Alana had ever seen on him.

"That looks good."

"What?"

"Your smile."

"If you let me, that was just the first of a lifetime full."

"I'll let you." She traced his smile. "It will be my pleasure."

"I think we're about to have an argument."

"Why?" She frowned, but wrapped her arms around his back as if to make sure he was really there and she was in his arms.

"Over who's going to get the most pleasure."

"Suppose we call it a tie." She smiled. She pressed her body against his. Heat radiated from the spot where his instant hardness came in contact with her and spread through her body. "I seem to remember a promise I made to you."

"What's that?" He cupped her bottom and pressed her tighter against him. Desire shot through him as a matching desire flared in her eyes. He rubbed against her and her moan made him smile again.

"I promised to see what I could do to make things all right for you."

"Oh. That promise." He leaned back enough to allow his hand to find the fullness of one of her breasts, then he stroked across the tip. "I think you've made a very good start." He nipped the side of her neck as his finger circled the now-hard tip. "Of course, I'll have to make sure that you're all right, too." He tugged gently on the already hard tip.

"Of course." Alana's voice was weak, hoarse, rough with desire.

Keith lifted her and her arms tightened around his neck. Their lips met and held as he carried her into the bedroom. He set her down, but still cradled her in his arms.

"I thought I was going to lose you." He pressed a kiss to her cheek as his fingers worked the buttons on her shirt free. "You don't know how afraid I was."

"That will never happen." She loosened his shirt buttons and shoved the shirt down his arms and onto the floor.

"Good." Her blouse fell also. Keith unfastened his pants

as Alana did the same with hers. It was as if they were in a race to see who could finish first. Both won.

"You are beautiful." He touched the dark tip pressing against the inside of her black lace bra. "And I love you so much."

Alana settled her hands at his waist. She eased a finger beneath the waistband.

"And I you."

"Shall we prove it?" Keith never gave her a chance to answer. He pressed his mouth to hers as he lifted her.

Protection in place, they began to prove their love to each other. A few hours later, they proved it again.


Alana awoke first. She lay with a smile, staring at Keith. His eyes opened and he returned her smile.

"It was not a dream, but then, I knew that. It's impossible to have two dreams at the same time."

"You had a dream?"

"Yeah."

"Sawyer?"

"Yeah."

"I'm so sorry."

He gathered her to him and brushed his hands up and down her back.

"Don't be. It's all right." He shook his head as he remembered Sawyer's words—the actual words Sawyer had said that day, not the ones his own mind had put together so many times, too many times since then.

"It wasn't your fault, Captain," Sawyer had said as Keith bent over him. "Things happen in war." Then he had closed his eyes for the last time. In this new dream, words were added: "Let me rest."

"Sawyer told me to let it go. I know it's crazy." He shook

his head. "Maybe it's wishful thinking on my part because I want this so badly."

"You believed that he was blaming you." Alana smoothed the crease from his forehead. "Why can't you believe this?"

He shook his head again. Then he shrugged. "I guess because it seems too simple."

"Sometimes important things are." She brushed her lips across his. He opened his mouth beneath hers. Then he pulled her into his arms, ready to show her once more how much he loved her.

He imagined he heard Sawyer say, "Live your life, Captain. You did well." Then he faded, and Keith knew he wouldn't be back.

Keith looked forward to his life for the first time since he could remember. He wanted the future. He wanted to spend it with Alana.

# Chapter 30

"Alana? Baby, are you ready?" Sarah Duke stepped behind the partition concealing Alana from the rest of the banquet room at the hotel. "The trio is in place and waiting for the signal." She patted the filmy lace covering the back of her daughter's head.

"I'm ready, Mom." Alana reached for the bouquet from the small table beside her. "Though I don't see why we bothered with live music. Or with music at all, since there are only a few guests here."

"Numbers don't matter. This will be your only wedding and it has to be perfect, with all the traditions." Sarah adjusted the scalloped lace framing the square neckline of the long gown a little, as if it weren't already perfectly placed. "You are more beautiful in this than I was."

"Dad would argue with you about that." Alana smiled, hoping it would help control the butterflies tickling her stomach. *Why am I so jittery when this is what I want?*

"Your father would pick his daughter." Sarah's smile softened for a few seconds as if she were back in her wedding day. Then she shook the memory off and returned to the present. "You don't look as nervous as I was."

"If that's true, then it's because I can internalize better than you do." She patted her middle. "My stomach is acting as if I had sent a gallon of espresso down to it, when in reality I didn't drink any coffee." She shook her head. "I was afraid it would make me nervous." She took a deep breath, let it out slowly, and then repeated the process.

"This is a life-changing event. You're entitled to a little nervousness, as long as that's the reason." She touched the side of Alana's face. "You do love him, don't you? This happened so fast. Are you sure this is what you want? It's not too late to change your mind."

"Change my mind?" Alana shook her head. "I never knew love could be this deep, this strong. I can't imagine *not* being with him."

"Good." Sarah nodded. "That's how it should be. Marriage should be forever."

"Speaking of forever, that's how long it's been since I saw Keith." Alana frowned. "Did you see him this morning? How did he look?"

"Yes, I saw him. He looks almost as handsome as your father did on our wedding day and just as nervous." She chuckled.

"I don't see why I couldn't see him before I came down here."

"Yes, you do. Tradition."

"Tradition doesn't say anything about talking with your"—her face broke into a wide grin—"husband-to-be." Her grin disappeared. "I didn't even do that this morning. Do you know how long it's been since I've seen him?" *How long since he held me in his arms? Since I felt his body against mine?*

"You talked with Keith just last night and, yes, I do know how long it's been since you've seen him. So does anybody who got within talking distance of you these last few days."

"One whole week. That's how long. Seven days."

"Alana, the man had to close up his apartment and move all of his things from Boston. He also had to finish any business he had up there. I think it's a wonder he was able to do all that in one week." She smiled. "Besides, after this you'll see so much of each other that you'll look for excuses to be apart."

"Sure. Just like you and Dad."

"Your dad and I have something special." Her smile softened. "I pray you and Keith do, too." She stepped back to take one last look at Alana. "Let's get this started before I start to cry."

"You never cry at weddings."

"I've never been to my daughter's wedding before." She frowned. "The dress is the something old, your shoes are something new, Yvette's earrings are something borrowed—"

"You got that right. She made it extremely clear about a dozen times that she wants them back."

"What's blue? We forgot the something blue."

"My underwear." Alana's eyes gleamed as if she had a secret.

"You have on blue underwear? Not the traditional white?"

"Midnight blue. White underwear doesn't do my tan skin justice."

Sarah shook her head, but she smiled. "Then I guess we're ready."

She stepped from behind the partition and gave a signal. The lights in the huge crystal chandelier dimmed and Alana knew Yvette was lighting the candles in front of the altar. The opening notes of the preliminary march sounded. Alana took a deep breath and slipped from behind the screen. She looked to the front, at the section of the room that had been made to look like a small wedding chapel.

Tommy was there. He had arrived two hours ago and Alana's father had introduced him around. Kadijah, Alana's friend from Philadelphia, was sitting beside

Corina. Both women smiled at Alana. Keith's sister, Tara, who had arrived a day ago, was standing with Yvette just outside the partition, ready to precede Alana to the front. Dave and Keith's friend Rassan were waiting to act as escorts for the two young women. Sarah smiled once more at Alana, then took her husband's arm and walked to their seats. Tara and Yvette followed.

Alana stood alone at the back, ready to make the walk to her new life, just as she had planned it. She didn't see any of others, though, and wouldn't have seen anybody else even if the room had been bursting with people. Her gaze was focused entirely on Keith, who was waiting to welcome her into his life, waiting to make his future hers.

The music changed to the introduction of the wedding march. When Alana failed to move, the trio repeated it to give her more time to get unstuck from Keith's stare and to remember how to walk. When it started the third time, Sarah smiled, shook, her head, stood, and walked back to Alana. She blocked her daughter's line of vision and leaned toward her.

"Honey, if you don't come to the front you can't get married, and if you don't get married you won't be his wife and the two of you can't ride in your hot-air balloon over the rainbow together." She nudged her daughter's arm. "Alana, everybody is waiting. Did you change your mind?"

"Of course not." Alana answered, but her stare held on Keith.

"Then let's go." Sarah hesitated, then wrapped her arm through Alana's and shrugged. "The heck with tradition."

Together the two walked to the front as the small group applauded.

Sarah placed Alana's hand in Keith's. Then she turned, again shrugged to the guests, then eased back to her seat.

Yvette's minister, Reverend Woods, stepped forward to

begin the ceremony and Alana handed her sister the bouquet.

The ceremony passed in a blur and all Alana remembered was that she and Keith promised their hearts to each other and exchanged rings.

"You may kiss your bride," was announced in a surprisingly short time.

Keith gently eased Alana to him, then carefully folded her close, as if afraid she would break. He brushed his lips across hers before claiming them in a fleeting kiss. "We'll save the rest for later," he whispered against her ear.

"I'll hold you to that," she murmured back.

Applause filled the room as everybody surrounded them. Yvette nudged Alana and gave her back the bouquet. "There are a couple of traditions left to follow before you guys take off. All single women, all three of us, please move to the center. Alana, you stand over here." She tugged Alana away from Keith. "For crying out loud," she said when they held onto each other's hand, "I'm only taking you over here, not miles away from each other."

After being positioned where Yvette was satisfied, Alana turned her back to the other women, but she remembered exactly where Yvette was standing and threw the bouquet at her. Yvette's hands went up instinctively and she looked surprised to see the flowers in her hand.

"Oh, well." She stared down at them, then shrugged. "Moving right along, next step. Alana, you sit here." She dragged a chair out and faced it toward everybody. "Come on, you two," she said when the newlyweds just stared at her. She pulled Alana, and Keith followed.

Alana sat and Keith stood facing her.

"I'm not sure I like this part," he grumbled. "You didn't put that thing up too high, did you?"

"I guess you'll have to find that out for yourself."

Hoots, shouts, and whistles came from behind him as he knelt in front of her.

Alana eased her skirt up to her knees and winked at him.

He glared at her when the garter wasn't in sight. Alana straightened one leg and slowly lifted it. Then she wiggled her foot slowly at him. Keith stared at it for a couple of seconds; then, without pushing the skirt up further, he slid his hand under it. Laughter sounded again as relief covered his face as he slid the garter down his wife's leg.

"Single men over here," Yvette directed. "Come on, you guys," she prompted when none of them moved. Finally Dave and Rassan walked to her as if through thick mud. "You too, Tommy."

He hesitated, then rolled his wheelchair over to the others.

"Okay, Keith. Do your thing."

Keith tossed the garter over his shoulder. None of the men put up a hand, but that was okay. The garter found its own place and tangled on Dave's boutonnière. There it hung. Everybody roared at the surprised look on his face.

"You're next." Keith smiled at Dave, who just stared at the object in his hand as if he had no idea what it was nor how it got there.

"Moving right along to the next tradition." Yvette nodded to the trio and slow music drifted from them. "Okay, Dad. You and Alana first."

Alan stood and walked to his daughter.

"Oohs" came from everyone as he softly kissed her cheek before leading her to the dance floor. After a few minutes he walked her over to Keith. "I'm leaving my daughter in your care. Be good to her."

"I will, sir. I will."

He drew Alana close as the music changed to *Always and Forever*.

Alana looked up into Keith's eyes. As they danced, everything and everyone faded away, leaving two people who had completed their journey through troubles and danger and were ready to face the future together.

An hour later, they left for their special champagne hot-air balloon flight. This time they would have a pilot with them. This time they would see what was below. When the ride was over, they would return to a honeymoon suite, take a private flight of love, and soar as high as their love could take them.

To the Readers:

I hope you enjoyed this fanciful trip to Florida. I spend a lot of time in the Orlando area and one of the things that triggered the idea for *Kindred Spirits* was the hot air balloons so readily accessible to anyone who wants to ride in these gentle giants.

Many mornings as I go for an early walk, I see the balloons drifting past. The morning that one almost landed in our community was the trigger for the idea for this novel.

Winter Garden is the site of our second home. If not for our grandchildren in New Jersey, we'd probably be living there full time.

That area is another world. For one thing, drivers actually stop for pedestrians in the crosswalks.

Keep watch for *Aloha Love* to be released in 2005. I'll take you on an adventuresome trip to Hawaii, our paradise on earth.

You can reach me at *agwwriter@email.com* or P.O. Box 18832, Philadelphia, PA 19119. If you would like a reply by mail, please include a self-addressed, stamped envelope.

Please keep on reading my books. Without you my writings would go no further than a stack of papers on a shelf in my home.

Alice
www.alicewootson.net

# ABOUT THE AUTHOR

*Kindred Spirts* is my seventh novel. When I retired from teaching I never dreamed that I'd reach this point. I never thought of writing a book-length piece of writing.

As a child growing up in Rankin, Pennsylvania (a small town outside of Pittsburgh), I wrote poetry and made up stories, but I never imagined that I would one day be a published author. I came to the Philadelphia area to attend Cheyney University, met Ike who was attending Lincoln University, got married and stayed in this area.

While teaching I wrote a novel using a typewriter and swore never again. After my school was designated a computer magnet school and I learned word processing, I decided to try again.

The historical novel that I wrote has yet to be published, but my first contemporary novel, *Snowbound with Love* was published in 2000 by Arabesque. *Dream Wedding, Home for Christrmas, Trust in Me, To Love Again* and *Escape to Love* followed.

I love to travel and I schedule book signings during my trips whenever possible. I enjoy meeting with book clubs and reader groups. I put my teaching experience to use by conducting writing workshops at conferences and for various groups.

I am busier in this second career than I was while teaching.